Praise for the R

HAR

"The reader will have a ... g
read with a well-crafted ... e
disappointed. New readers will want to glom the backlist so they don't miss a single minute." —*Fresh Fiction*

"The Renaissance Faire Mysteries are always an enjoyable read . . . Joyce and Jim Lavene provide a complex exciting murder mystery that amateur-sleuth fans will appreciate."

—*Midwest Book Review*

DEADLY DAGGERS

"The Lavene duet can always be counted on for an enjoyable whodunit . . . Filled with twists and red herrings, *Deadly Daggers* is a delightful mystery." —*Midwest Book Review*

"Will keep you entertained from the first duel to the last surprise . . . If you like fun reads that will let you leave this world for a time, this series is for you."

—*The Romance Readers Connection*

"Never a dull moment! Filled with interesting characters, a fast-paced story, and plenty of humor, this series never lets its readers down . . . You're bound to feel an overwhelming craving for a giant turkey leg and the urge to toast to the king's health with a big mug of ale as you enjoy this thematic cozy mystery!" —*Fresh Fiction*

GHASTLY GLASS

"A unique look at a renaissance faire. This is a colorful, exciting amateur-sleuth mystery filled with quirky characters who endear themselves to the reader as Joyce and Jim Lavene write a delightful whodunit." —*Midwest Book Review*

continued . . .

WICKED WEAVES

"Offers a vibrant background for the mysterious goings-on and the colorful cast of characters."

—Kaye Morgan, author of *Celebrity Sudoku*

"This jolly series debut . . . serves up medieval murder and mayhem."

—*Publishers Weekly*

"Fast-paced, clever, delightful."

—John J. Lamb, author of *The Treacherous Teddy*

"A creative, fascinating whodunit, transporting readers to a world of make-believe that entertains and educates."

—*Fresh Fiction*

"[A] new, exciting . . . series . . . Part of the fun of this solid whodunit is the vivid description of the Renaissance Village; anyone who has not been to one will want to go . . . [C]leverly developed."

—*Midwest Book Review*

"[A] terrific mystery series . . . A feast for the reader . . . Character development in this new series is energetic and eloquent; Jessie is charming and intelligent, with . . . saucy strength."

—MyShelf.com

"I cannot imagine a cozier setting than Renaissance Faire Village, a closed community of rather eccentric—and very interesting—characters, [with] lots of potential . . . [A] great start to a new series by a veteran duo of mystery authors."

—*Cozy Library*

Berkley Prime Crime titles by Joyce and Jim Lavene

Peggy Lee Garden Mysteries

PRETTY POISON
FRUIT OF THE POISONED TREE
POISONED PETALS
PERFECT POISON
A CORPSE FOR YEW

Renaissance Faire Mysteries

WICKED WEAVES
GHASTLY GLASS
DEADLY DAGGERS
HARROWING HATS
TREACHEROUS TOYS

Missing Pieces Mysteries

A TIMELY VISION
A TOUCH OF GOLD
A SPIRITED GIFT

Treacherous Toys

Joyce and Jim Lavene

BERKLEY PRIME CRIME, NEW YORK

THE BERKLEY PUBLISHING GROUP
Published by the Penguin Group
Penguin Group (USA) Inc.
375 Hudson Street, New York, New York 10014, USA
Penguin Group (Canada), 90 Eglinton Avenue East, Suite 700, Toronto, Ontario M4P 2Y3, Canada (a division of Pearson Penguin Canada Inc.) • Penguin Books Ltd., 80 Strand, London WC2R 0RL, England • Penguin Group Ireland, 25 St. Stephen's Green, Dublin 2, Ireland (a division of Penguin Books Ltd.) • Penguin Group (Australia), 250 Camberwell Road, Camberwell, Victoria 3124, Australia (a division of Pearson Australia Group Pty. Ltd.) • Penguin Books India Pvt. Ltd., 11 Community Centre, Panchsheel Park, New Delhi—110 017, India • Penguin Group (NZ), 67 Apollo Drive, Rosedale, Auckland 0632, New Zealand (a division of Pearson New Zealand Ltd.) • Penguin Books (South Africa) (Pty.) Ltd., 24 Sturdee Avenue, Rosebank, Johannesburg 2196, South Africa

Penguin Books Ltd., Registered Offices: 80 Strand, London WC2R 0RL, England

TREACHEROUS TOYS

A Berkley Prime Crime Book / published by arrangement with the authors

PUBLISHING HISTORY
Berkley Prime Crime mass-market edition / September 2012

Cover illustration by Ben Perini.
Cover design by Lesley Worrell.
Interior text design by Laura K. Corless.

ISBN: 978-0-425-25158-4

BERKLEY® PRIME CRIME
Berkley Prime Crime Books are published by The Berkley Publishing Group,
a division of Penguin Group (USA) Inc.,
375 Hudson Street, New York, New York 10014.
BERKLEY® PRIME CRIME and the PRIME CRIME logo are trademarks of
Penguin Group (USA) Inc.

PRINTED IN THE UNITED STATES OF AMERICA

10 9 8 7 6 5 4 3 2 1

One

Christmas at Renaissance Faire Village and Market Place was like a greeting card come to life. The Village staff had created a winter wonderland that would last about four weeks, until Christmas Eve at six P.M. There was a light snow blanketing most of the ground and the rooftops. Icicles hung from the trees.

An ice skating rink was set up in the middle of the Village Green. Already, children were skating there—amazing considering the temperature was a balmy sixty degrees. After all, the Village was located in the heart of Myrtle Beach, South Carolina. Even in the winter, there was rarely cold weather here, much less snow and ice.

Of course, none of it was real—from the icicles to the sparkling white snow. The skating rink was frozen from beneath with cooling coils that would maintain the six inches of solid ice even if the temperature around it were eighty degrees. I wasn't sure how they'd managed the icicles.

I knew the snow was made several times a day to keep it fresh.

There were wreaths on all the doors and candles in every window. Carolers in beautiful costumes wandered down the cobblestone streets and through the paths, adding a touch of spirit to the festive season. The scent of pine from Sherwood Forest mingled with the smell of cinnamon rolls baking at the Monastery Bakery. It felt like Christmas should in a Renaissance Village. That was all that mattered to me.

It was my first time attending the Faire during the holidays. Normally, I'd be back in Columbia teaching history and grading papers. But not this year. This year, the University of South Carolina had furloughed me for the next six weeks. I had yet to discover if I'd still have a job after the first of the year.

I probably should have gone out and looked for work that paid better, or at least came close to what I made as an associate history professor. But the opportunity to spend Christmas at the Village was too hard to pass up. I'd seen the pictures and heard the stories since I'd started coming here when I was in college. This was my first opportunity to experience it in person.

"Jessie!" My good friend and the Faire's resident giant, Bart Van Impe, greeted me at the snowy entrance to the Village. "Think fast!"

He threw a snowball at me as I came under the Main Gate. I moved too slowly and it caught me in the shoulder. Bart, and several of the lord and lady greeters, had a good laugh at that. I didn't mind. I was amazed that the cold wet stuff *felt* like real snow.

"This is great! How do they do it?" The snowball was definitely real, and a little hard. My shoulder stung where it had hit.

"Every hour, real snow falls from the castle," Bart explained. "Maybe *falling* isn't the right word. It's more like *shooting* out of the castle. Sometimes you can get enough of it together to make a ball before it melts."

"And you threw yours at me," I joked. "How thoughtful of you."

He threw his massive arms around me and hugged me tight, lifting me off the snowy ground. "How are you doing? Chase sent me to meet you. He was otherwise detained. You know. Everyone wants him, right?"

"I'm fine," I replied, keeping it to myself that my car had broken down on the side of the road on my way from Columbia, my landlord was opting to change my apartment into a condo, and I was probably going to be one of a vast group of job hunters next year. Why ruin our reunion? I hadn't seen him in months. "What's Chase doing?"

"He was breaking up a fight over at the Dutchman's Stage. Two of the comedians got into it. I think one of them threw a punch at Chase. Stupid man. But you didn't hear that from me."

That wasn't surprising. Chase Manhattan was the Village bailiff—judge, jury, and police officer all rolled into one. He was also my boyfriend.

"It's good to see you, Bart." I hugged his mammoth form dressed in brown tights and a red tunic with a blazing red and white cape across his shoulders. "How's Daisy?"

He shrugged. "She threw me out last night. She'll get over it. That's just the way she is. I love her anyway. I only wish she crocheted instead of making swords. It would be a lot safer when we fight, you know?"

I laughed, understanding the problem but glad they were still together. "I don't know. I've heard people can be vicious with those crochet hooks."

He laughed, his wide shoulders and broad chest heaving with the force of it. His large, plain face and sometimes deliberate manner hid a sharp intellect and a warm heart. "That's true. May I walk with you to the Dungeon to await the bailiff, my lady?"

"Thanks, but I think I'll check in with work. I'm apprenticing with the new toy maker. Have you met him?"

"Sure. He's jolly and nice. Daisy said he's as round as an apple, but I think it's just because he wears those big red suits. They aren't very flattering on him."

"So he's more like Santa than Father Christmas?"

I smiled at two of the monks I recognized from the Monastery Bakery. They acknowledged me with a nod, appropriate for them. The Brotherhood of the Sheaf made the best cinnamon rolls and bread I'd ever had. The mere smell of them made my stomach grumble.

"I don't know. They seem to love him. Everyone really loves his toys. He has all those little elves helping him every day. It's a nice touch for the holiday."

The Village had located the toy maker in one of the brick manor houses on Squire's Lane, not too far from the Main Gate. It was the first time I'd ever seen the houses open. They had dressed up the three stately homes with wreaths and lots of fake snow. There were colorful ornaments on all the nearby trees. Children were waiting with their parents in a line that stretched around Mirror Lake and up toward the castle. Obviously, a *very* good attraction for the season.

"I'm going to go in and say hello," I told Bart. "Thanks for meeting me. Maybe we can have lunch or something later."

"That sounds nice. I'll tell Daisy you're here. That will give me an excuse to talk to her without *really* talking to her. That's the way we make up. Bye, lady."

As usual, Bart wasn't much help in describing what was going on. He always kind of wandered around a topic until it was hard to decide what he was talking about. It didn't really matter in this case—I was about to dive right into the holidays. My bruised spirit needed all those well wishes and special treats that come with this time of year.

"No, you'll have to wait in line with the others," a heavy-set woman said at the side door. She was dressed like I'd expect Father Christmas's wife to be—deep shades of burgundy velvet with a long skirt and white trim.

She looked a little frazzled, her snowy white hair standing up around the matching burgundy velvet hat she wore. She had a pretty face with pink cheeks and bright blue eyes, silver-rimmed glasses set on her nose. It was easy to imagine her making cookies for the elves.

"I'm Jessie Morton," I said. "I'm your apprentice. They should've told you I was coming for the season. I can help make toys, run the shop—"

"You're hired!" She pulled me inside with surprisingly strong fingers. "Thank God you're here! We're terribly understaffed for this crowd. I don't know what those executives are thinking! I'm Christine Christmas. Let's get you an elf suit. You can take over the photography. Right this way."

I didn't exactly have photography in mind. But every apprenticeship I'd ever done had required some flexibility. I'd done some things during apprenticeships that I wouldn't have done at any other time. I was as familiar with Lady Visa and Sir MasterCard as I was with a duster and a mop. I'd coddled lords and ladies by fetching tea, giving foot rubs, even listening to their problems. There probably wasn't a floor in the castle that I hadn't scrubbed.

I had no regrets. I was very close to finishing my dissertation—"The Proliferation of Medieval Crafts in Modern

Times." Once I received my doctorate, I'd be able to go anywhere, do anything. Maybe make enough money to put some aside for things like broken-down cars and electric bills, not to mention new apartment hunting. All the stresses of real life outside the Village make-believe.

I'd worked hard on my dissertation through the past few years while managing to have a good time, too. I could make and shoot arrows, blow glass, weave baskets, make hats, and forge swords (which was how I knew Daisy and Bart so well). I was even partially responsible for getting the two of them together. Playing Cupid was more a hobby, but I excelled at it.

I pulled on the ivy green tights and tunic, then stuck the Robin Hood-like hat on my head. I looked in the mirror—there was a six-foot elf with blue eyes staring back at me, strands of flyaway brown hair sticking out around the hat. I wasn't sure if they'd be able to find any size-twelve elf shoes for me.

Christine knocked impatiently on the bathroom door. "Are you almost ready in there? These kids are going wild."

I wasn't really good with kids, though I'd become better while working at the Village. I got impatient with the younger variety too easily. I could handle the college kids, but sticky hands and runny noses weren't my favorite things.

As I emerged from the bathroom, Christine gave me a quick once-over. "Those tennis shoes are going to have to do. We don't have any adult-sized elf shoes."

Before I could ask if she had any kid-sized elf shoes, two children came up and tugged at her skirt. They were dressed like me, except they had tiny elf shoes with jingle bells on the toes.

"Mom, we're almost out of candy," the boy, maybe nine or ten, said.

"And we're completely out of coloring pages," the girl, eleven or twelve added. She had a sprig of holly in her very blond hair.

"All right. We'll take care of it in just a moment! Merry Beth, you take this lady to the camera. She'll be taking pictures. Garland, you go to the workshop and pick up more candy and coloring pages. Be quick now!"

Merry Beth took my hand as Christine headed in the opposite direction. "It's very nice to meet you," she said. "I hope you'll stay longer than the other photographer they sent. He couldn't handle it. I'm not surprised!"

"It's very nice to meet you, Merry Beth," I replied to the pretty girl at my side. "My name is Jessie Morton. I doubt that I'll be here taking pictures long. I'm the toy maker's apprentice for the next few weeks."

She smiled and pushed her long hair away from her face. "I think that's what happened to the last photographer. I'm not sure he was supposed to be taking pictures either. In fact, I think he was just here to make a delivery. Mom is desperate. She'll make anyone take pictures."

"Why not you?" She seemed capable and mature to me. "You're old enough, right?"

"Thank you. I keep telling her that. I'm not a little kid anymore. I can do all kinds of things now that I'm eleven."

We stopped walking as we reached a big room containing a large, gilded chair, a huge, decorated tree, and an old-fashioned instant camera—the kind my grandmother had once had on a tripod. The rest of the room was filled with children, noisy, crying, demanding children.

They gathered around the beautifully decorated tree, which reached the high ceiling and had a star on top. They ran restlessly around the camera. Their parents seemed to have given up on any order while they waited to see the toy maker. The only place they didn't go was on the thronelike seat. Probably afraid Father Christmas wouldn't like it.

I was about to ask where the man himself was when another door opened and he bounded into the room. I was immediately caught up in the old poem about Saint Nick. *His eyes—how they twinkled! his dimples: how merry, / His cheeks were like roses, his nose like a cherry.*

He was the perfect Father Christmas. Leave it to the Village to hire the best. The fact that he was also a talented, highly regarded toy maker was icing on the holiday cake.

I'd never seen such a beautiful outfit before. It had to be his own and not a rental. The long coat was embroidered with gold thread and had bright gold closures on the front. It was made, as were his trousers, of the plushest velvet.

His beard and mustache looked real, too, soft and white. Seeing him was enough to make my heart sing a few bars of "Santa Claus Is Coming to Town."

He was probably a little more seventeenth-century Saint Nicholas than Renaissance, but the costume was good. As always, Renaissance Village erred on the side of what looked best and would sell tickets, even if it wasn't historically accurate.

He came right up to me and took my hand in his white-gloved one. "You must be Jessie, my new apprentice. It's very good to meet you. I apologize for the delay in taking you to the workshop. The Village didn't tell us they were opening the Father Christmas visitation today. I'm a little short staffed, even with my brood."

His blue eyes smiled at me in a kind way, and his voice held the enthusiasm one would expect from the jolly old elf.

I looked around the room and saw more elves—eight in all, varying in age from older teen down to preschooler—

walking around and talking with the children there to have their pictures taken. "Are all of those elves yours?"

He laughed in a low-key yet contagious way. "It gets cold up there at the North Pole, you know. And Mrs. Christmas and I share a great love."

"I wasn't criticizing. I think it's wonderful!"

"You wouldn't think so early in the morning when they're all looking for breakfast. Or at night when they have to get along with one bathroom." He chuckled. "But it makes them closer, Jessie. Do you have family?"

"One brother. My twin, actually. He and I are kind of close. He works here, too."

"That's the way to be. I hope you'll be happy here with us for the next few weeks. We could certainly use your help. It gets really crazy around this time of year."

I couldn't believe he'd taken the time to talk with me while the line of children grew longer. It was a nice gesture. Nothing melodramatic or strange here like some of the other people I'd worked for in the Village. I couldn't wait to see Chase and ask him about Father Christmas's history.

Or maybe not. I wasn't sure I wanted to spoil what might be an illusion. Very few people at the Village were what they seemed to be.

"I guess I better get up there and hear some wishes." He put his head back and laughed again. "I'm sure we'll get along famously. I have so much to share with someone interested in learning to make toys. When we're done here, we'll go on to the workshop. Thank you for being here."

He started to walk away, and I remembered that he hadn't told me his real name. "What should I call you?"

"Why Father Christmas, of course. You might know me by other names—Santa or Saint Nick. But here, I'm Father

Christmas. Chris Christmas, in fact." He smiled, went to his chair, and sat down.

The effect was completely charming. I was swept away by it.

Garland was there a minute later, distributing coloring pages and candy to his brothers and sisters. They all began weaving through the crowd, passing out the goodies while the first child came to sit on Father Christmas's lap.

The little girl had been wailing when she and her mother approached the big chair. She stopped crying immediately and had a contrite look on her face as he lifted her. They discussed what she wanted for Christmas at length, despite the crowd. She got down, smiled, and waved, and the next child came up.

It was so heartwarming that I totally forgot I was supposed to be taking pictures of it. A small elf hand pulled at my tunic. "You have to take the picture while they are *on* his lap," Merry Beth suggested. "Once they're gone, it's too late."

Not like I didn't know that. I had just been transported into holiday heaven for a moment where my brain wasn't working. It was as though this man was the real thing and all I could do was stand and marvel at seeing him. He had a huge amount of charisma. Good line of work for him.

The camera was tricky. It wasn't made during the Renaissance, but it was old enough to be classified as an antique. I wasn't even sure how to use it. My cell phone might have been better.

I tried to secure it on the tripod, but the connection was the wrong size. I finally held it with one hand and managed to snap the picture with the other. Immediately, a developing photo (not very good) was spit out.

The second child's mother raced over and jerked it away

from me. "I'll take that. No telling what you people would do with my daughter's picture. And don't forget, it's free. I don't have time for a sales pitch either."

Too bad Father Christmas didn't seem to have the same calming effect on the adults that he did the children. As each child sat on his lap, I took the picture and a greedy, rude adult snatched it from me. Where was the holiday spirit?

Some parents asked if I had copies or knew where they could purchase them. I thought it was obvious that I didn't. I was lucky to have even one photo to hand them with the old camera I was using. Others tried to give me money for the picture. I waved it away. One man threw a ten-dollar bill at me. I stooped down to pick it up.

Merry Beth's little hand was there before mine. "All tips go in the jar. We split eight ways—well, nine including you."

I was fine with that. Not like I was expecting tips. It was obvious this session was nothing new for Father Christmas's children. Even the youngest ones seemed to know exactly what to do.

As the photo session continued, the tip jar that Merry Beth had brought out grew increasingly full. This looked like a lucrative idea. I was glad for Father Christmas and his wife. It couldn't have been easy raising so many children. It was good for the Village, too.

I was surprised when a very pregnant Queen Olivia came into the room with her usual entourage of ladies-in-waiting, gentlemen courtiers, and, in this case, a jester or two dressed for the holiday in red and green with jingle bells on their hats.

The queen was the top figurehead of the Village, along with her husband, King Harold. Whatever they wanted usually happened. Their word was law, in an almost real sense of the word.

Despite her increasing girth, the queen was dressed to the hilt in fine blue satin and a silver gauze stole, which she wore draped across her shoulders. The others in her party were dressed well, too—but never the equal of their queen. There was an unwritten law about that.

There was a strange, sort of awkward moment when the queen finally came face-to-face with Father Christmas. They just stood there and stared at each other. I wasn't sure what that was all about, but it felt like *something*.

"Olivia," he said with a smile. Then he gave her a deep, respectful bow and everything moved forward. It was hard to describe but odd somehow.

"Carry on," the breathless queen proclaimed. "We only wished to see how the event fared. It appears to be going quite well."

There was always excitement and interest when the queen visited any shop or amusement in the Village. The parents of the Father Christmas-bound children were no exception, taking plenty of pictures and asking for her autograph.

The children were another story. They just wanted to see the man in the big chair whom they instantly recognized as one of their icons, even though his costume was a little different than what they were used to. The queen wasn't interesting enough for them—not when there were toy requests on the line.

After a few minutes of preening in front of her audience, Queen Olivia took her leave in grand theatrical style. There was a chorus of admiring sighs after she swept out of the manor house, but she was quickly forgotten in the renewed push forward to visit Father Christmas.

"She's quite a character," Father Christmas said with a rich chuckle. "I knew Livy and Harry a long time ago. They were the best salespeople ever born. No wonder Adventure

Land snapped them up to run Renaissance Village. The things I could tell you!"

I'd never met anyone who knew the king and queen before they were royally installed in the good life presiding over the Village. "I'd love to hear it," I said, thinking of the possible future leverage that quirky stories from the past could lend.

"Not now!" Christine chided with a deep frown marring her attractive face. "You have a whole house full of children waiting to see you, Chris. You need to sit down and get through this."

He kissed her lightly on the cheek—to the *awws* and camera flashes of the visitors. "I'm heading that way right now, love. We'll get through it just fine. We always do, don't we?"

Christine stood near me as we both watched the man in demand go back to his seat and start receiving children again.

"This gets harder every year," she confided. "Sometimes I don't know how we'll make it through another Christmas. But it's his life. How could I take it away from him?"

Two

I knew it! Things could never be that simple and good.

I sensed trouble in this holiday paradise. It seemed that Father Christmas didn't feel the pressure his wife did. Or she protected him from it. Either way, she was bearing the brunt of some pressures that he didn't seem to notice.

I had hoped things were exactly as they seemed, but that rarely happened. Especially here in the Village, where everyone concealed their true identities. There were always deeper secrets.

I didn't have much time to think about it. Chase paid me a surprise visit. Between shots of crying or angry children, he managed to sneak up behind me and hug me tight.

"Welcome back!" he said after a big kiss that received appropriate notice in the form of flashing cameras and ribald teasing from visitors. "I was wondering if we were ever going to see each other today."

Chase was six foot eight, two hundred and fifty pounds

of Village justice and sex appeal. I noticed his new costume right away. Gone was the usual leather tunic, replaced by rich black velvet with a dashing black cape. I supposed he looked a little strange to some, kissing a large elf.

"You've traded up in the world," I said, so pleased to see him that it was all I could do to concentrate on the pictures I was taking. "I hope I see a costume as nice for the season."

"You don't like this cute green elf costume?" He laughed at me. "You look really sweet and in the holiday spirit. Why would you want to change?"

Chase and I had known each other for years. Even before we'd started dating, we were friends. Because he was the bailiff and had a permanent apartment above the Dungeon, I was always guaranteed a place to stay while I was at the Village. Not that I would have cared where it was if I could be with him. Sappy, I know. But he was the light of my life.

"I guess that means I'm stuck looking like the jolly green giant for the next six weeks." I snapped a picture of a cute little girl with pigtails as she sat on Father Christmas's lap. I had the hang of it now.

"But you'll have *me*." He smiled and winked at me. "How long are you going to be here?"

"At least until the Main Gate closes," Christine intervened. "Don't you have somewhere else to be, sir? We're very busy here. Jessie can meet you later."

"Maybe." He looked back at me, not at all abashed by her. "You must get lunch, right? Even Santa takes a break."

Christine put her hands on her ample hips. "I'm sure everyone gets a break sometime. In the meantime, we're trying to work here. I'd hate to complain to anyone about you interfering with our busy, important schedule."

Chase sobered immediately and bowed slightly to her. "You're correct, madam. I would hate for you to complain as well. I beg your pardon."

She gave him a satisfied nod and turned away to go back into the crowd. Chase picked me up and spun me around, one of his favorite pastimes, before he whispered that he would return promptly at noon.

I had to laugh. Christine didn't realize that everyone in the Village loved Chase, and she'd have to go past the CEO of Adventure Land, who lived at the Village under the guise of Merlin the Wizard, to find anyone who would chastise him in any way. He was just too modest to admit it.

My heart was pounding in that old familiar way that happened whenever I was around Chase. I never tired of seeing him and knowing that he was mine. It was what kept me going when I was teaching history in Columbia and couldn't be with him. It was my own personal curse that I couldn't let go of that other life and be here with him all the time.

Then the old camera ran out of film, and no one could find any to replace it. I couldn't see the end of the long line that stretched out of the manor house. It wasn't lunchtime yet. Christine looked ready to explode.

"I told you we needed a new one," she whispered in an angry voice to Father Christmas. "There's never enough money for the important things. Now what do we do?"

His kindly face didn't change. He put one arm around her that she hastily shrugged off. "We take a break and go get a new camera," he said. "Not to worry. We've made enough this morning to get a much better one." He nodded toward the tip jar.

A tall, thin likeness of him—minus the white hair and beard—offered to get the camera. "Let's go ahead and invest in one of those that connect to a computer, Dad. That would be the best thing."

"You see, Christine." Father Christmas put his arm around the young man's shoulders. "Jolly will look out for us. The two of you take the money and get what he needs. I'm sure there's some electronic warehouse store around here somewhere."

"Call me Charlie, Dad." Jolly was wearing an elf suit like mine but apparently was having issues with being part of the holiday retinue. "You know Jolly embarrasses me."

"But that's your name." His father laughed. "Charlie is just your middle name. And your uncle's name at that."

"Whatever." Charlie/Jolly turned away.

"And what are you going to do while I'm out shopping?" Christine demanded.

"I'm going to show Jessie the workshop, and we'll get started on her apprenticeship."

Those words were always music to my ears. But Christine didn't look too happy with his answer.

I didn't want to get stuck in a family brawl either. "If it's all the same to you, I'd like to run and get my suitcase and check in with the Village." By *the Village*, I meant Chase. "I could grab lunch for both of us and meet you at the toy shop later."

He nodded. "I understand. That was quite a handsome young man who was here looking for you earlier. That's fine. The workshop is right next door. We're hoping to have it set up and open by tomorrow. Then part of my time will be here with the kids and the other part will be making toys."

"You should come with Jolly and me to the store so you can see what we're buying," Christine said to him. She eyed me suspiciously. "Nothing *that* important is going on here while I'm gone."

"That's okay. I trust your judgment. And I'll take one of those big turkey legs, Jessie," he said, apparently unconvinced. "And a big ale to wash it down. I can't afford to lose weight, not at this time of year."

Christine gave him one of the looks wives are famous for, then stormed out with Jolly for the store. The other Christmas children, with the help of a few Village security guards, were emptying the manor of the remaining crowd. Merry Beth was handing out little pieces of paper that would ensure the people who'd been waiting would get in first once the camera was replaced and Father Christmas returned.

I didn't care. The satchel of clothes I'd left in the car was forgotten. I took out my cell phone—totally against all the rules—and called around the shops and restaurants until I had located Chase. It took less than ten minutes for both of us to end up at the Dungeon together.

"What about lunch?" he asked in a mischievous tone that said he already knew my answer.

"I think I'll have dessert first," I told him, playing with his long brown braid that casually rested on his shoulder. "Right now."

Chase and I had a little time left over for lunch at one of our favorite eating spots, the Pleasant Pheasant. He brought me up to date on everything that had happened in the Village since I'd seen him a few weeks before.

"Olivia's baby is due before Christmas," he told me. "Her staff have practice runs getting her from the castle to the Main Gate almost every day, and every time, they make some mistake or bad decision. It would be funny if it weren't for the fact that she's really having a baby. I don't see anything getting better."

"As long as they don't expect you to deliver it and don't let Wanda Le Fey near it, at least the baby should be fine." I sipped some cold ale and remembered that Father Christmas also wanted some with his turkey leg.

"I get the whole bad-blood thing between you and Wanda, but why would it be bad for me to deliver the baby? I have emergency medical training."

I shivered when I thought about Wanda—the Village's resident nurse—and all the evil things she'd done to me in the past. Her cold blue eyes affected me even when she wasn't around. "I think Livy would take it the wrong way if you deliver her baby."

"You mean she'd want to name the baby after me, that kind of thing?"

"No." I stole his last two French fries. "I think she'd feel like you two were having a relationship. You know how she is that way. Having a baby is a very intimate thing."

He laughed. "I think motherhood has changed her. Just watch her for a while. She's a different woman."

"You mean since Harry announced the baby was his and he wouldn't demand a paternity test? I wouldn't call that change exactly. Just a reprieve."

He shook his head, the light from the window near us catching on the gold ring in his ear. "What about you? I guess the car made it down here. I wish you would've let me come and get you. Have you heard anything about your job?"

"Mostly that it probably won't exist in January. Everybody has to make cuts. I seem to be one of those. And don't ask about the apartment. I moved everything into storage. Not that there was much to move."

I tried not to fixate on the fact that I was almost thirty-five and had so little. Outside of a few old posters and a table that had belonged to my grandmother, who'd raised me and my brother after our parents' deaths, everything else had gone to Goodwill. Nothing in that small space had meant much to me. It seemed as though my whole life was here in the Village with Chase.

"I don't want to make you feel that I'm pushing you into something, but you know you can stay here. I know it's not the same as living away, but you love it here. I'd love you to be here all the time."

It wasn't my favorite subject. My plan was still to get my doctorate and move up the ranks of academia until I could afford a new car and a better apartment. I'd tried not to let my focus wander too far beyond that goal.

"I appreciate that." I held his hand on the table and looked into his beautiful brown eyes that reminded me of dark, sweet chocolate. "But I've worked too hard just to let it all go. I can't give up when I'm so close."

He shrugged. "You could work on it here, Jessie. Everyone works online now."

"I'll think about it. Thank you for offering."

"You know I'm not just saying it because you need somewhere to go. I love you. Stay here with me. You can get as many doctorates as you want to. You won't ever have to worry about anything again."

I was about to start crying. I loved him, too, and wanted to stay there, but I wasn't sure my plans would work out if I did. It wasn't that I didn't want to lean on Chase and his wealthy family. Well, maybe it was. I wanted to do this on my own. I wanted to be able to take care of myself, and occasionally my brother, Tony. I knew it didn't make any sense, except to me.

"I have to go." I got to my feet, almost knocking my

empty ale mug off the table. "I'll think about it. Really. But I better get that turkey leg back to my new boss. I'll see you later."

I ran out of the Pleasant Pheasant with my cardboard container of ale. I didn't want to imagine what Chase must think. How many times had I turned him down? Would he get tired of it one day and never ask again?

I wanted to stay on course, stay focused. I needed to know that even if Chase and I broke up, I could take care of myself. I didn't want to be like my mother when my dad left her—like wet gingerbread. I had to finish my doctorate. Then I could think about being with Chase all the time.

I looked at the old sundial outside the Pleasant Pheasant. Father Christmas would think I'd changed my mind about making toys since I'd been gone almost two hours after we'd had to break for lunch. I had to do better than that if I wanted to keep my apprenticeship.

I hailed a turkey leg vendor wearing a bright green mob cap and matching gown. I recognized her from another position she'd had in the Village. "Is that you, Arlene?"

"Yes!" She smiled brightly, then frowned. "I'm sorry. I don't remember your name. You used to work in the castle kitchen, right?"

"Yes. I'm Tony's sister, Jessie. You were Lady Godiva."

"That was me—two kids ago. My husband makes flutes. He's opening a shop here over the holiday, and we'll see how it goes. I just wanted to do something to help out with expenses. Nothing that requires a skin-colored body suit, but turkey legs are good."

"I'm glad you're back." I took the large roasted leg and paid her. "Did you ever think you'd come back here to live with your husband someday?"

"No. Not really. This never seemed real to me, you

know? But it's probably a good place to be a flute maker. Where else would you get this kind of traffic?"

We said good-bye and I continued past the Dutchman's Stage and Peter's Pub. Maybe I was wrong to be so harsh on people who chose to live here. It didn't matter to Chase—but he was also a patent attorney who made money doing online research for his clients. I wasn't sure where a history professor would fit in with jugglers, fire-eaters, and shepherds, even with a doctorate.

I waved to Andre Hariot at the Hat House. He was decked out festively in a gold and red tunic with matching gold tights. His hat was a thing to behold—a creation of red berries, gold garland, and some kind of evergreen that draped down close to one of his eyes. Andre was an extraordinary hatmaker.

The crowd had paid full-price entrance to the Village to see Father Christmas. They were still milling around playing games, having their fortunes read, and eating. Knife throwers were showing off their skills, and the pirate ship, *Queen's Revenge*, was shooting off its cannon on Mirror Lake. It wasn't like the visitors wouldn't get their money's worth while they waited.

I finally reached the third manor house of Squire's Lane where the toy workshop was located. The front door at the top of the stairs was closed. There were no lights on inside. I went back down to the basement door and managed to knock despite the cardboard cup of ale and greasy, napkin-wrapped turkey leg I was holding. No lights were on inside here either, but the door was open. I went in to take a look around.

The workshop was filled with hundreds of toys of every kind. They were stacked on shelves, spilling out of crates, and lying half finished on long worktables. Most of them were hand carved, but by so deft a hand that the figures, animals, trains, and cars, almost came to life. Some of them were in the process of being painted. Others were in the wood-finishing stage. The workshop smelled of wet paint and sawdust, exactly what I'd expected.

"Hello?" I called out into the large, shadowed room. "Is anyone here?"

I heard a sound behind me. I turned my head just in time to have a crashing blow hit me hard on the side of my face. I went down like a wet deck of cards, turkey leg, ale, and all. I didn't see who'd hit me, but I heard him or her run from the workshop, slamming the door behind them.

My head was swimming. I was conscious but couldn't move from the spot on the floor where I'd fallen. I looked to the side. Something large and burgundy velvet covered lay close beside me. I sat up, dizzy and light-headed, sick to my stomach. There was no mistaking those hand-tooled boots or the regal gold embroidery on the costume.

Father Christmas's happy holidays were over.

Three

Detective Donald Almond was assigned to the Village from the Myrtle Beach Police Department. He was a big man with a chin that folded into his neck, and he always looked like he needed a haircut and a shower. His clothes appeared to be ones he'd slept in the night before.

He shook his head as he came into the workshop. "Jessie Morton. Why am I not surprised? Is your middle name *trouble*?"

I didn't move my head since the ice and three pain relievers were barely keeping my headache down to a dull roar. I was going to have a heck of a bruise on the side of my face, too. "Believe me, it wasn't my idea to be here for this."

I'd called security as soon as I could. Chase and two of his men had rushed over. They'd tried to revive Father Christmas. No use. The paramedics came, and Chase called Detective Almond right away.

"And whose idea was it to mess around with the victim?"

Detective Almond asked as he walked around the room looking at the toys and tools scattered everywhere. "It never helps to change the scene of the crime. You've probably destroyed evidence that might have led to our killer."

"That was my decision." Chase shifted from where he'd been sitting on the floor with my aching head on his lap. "We didn't know if he was alive. I wanted to give him the chance to survive."

"And how'd that work out for you?" Detective Almond sneered.

"He couldn't be revived. He'd been gone too long." Chase smiled at me in a sad way. "Whoever did this knocked Jessie down as he or she was leaving. It hasn't been that long since it happened. Chris was still warm."

Detective Almond nodded, taking it all in. "Anything else suspicious? I mean besides that bullet hole in his neck."

"What's going on?" Christine stormed into the room. "Where's my husband? What have you done with him?"

"And who are you?" Detective Almond asked.

"I'm his wife! I demand that you let me see him."

"I'm sorry. He was killed, ma'am. We'll be investigating his death." Though Detective Almond's words were forthright, his tone was apologetic. "I'm afraid he'll have to be taken to the morgue for an autopsy. This room will have to be cut off from the rest of the Village until we figure out what happened—unless *you* have something to share."

Christine lost her anger. She stared at the bloodstain still on the concrete floor where her husband had breathed his last. The paramedics still stood next to his body, covered by a black bag, at the side of the room. The reality of it seemed to strike her. She didn't say anything else. Her lips trembled.

Detective Almond nodded to one of the three men he'd

brought with him. "Officer Duncan will take you to the morgue, ma'am. We'll have some questions for you, too, I'm afraid. But he'll bring you back again when it's over. I'm truly sorry for your loss."

"What about my children?" she muttered hoarsely as she started to follow the officer.

"I'll take care of them." The words were out of my mouth before I'd really thought about what I was saying. My head was throbbing and I still felt sick. How was I going to take care of them? I grabbed Chase's arm. "*We'll* take care of them until you get back. Don't worry."

"*We?*" Chase looked surprised.

"Before you two go off to fluff your nest," Detective Almond added, "I need to talk to you outside a minute, Manhattan. Jessie, don't forget I want to see you at the station ASAP. Make sure she gets there." He nodded sternly at Chase.

"I'll make sure she's there," Chase promised, equally solemn.

Sometimes he took his bailiff persona a little *too* seriously.

Detective Almond had the other two officers stay in the room with the paramedics while he and Chase walked outside to talk. I didn't know what to do—I didn't want to interrupt them.

I needed to find the children. Someone should tell them what had happened before they saw a tweet or some other Internet posting about it. I assumed Jolly must know since he'd been with Christine. My heart ached for them.

On a selfish note, I couldn't believe the toy maker was gone before I'd even managed to mangle one toy. It had to be my shortest apprenticeship ever.

I found the bathroom in the back of the workshop and washed my face. I was right. There was going to be a major bruise on my face.

As I finished looking at myself in the mirror, I noticed a bit of bright green fluff caught in my earring on the side that had gotten hit. With a gentle tug, I pulled the fluff off the earring and looked at it—it was felt. Of course, bright green felt wasn't much of a clue right now. Everyone in the Village was wearing it as part of their costumes. It even matched the elf costume I'd been wearing earlier when I was helping out with the Father Christmas photos.

But I'd changed back into jeans and a sweater after I'd gone back to the Dungeon. I wasn't officially working yet. It definitely wasn't from my costume. The color was easy to spot.

It had probably come from the person who'd mowed me down trying to get out of the workshop after killing Chris. I had to decide whether to turn it over to Detective Almond. Not much of a decision. It might be better if I hung on to it. He tended to ignore me.

Chase and Detective Almond came back into the workshop. Detective Almond told his men to stay there. A crime scene unit and transport for the body was on its way. "Don't worry," he told Chase. "I don't expect you to do all the heavy lifting on this, Manhattan. I'll try to find some men I can send in undercover to keep an eye out. But you know what happened last time I sent someone in."

I knew. The undercover officer had gone rogue and become a pirate. I wasn't surprised that Detective Almond was reluctant to take that risk again. Many people who came here to do a normal job ended up in costume permanently.

"That's fine," Chase said. "But I can already see the

publicity for this—*Santa killed at Renaissance Village.* And whether I like it or not, Adventure Land won't discourage the crowds who want to see where it happened."

Detective Almond shrugged. "We all have our crosses to bear, son. Do the best you can."

Merry Beth looked around the corner of the doorway. "Is everything okay down here? Where are Mom and Daddy?"

I almost broke down at that point. Seriously, all of those kids losing their father. They were so young. And what an awful mom substitute I was, hanging out there looking at green fluff while those poor kids were wandering around the Village.

I took Merry Beth's hand. She looked at me a little strangely, but I held on. "If you two are done talking, Chase and I need to get all the kids together. They shouldn't just be out there alone."

"We're fine, Jessie," Merry Beth assured me with that impressive maturity. "We do this all the time when Daddy travels. Aren't my Mom and Jolly back from the store yet?"

"Go on," Detective Almond said. "Take care of things. We'll talk again later."

Chase and I walked out into the late afternoon sunshine with Merry Beth. I wasn't even sure where to start to look for the other kids. The Village was a big place. They could be anywhere.

But they weren't too far away. They'd been waiting outside the workshop for their sister.

I wasn't sure how much to tell them. I knew the news would be all over the Village in a short time. But I didn't want to take something away from what their mother would say. Still, they had the right to know where she was and what had happened, even if it was only the basics.

"Something has happened to your father," I said as we

stood together outside the manor houses. "Your mother is trying to find out what she should do. She'll be back soon. You'll be with Chase and me until she gets back."

"Something like what?" Garland asked quietly. "Is he sick?"

"He's probably been fooling around again," Jolly answered. "This is what it's usually like when that happens. We don't see him for a while, then he and Mom make up. We all go away somewhere else again."

"You don't know that for sure," Merry Beth said. "We shouldn't judge until we know."

The next boy down in age, Nick, shrugged and walked away from the group. The four youngest sisters, Joy and Star (obviously twins about six or seven) and Faith and Holly (three and four, maybe?) stood together holding hands.

"The Main Gate is closing early because of what happened so they can get the body out," Chase said. "Why don't we go down to the other end of the Village. They'll be feeding the camels and elephants soon. You could help if you like."

Even Jolly was excited by that idea. I smiled at Chase as we left word with the police officer standing guard over the crime scene. Christine would know where the kids were when she got back. We took a walk down the cobblestones.

Chase would make an incredible father, I decided, though I wasn't sure if he would ever want the job. His own family was a little dysfunctional, like mine. I certainly never thought much about having my own children.

Tom, Tom the Piper's Son was in the middle of practicing stealing a piglet close to the manor house. A Village madman was counting up his take after having spent the day begging for spare change from the crowd while beating his pot with a large wooden spoon. Two ladies, dressed in the height of Renaissance fashion, went by with only a spare glance for Chase.

Their expressions had changed when they saw that he was with his large family and wife.

Life in the Village went on. By nightfall, everyone would know that Chris Christmas had been found dead in his workshop. No doubt it would put a pall on festivities, even though he was just a visiting resident.

"Who do you think killed him?" I asked Chase quietly as we passed the Dutchman's Stage where a knight and a pie maker were rehearsing a comedy routine for the next day.

"I don't know. I hope we find out quickly."

"I found this." I showed him the piece of green felt I'd found in my earring. "I think my attacker, aka Chris's killer, left it there when he or she hit me."

He looked at it. "You should give that to Detective Almond when we go see him tomorrow. It could be important."

We paused to let the kids marvel at a sword swallower practicing his routine near the tree swing, and I explained my theory about everyone in the Village wearing green felt.

"That may be true," he quietly agreed. "But he can have it analyzed and might be able to find out exactly where it came from. This is a murder investigation, Jessie. You can't hold anything back."

Like I said, too serious. And becoming too much like Detective Almond.

Once we arrived at the elephant and camel ride enclosure, the kids ran off to have fun with the animals, forgetting all about us.

Tom Grigg, the undercover police officer turned pirate, found us there. "I heard about Santa," he said, playing with his saber. "What happened?"

"Father Christmas," I corrected. "And he was shot."

"Once in the back of the neck, I think," Chase added. "He was dead when I got there. But the killer may have run past Jessie in the workshop. He knocked her down."

Grigg turned interested eyes toward me. "You didn't see anything?"

"Nothing." I didn't tell him about the green felt. I tried hard not to stare at his new mustache and failed. "Have you heard anything else?"

He shrugged his shoulders beneath the tattered red shirt he wore. "Only that San—Father Christmas liked the ladies. He goosed a few of the serving wenches at the tavern last night. His wife came and dragged him home by the ear about midnight."

I supposed that was what I had sensed between him and Christine earlier in the day. It totally destroyed my lovely vision of their happy family life. Eight kids with Christine and he was still fooling around. There should be some way to tell when men were like that—a big black spot on their forehead or something. They shouldn't be allowed to be charming and nice.

"You might remember something," Grigg said to me, "after the shock wears off. It happens to victims. Let's just hope the killer doesn't think so, too. He might come after you."

"What makes you think it was a man?" I asked.

"Angry husband, maybe. Jealous boyfriend. Who knows?"

"Same thing for angry wife, jealous girlfriend," I said. But as I said it, I hoped that wouldn't be the case, at least about the angry wife. I hated to think about the kids losing their mother, too.

I saw Christine walking across the King's Highway toward us and cautioned Grigg to keep his mouth shut. He nodded and walked away.

She'd been crying, of course. Her eyes were bloodshot, her face pale. As soon as the kids saw her, their enchantment with the animals was over. They'd all been putting on a good face for us. Now they broke down and ran to her in tears, wanting to know what had happened.

"Thank you for taking care of them," she said to me and Chase. "We need some time to talk. I'll see you tomorrow."

We watched them leave, sliding our arms around each other for comfort.

"Well, I think that's it for tonight," Chase said. "Let's catch some dinner and go to bed. You need some rest so you can be up and running after those kids tomorrow.

"Thanks. All of that sounds fine. Maybe better than fine. What a day."

But I tossed and turned restlessly all night in bed thinking about Chris. Every time I closed my eyes, I saw Chris again, lying beside me on the floor. I scoured my memory, trying to make out the person who'd smacked me down as they'd made their escape. There was nothing.

I hoped the killer didn't think I knew who he or she was. But it was incentive for me to begin thinking about who it *could* be. Who would want to kill Chris?

It was a long night, not the pleasant one I'd planned for my first night back with Chase. I must've finally gone to sleep toward dawn because it was daylight when I woke.

Chase was smiling at me, holding a plastic tray with a red rose, a cinnamon roll from the Monastery Bakery, and a hot mocha latte.

"It's about time." He barely waited for me to sit up. "I've already done my rounds, helped catch a runaway camel, and assisted Galileo in setting up his new telescope. I didn't think you were *ever* going to wake up."

It was a lot to take in—especially before coffee. But my

head didn't hurt anymore and even a little sleep was better than none.

"Any news about what happened to Chris?" My mind was still focused on that subject. "Did they find anything that might help?"

"I haven't heard from Detective Almond, if that's what you mean. As far as the Village is concerned—Adventure Land hired a new Father Christmas last night." He grimaced. "I know. But the show must go on. It was a single-day record for us on ticket sales. That's a big draw."

"How is that possible so fast? And what about Christine?" I nervously nibbled on the cinnamon roll. "Tell me they didn't just kick her to the side of the cobblestones with her eight kids."

"She and the kids are all going to help with the pictures and making toys. The new Father Christmas is only for show. He doesn't make toys. I think he might be a male model. Older variety, like those kinds on commercials for Viagra."

I didn't really care about Adventure Land's decision to hire a new Father Christmas. I was sure they would replace all of us as needed. But keeping Christine and the kids was awesome. "That's wonderful! I was afraid they'd be gone."

"Probably not. Adventure Land paid them a lot of money up front to be here. It's part of their contract. They have to stay. It's not going to be easy for them."

"Maybe. But at least they have somewhere to go until they can decide what else to do. Thanks." I kissed him and handed him the tray so I could get out of bed.

"Where are you going?" He ate a piece of my leftover cinnamon roll.

I grabbed the coffee and the rose. "To help make toys. That's what I came for."

"Maybe you should take it easy today. We could talk about you staying here."

"I'm just going to jump in the shower and get right over there," I explained. "I'm sure Christine could really use my help. We can talk later. Maybe at lunch."

I hurried into the shower, glad there was plenty of hot water. Sometimes when Chase and I showered together, the water heater ran dry. Not that it mattered in that case. And cold water could be really good if it was hot outside.

But I didn't want to talk about moving here or anything else having to do with my other life as a history professor. I'd had enough trauma in the last twenty-four hours, with Father Christmas dying before I could even make a single toy. It looked as though I would get another chance, though, since Christine was also a toy maker. I wanted to concentrate on that.

When I got out of the shower, Chase was gone. He'd left a little note on my costume, which he must have procured from Portia at the costume shop. He really was a wonderful person to go through that ordeal for me.

Love you. See you later.

It made me smile. Chase always made me smile. I couldn't imagine facing life without him. While I was teaching, time dragged and I was miserable. I spent hours just thinking about being here with him. He'd said he loved me. I was crazy about him.

I thought about him as I dressed in my red, green, and white gown with a ruffled petticoat under it. There were even matching slippers. I looked at myself in the mirror and twirled around a couple of times. Life was good. I was happy just the way things were between me and Chase.

I answered the quick knock at the door, wondering if

Chase had forgotten something. Instead it was my twin brother, Tony.

"Hi, sis!" He smiled and hugged me. "How long have you been here?"

"Since yesterday." I was happy to see him. We're almost exactly the same height. Both of us have brown hair. He's got my mother's brown eyes, and I've got my father's blue ones. "How have you been?"

He looked away, playing with Chase's sword collection that was mounted on the wall. "I have a little problem, Jessie."

"How much?"

"Not much. Maybe a couple hundred would get me through. You know I'm good for it. Since I started working on all the computers around the Village, I've been solid."

"What happened?"

"I needed a car. There was this hot little fairy—"

"There always is. Was she too good to ride the bus?"

"Sort of. We broke up when I wrecked the car."

He smiled, like always. I shook my head and sighed. He was just like our father—a man I could barely remember since he and my mother were killed right after they got divorced. The one thing I could remember was my mother crying because he was always on the hunt for some new woman and he could never hold a job.

Just like Father Christmas, I supposed.

I prided myself on being more like my mother. She'd been responsible, hardworking, hadn't let daydreams keep her from putting food on the table.

I'd spent my whole adult life getting Tony out of scrapes, loaning him money, and finding answers to his problems.

I knew that was why I was reluctant to stay in the Village with Chase. In the few years we'd been together, Chase had never exhibited the awful traits of Morton family males. He might not ever. But I couldn't trust that life with him would flow smoothly. If he let me down, I wanted to be able to bounce back. I needed to be able to take care of myself, just like Christine.

"I'm sorry," I told Tony. "I don't have any extra money. I lost my job, my apartment, and I think the roadside mechanic who got my car going duct-taped it together. I don't have anything right now."

He looked amazed. "No nest egg? Jessie, you always have a nest egg for something or other."

"Not this time. I'm sorry. I have to go to work."

"But they'll take the car if I don't pay for it, even if it is wrecked. I don't need much. I can pay you back by Christmas."

By this time, we were walking down the short flight of stairs from the apartment and out of the make-believe Dungeon where the plastic prisoners bemoaned their fate behind prison bars.

"I don't have any money, Tony. You might have to get a part-time job outside the Village."

"What about Chase? He has money, right? Couldn't you borrow some from him?"

"I probably could. But I'm not going to. Grow up. Figure out your own answers for a change."

He stared at me as though I were speaking another language. I supposed I was for him. The language of *not happening*. It wasn't something he recognized.

"Okay. I understand." He stared off into the distance past the Village Square and the King's Highway. "Where are you working anyhow?"

I told him about Father Christmas, his wife and children. "I should still be able to learn how to make toys. If not, I guess I'll be wiping down tables at one of the pubs. I can't afford to turn anything down right now."

"That's interesting," he said. "I just heard yesterday that some of the older residents knew that Santa guy. They said he'd worked here before."

"Which older residents?" I asked. Tony was always a great source of gossip, if not much else.

"You know, the really old ones—Merlin, Roger Trent—the old ones."

"Thanks." Maybe that would give me a place to start anyway. The Village had been open a lot longer than I'd been coming there. I recalled that moment between Chris and Livy when I thought something weird was happening between them. Maybe they knew each other. "I'm sorry about your car," I said sympathetically before we parted. "You know I'd help if I could. I'm just in bad shape myself right now, Tony."

"Marry Chase," he urged. "Live happily ever after. Forget all that crazy stuff about being on your own. Chase is a good guy, Jessie. He never messes around while you're gone. Go for it."

He smiled and left. I wondered why he thought I should get married when he seemed so unlikely to do it. Maybe because I'd have money to lend him again. Or maybe because he really cared about me. I hoped it was the latter.

I stopped walking to let a little goat cart go by. It was followed by a colorful goat girl with her crook and several other goats. Behind her was the Green Man, who was practicing on his leaf-covered stilts. He made me think about Bart, who'd played the Green Man once. He was so tall, he hadn't needed stilts. He was strong, too, like the proverbial ox.

I hoped he and Daisy were speaking again this morning. I'd try to get over to Armorer's Alley later for a chat.

I had to stop thinking about Chris's death, I reminded myself. Nothing good ever came of it. Detective Almond was going to take care of everything. Christine and her family might never know who killed Chris, or why. But that wasn't my job. My job was to make toys and stay out of trouble.

I could stay at the toy workshop, learn a new craft, and not let it bother me. It wasn't like the Village would pay me more because I found out what had happened.

I kept repeating that mantra over and over as I passed familiar faces like Fred the Red Dragon and Brother Carl, head of the Brotherhood of the Sheaf. I waved to each of them, always glad to see them. They were like family to me.

Chase had told me that the police had moved as much as they could of the toy-making materials from the old shop, which was still being investigated by the crime scene people, to the basement of the second manor house. No one would be able to access the place where Chris was killed until the police were finished.

I went to the basement door of the new workshop and entered, but I wasn't prepared for the sight that greeted me. Christine and all the children, dressed in their costumes, were hugging each other and crying. They all looked up when I walked in.

"You have to help us, Jessie," Christine said. "We have to find out who killed Chris."

Four

How was I supposed to ignore that? All of my mantra work went out the window. That left behind my own suspicious nature. Someone killed Chris, taking him from his family. We had to do something.

"What did the police say?" I asked, closing the door behind me.

Everyone started talking at once. Christine had to quiet the children down before she could answer.

"Basically nothing," she said finally. "But they asked me plenty of questions. Now they want to question all the kids. I think they have a theory, but they won't tell me what it is. I don't know what to do. Do you think they can find Chris's killer?"

"I don't know. They don't know the Village."

"Exactly! Which is why I think we should turn to you and Chase for help," she explained.

I looked at all the tearstained faces. This was the right

thing to do, even though Chase wasn't going to like it. "Chase works with the police. He doesn't like to do anything without them. But you and I can look around and ask questions. I already have a few I'd like answered."

"That sounds like a good place to start," Christine agreed. "I think we should write a journal or something where we can chronicle our search for what happened to my husband."

"We want to help, too," chorused a few of the older children.

"Us, too," the twins, Joy and Star, said at once.

"So what about the journal?" I encouraged everyone to take a fresh look at what had happened to Chris. "Let's think about what we know for sure."

Christine brought out a lovely, hand-bound notebook. We all sat down at one of the workshop tables, and she began writing down everything we could think of.

"I left him in the workshop to meet with Jessie," Merry Beth said. "He was alone, getting ready to set up and make some toys."

"Did anyone else come to the workshop after that, before I got there?" I asked the group.

Heads shook, indicating they hadn't. "But we weren't watching the whole time," Garland admitted.

"Jolly, you were down there talking with Daddy right before you and Mom left for the store," Merry Beth said.

They all turned to look at Jolly. "What?" he demanded. "I just wanted to ask him not to call me Jolly again in front of people. That's all."

"You think you have a bad name. What about me?" Garland said. "I'm a Christmas decoration!"

The kids started talking about how much they all hated their seasonal names. Christine finally broke it up and they quieted down. "Your father and I did the best we could to keep you happy, healthy, and fed. We chose your names to go with the important calling your father had. I don't want to hear a bunch of complaining."

No one said anything else about it. I felt this discussion wasn't getting us very far. I wanted to ask Christine about Chris working in the Village before and if he'd left behind any jealous girlfriends, but I didn't want to do it in front of the kids. Those topics were too adult for them.

Christine looked at what she'd written. "This isn't much help, Jessie. What else should we do?"

"What about enemies?" I asked. That seemed a safe subject. "Did Chris have any enemies?"

They all took a moment and thought about that. "Do bill collectors count as enemics?" Merry Beth finally asked. "They seemed to call and threaten Daddy a lot."

"This is neither the time nor the place to discuss problems with our finances," her mother chastised.

"Actually, this is the best time and place for it. Were there a lot of bill collectors?" I asked Merry Beth.

"I'll say!" Her bright blue eyes opened wide. "People called all the time. They said some really bad things sometimes when I wouldn't let them talk to him. I don't really understand all the details." She glanced at her mother.

"We owe some bills," Christine confirmed. "It was this stupid life he wanted to lead. Always moving around from one place to the next. I kept saying, 'Let's settle down someplace with plenty of tourists, like Dollywood or Williamsburg.' People would have respected him for his craftsmanship."

"Why did he want to keep moving?" I asked. "Was he afraid to stay in one place?"

"It was like a hobby for him," Jolly said. "Once I saw

him throw a dart on a map and that's the next place we went. You remember, Mom. Six hot months in Arizona without any kids around, just old people who wanted to sit on Dad's lap."

Christine passed her hand across her eyes. "I'm sorry you saw that, Jolly. But your father loved you and all the rest of us very much. He was always trying to find the perfect place. It wasn't easy for him."

"But did he ever borrow money from someplace outside of a bank or other financial institution?" I was hoping to get away from Chris's character flaws—at least from his family's point of view. At the rate they were going, there would be nothing good left for the younger kids to remember.

Christine thought back. "The Santa Fund loaned us money a few times. But that's what they're for. Sometimes it can be tough between jobs. Everyone pays in something, and then they can use it during the bad times."

That didn't seem to be anything like a loan shark, which was what I'd been thinking. There wasn't much to put in the journal. There didn't appear to be any good reason for killing Chris.

"Do you know anyone here in the Village?" I asked. "Chris mentioned working with Queen Olivia and King Harold. Did he have a good relationship with them?"

Christine raised her eyebrows and shot back, "A little *too* good, if you know what I mean. I told you we had a few problems in that general direction, Jessie. But that was a long time ago. I'm sure your king and queen remember Chris, but I can't imagine either of them wanting to hurt him. They probably had some input in his coming here, but certainly not to kill him."

I wrote Olivia's and Harold's names in the journal anyway. Sometimes hard feelings lasted a long time. If Chris and Olivia were messing around when he was first at the Village, anything was possible.

I couldn't imagine Harold sneaking down here and killing Chris—it would take a few knights to assist him—so that was probably a dead end. Livy, well, that seemed like another implausible idea.

I was about to ask another question when the door to the workshop flew open and a crowd began to spill into the basement area.

"Oh my heavens!" Christine put her hands to her face. "I completely forgot that the new Father Christmas was visiting the shop this morning. Quick! Everyone look busy."

I sat down at the nearest table and hid the journal under some thin pieces of wood. I wasn't sure what to do to look busy, but the Christmas twins, Joy and Star, sat on either side of me and started right in making fire trucks. They were young, but they knew exactly what to do.

"And here is my workshop." The new Father Christmas led the way for a pack of reporters. "I enjoy spending time here making toys for the good girls and boys."

Chase was right. The actor Adventure Land had hired to take Chris's place looked more like the Burger King than a Christmas figure.

True, he wore a long red velvet cape and matching outfit, much like the one Chris had worn. His black boots were shiny, and the brass buttons on his jacket were polished. But his face looked molded, unreal. I didn't know if they'd put too much makeup on him or what. He looked like a large plastic doll.

Of course, the only reason a mob of reporters from the Myrtle Beach area were interested in the Village was because someone had died there under mysterious circumstances. While the new Father Christmas went on about the toys and the spirit of the holiday, the reporters were asking questions about where the body had been found. They took long videos of the children and Christine, speculating on when the police would release information on the case.

"Do you have any problem with taking over the role from a man who was murdered just yesterday?" A reporter whose badge said she was from Charleston got right to the point.

New Father Christmas grinned. "It's very sad when someone dies. Believe me, I have mourned my predecessor extensively. But life is short, and there are thousands of little children who are still waiting to talk to their favorite person in the whole world—me."

Everyone kind of smirked at that. The reporters threw more questions at him, which he answered in ever more irritating ways. When one of the reporters asked him to comment on why he thought someone would want to kill Chris, that was enough for Christine.

"My husband was a good man. I won't have you defaming his name and reputation. None of you have the right to ask questions about him. You should all leave."

Everyone was stunned by her outburst—until they realized who she was. Then the reporters turned on her, the cameramen zooming in on her tearful face, as though she were an alien newly arrived from outer space.

Christine, probably realizing what she'd let herself in for, jumped up and walked quickly out the door. The reporters followed her like flies buzzing after a garbage truck. She'd probably saved her children a lot of embarrassment—the reporters would've been happy to question them, too.

The kids and I were left in the basement workshop with the new Father Christmas, who tried in vain to call back the reporters, promising them a show they wouldn't forget.

When he saw the reporters weren't interested, he turned on the rest of us as his only audience.

"I can see all of you have been hard at work." He smiled and sounded like a kindergarten teacher on the first day of school. "Father Christmas—that's me now—will be making stops in here from time to time with visitors. Try to keep your toy making tidy, okay? We want the visitors to be happy."

Jolly got up and walked out. I didn't blame him. It was bad enough they'd lost their father yesterday. They shouldn't have had to put up with a comedian making jokes about him.

"That elf doesn't look very happy," New Father Christmas said to me. "I guess that leaves you in charge since you look like the only one here over the age of twelve. How would you like to be my liaison with the elves?"

"We're not elves," I flatly told him. "And these children belong to the Father Christmas you're replacing. Have some compassion."

He smiled and looked around. "I guess none of you are into this today. You know what? That's fine. We'll all learn to get along. You'll see. Now, you, elf liaison, you go get Father Christmas some coffee. Double shot. Nonfat milk. I'll be upstairs."

"I'm not an elf," I repeated, a little more emphatically. "I'm not your liaison, and you can get your own coffee. Go away."

The new Father Christmas finally convinced Merry Beth to go to the Monastery Bakery for coffee. I told her she didn't have to go. She said she'd rather get coffee than sit there any longer.

She wasn't gone more than a minute before Queen Olivia, in a gold and white maternity gown, came briskly into the workshop. "Have we missed the press conference?"

New Father Christmas shrugged. "They were here. Now they're out there, chasing the widow, I believe." He smiled at the queen as he took in her crooked crown and the jewels slightly askew on her bosom. "You missed the excitement, my good lady."

It was said in a perfectly charming voice, but one did not address the queen as *my good lady*. I knew there was going to be fireworks. I got the rest of the children together, and we put our arms around one another. I wished Christine would hurry back. I didn't know a lot about taking care of young children, and the two oldest ones were gone.

Queen Olivia's page joined us in the workshop. Obviously the two of them had hastily garbed themselves to seek out some publicity for the Village. Too bad they were too late.

But the page's arrival saved us from one of the queen's rampages. "Tell this buffoon, my royal page, that he must never address us again without proper knowledge of protocol or we will feed him to the sharks in Mirror Lake."

She looked very regal except for her enormous baby bump. The tone was accurate, but I could've sworn I saw some tears welling in her eyes. Who knew maternity would soften Livy's nature? Apparently Chase had been right.

But Father Christmas was fast on his feet. He made a deep bow to the queen and kissed her royal hand. "Please excuse that a newcomer such as myself would be awed by your presence, Your Majesty. Allow me to present a small token to your most wonderful self."

It was a little hokey, but the queen seemed to enjoy it. Father Christmas handed her a small, wrapped gift from the pile of finished toys near the door. It could've been anything from a boat to a dinosaur. His choice was a good one—a pretty dolly with red hair that almost matched Livy's own bright color.

"You are a magician, good sir. We shall allow you to escort us from here to the Good Luck Fountain where we are judging an art show in a few moments. Page, tell the trumpeter to announce that we are ready to leave." She looked my way and almost smiled. "We are happy to see you at this time, Lady Jessie. We hope you are enjoying your stay."

That was the first time the queen had *ever* wished me a good time. She rarely acknowledged anyone besides one of the attractive Village men. She had a thing for Chase, which annoyed me. Not much I could say since she was the queen. Better her than young, sexy Princess Isabel.

I nodded to her. She put her hand on New Father Christmas's arm, and they waltzed out the door together. At least that was over.

The kids were upset. Star and Joy were both crying for their parents. I hoped Christine would realize what was going on instead of spending all her time with the media people. I knew what she'd done had been for the best—but now I was wondering what to do next. Maybe I should buy them a turkey leg.

Garland saw his mother before I did. The children deserted me en masse and ran to her. Christine's face was red from crying as she hugged her children.

After a few moments, she looked up at me. "Thanks for staying with them, Jessie. And you know how you were wondering if there might be anyone here with a reason to kill Chris?"

"Did you think of someone?" I asked as I searched for the journal.

"Yes. You just met him. If anyone had a reason to see Chris dead, it's the new Father Christmas."

Five

Christine didn't want to discuss the issue around the children. I didn't blame her—although the curiosity almost killed me.

We made some toys. Chris had left behind setups for dollhouses, rocking horses, cars, trains, fire trucks, you name it. The setups were like kits that included pieces for the toys. Basically, the pieces had to be glued, stapled, or nailed together. Then the completed toys were painted and detailed.

It looked like there were enough setups for weeks until the fast-moving children got started. They really knew how to put things together. It was easy to see that they had been working at this their entire lives.

Jolly came back while we were working. He and his mother had a quiet conversation as she was working on new setups. Because creating the new wood pieces required using a saw, the children weren't allowed to participate.

After the mother-son talk, there were some tears and lots of hugging. Eventually Jolly and his mother came to an understanding, and Jolly took over cutting the wood. I thought this might be a good time for Christine and me to discuss her accusation about the new Father Christmas. But then Merry Beth returned after delivering coffee and the whole thing started all over.

I could only imagine what this small tribe must have been going through. Not only losing their father and husband but also having their tragedy made so public. I remembered not wanting to go to school after my parents died because people would ask about them. I knew I wouldn't be able to talk about them without crying. I didn't want people to laugh at me for that.

It seemed to be therapeutic for the children and Christine to continue working here. It was what they knew, what made their lives normal. We all worked in harmony for more than an hour before Christine called a halt for lunch.

The largest jar of peanut butter I'd ever seen was hauled out of a pantry and paired with jelly and bread. The children made sandwiches the same way they worked. Even Faith, the youngest, had a role. She spread jelly on one side of the bread while Joy and Star spread peanut butter on the other side. Holly put the two pieces of bread together.

For a while they were just happy little kids, teasing and giggling, while they made and ate their lunch in the workshop. Their spirits had definitely improved from the unhappy, teary-faced state I'd found them in when I'd arrived that morning.

Christine had been right about what they'd needed. It was hard to hold in all the questions I wanted to ask, but she had prepared for that, too.

"After lunch, I want everyone to wash up and you're

going to spend some time playing outside in the Village. Jolly and Merry Beth have some money for snacks and drinks. The nice people at Adventure Land gave me passes for all of you to ride the camels, go to the joust—whatever you want to do."

There were eight cheers that went up from the kids, who barely waited to thank her before going to wash their faces and hands. For once, I was proud to be part of Adventure Land. Despite the board of directors' scheming and money grubbing, Merlin's soft heart must have prevailed.

"Is Jolly in charge?" Merry Beth asked in a tone that said she wasn't happy about the idea.

"He is the oldest," her mother said. "But I'm giving you the cell phone. Keep it in your pocket, and if there's a problem, call me."

That satisfied the girl. She hugged Christine and took the badges each child had to wear to get in all the attractions for free. Seeing the family working together in this way made me tear up. Christine was a wonderful mother, able to handle so much and keep it under control. I couldn't even imagine how hard that must be with eight kids under the age of eighteen.

When all the kids were clean and had their badges pinned on, they kissed their mother good-bye and headed out for Renaissance fun, slamming the door to the workshop behind them. I wished I was going with them.

No sooner had the door closed than Christine collapsed into one of the wooden chairs set at the painting table and began crying. "How am I ever going to do this without Chris?" She looked up toward the ceiling. "How could you leave me like this?"

I hugged her even though I knew that wasn't the answer she was looking for. I had no idea what to say to help ease her pain. It wasn't like this was something that could be resolved by a hot cup of coffee or some chocolate. Those were the extent of my normal therapies.

"I know it wasn't his fault." Christine wiped her eyes with her ever-present white apron. "Now that I know that Edgar Gaskin is here, I'm more sure than ever that we know who murdered Chris."

I dropped into the chair beside her, reaching for the journal we'd started earlier. "Edgar Gaskin?"

"The new Father Christmas—you've met him now. He's taken Chris's job as he took his life."

There was so much bitterness in her voice, I had to ask why she felt so strongly about him. "It seems unlikely that he'd kill Chris and take his place here. That would be kind of obvious, wouldn't it?"

"Not for *that* man! He threatened Chris a few years back when Chris exposed him. Edgar had been stealing money from the Santa Fund. Chris caught him at it. Edgar replaced the money, but the Santa Fund board decided he could never be in a position of authority for the group again."

"What did he threaten Chris with?" I wrote it all down, wishing I had a keyboard instead of a pen.

"They got into a fistfight that was all over the evening news in Chicago," she explained. "It's not often you see Santas brawling on the street, especially during the holidays. Edgar swore he'd get back at Chris. Nothing happened immediately. We forgot about it. But I don't think it's a coincidence that Edgar has taken Chris's job."

I looked at what I'd written in the journal. "I was wondering about Olivia and Harold. I know that you and Chris knew them. Do you think they could be involved?"

"I don't really know them personally. But I know of them. I can't imagine Harold still being upset about Chris sleeping with Olivia. I met them when we first arrived, and they seemed very polite. I was mad when Chris told me who Olivia was, but I got over it. That was a long time ago, before Chris and I were married."

I stopped writing. "Was Chris married before you?"

"Yes. He was divorced."

"Do you know her name? Does she work here?"

"Her name is Alice. I've never met her. If she works here, Chris didn't know. He would've said something. He was good about preparing me, like with Olivia. We had no secrets, even about the unpleasant things."

"I guess I was just looking for some common denominator. I've heard that Chris wasn't new here. He might have known his killer."

"Well there's no point in looking further than Edgar," she told me. "If we check into his whereabouts the last few days, no doubt we'll find out what happened."

I closed the journal, not wanting to cause her any more stress. And she knew Chris's life better than I did. Edgar seemed a likely suspect—more likely than Livy, whose affair with Chris had ended years ago. I couldn't imagine Harry even recalling the number of people either of them had slept with since they'd come to the Village.

Their infidelities were legend. Harry flirted with the ladies-in-waiting. Livy secretly met knights outside the castle. Everyone knew about it, and it hadn't seemed to matter to the couple—until last year.

There had been a change between them last year that had produced their first offspring. At first, Harry had been reluctant to acknowledge the baby was his. Something had changed his mind, though even the most prolific gossips in the Village didn't know what that was.

Since then, they'd been the perfect couple, outfitting their royal nursery and sweetly spending their hours together waiting for their heir. No one who hadn't known them before Livy's pregnancy would ever guess what they'd been like previously.

"I'll see what I can find out about Edgar's arrival at the Village," I promised. "If he got here before Chris died, Detective Almond might be willing to listen to that theory."

"I can call the Santa Fund, too," Christine added. "They know where any working Santa is, even between jobs. It's how they keep in touch to help them with employment."

I helped Christine make more pieces to put together for the toys. The family had a quota they'd promised to fill for the season. Christine said a number of the toys were already on back order from their website. Apparently, they did everything they could to support their family as Christmas characters.

We got a call a little later from the Father Christmas photo area. Even though Adventure Land had brought in extra hands, they needed help with the crowd that wanted to sit on Father Christmas's lap. Christine wanted the children to have the rest of the day to themselves, so I volunteered my services.

As we walked from the workshop to the photo area in the next manor house, we saw one of the dry runs for Livy's future trip to the hospital. Like everything else the royals did, it involved a parade of support workers going from the castle to the Main Gate.

"How pregnant is the queen?" Christine asked, smiling at the spectacle.

"She's supposed to be due at Christmas. I'm surprised they aren't planning on picking her up in a helicopter and flying her there."

"Maybe they couldn't fit the jugglers and ladies-in-waiting into a helicopter," she said. "I admire her style. I had Jolly in an elevator in a department store in Dayton, Ohio. Chris delivered him. I always waited too long. Of course, they all had to be born after Thanksgiving, our busiest time of year."

I laughed at that, thinking how unique her life had been with Chris. Maybe it wasn't so bad living outside what most people think of as normal society. Harry and Livy had certainly done it for many years. I knew quite a few couples who lived and worked in the Village. Their lives weren't the same as those of nine-to-five workers, but they were good nonetheless. I wished I could convince myself that living here with Chase, giving up my hope of tenure at some big college, didn't signal disaster.

We were walking close to the cobblestones to avoid a group of children. They were having pictures taken with various Village characters, including Merlin the Wizard.

I noticed a knight coming down the cobblestones at a high rate of speed. Visitors and Village residents got quickly out of the horse's path. It appeared that the rider had lost control of his mount—until he took a sharp turn directly into our path, scattering the children.

"What in the world?" Christine asked as he came closer and his lance went down in a fighting position. "Jessie, I think this rider might be in trouble."

But I realized with terrible clarity that the rider wasn't in trouble—we were. He seemed to have complete control of the horse, and he was directing the animal right at us.

"Get out of the way!" I yelled, pushing her into one of the small walkways between the manor houses.

Christine yelled but moved quickly, especially considering the long skirts that kept us from actively running from the horse. A pretzel vendor, not realizing the situation, wandered between us and the horse, giving us a few precious seconds to get out of the way.

Pretzels flew everywhere as the horse collided with the small cart. The vendor was flung back away from the horse's hooves. The knight's lance got caught up in the yellow and white spokes of the cart. The pretzel banner tangled in his armor.

The rider never broke his stride. Christine and I were just inside the narrow pathway as the horse galloped by. I could feel the breeze from the fast-moving animal and see the flecks of foam on his mouth. I realized the knight must have ridden him hard for quite a while. Where on earth had he come from?

The horse and his rider continued on their course of destruction and mayhem, swerving back on the cobblestones past the startled visitors emerging from the privies and the first aid station. Then they charged through the Main Gate and into the parking lot, never slowing as they continued out of view.

"What was that all about?" Christine asked, brushing grass from her gown. "Do they gallop through like that every hour or something?"

"No. That's not like the Sheriff of Nottingham catching Robin Hood," I assured her. "That was dangerous and reckless. I don't know who it was, but it looked like he swerved toward us on purpose."

She blinked several times, and her normally pink face grew pale. "That's ridiculous. Why would someone want to hurt us?"

"I think that's something we should find out." I thought about what Grigg had said. Maybe the killer was after me because he or she thought I could identify him or her.

Security guards were already in the area. They began

helping people to their feet, cleaning up the pretzels that had spilled, and assuring everyone that they were sorry for the accident.

I knew Chase wouldn't be far behind. He'd be there to calm everyone down and hand out free passes to those who wanted them. A runaway horseman hurtling through the Village wasn't something Adventure Land wanted the media to find out about. As it was, there were probably a few people with video phones who had already sent the event to YouTube.

"I'd better get upstairs," Christine said.

"Wait a minute. Let's talk to Chase about this," I said. "He'll want to know about the rider coming at us."

"They need me up there," she replied. "Besides, I don't think he was coming at us any more than he was that poor pretzel vendor, Jessie. It was just panic, that's all. We're fine. I'm sure they'll sort it all out."

I was amazed that she couldn't see that the pretzel vendor was just unlucky enough to have been between us and the rider. Maybe she couldn't handle any more drama right now. I could understand that. But Chase needed to know what had really happened.

"All right. I'll talk to Chase, then come and help out." I looked at the line of visitors standing on the manor house stairs waiting to have their picture taken with Father Christmas. With all those children on hand, the Village was fortunate the stampeding steed had not caused serious harm.

"That was insane!" Merlin said as Christine smiled and walked past the children on the stairs. "Who let that madman ride that horse through here in such a manner? I'll have someone's head for it!"

Most people in the Village didn't realize that Merlin,

who lived in the apothecary near the castle with a stuffed moose head named Horace, was the corporate head of Adventure Land. He was another example of a person who lived in the Village but still managed to have a somewhat normal life—as normal as any corporate head who wore a purple robe with stars and a pointy hat.

"I think he was going after Christine and me," I said. "He put his lance down in attack position when he saw us."

"Why would some knight want to hurt you two? Not very chivalrous!" Merlin looked around the crowd and shook his head. We could both hear the sound of an ambulance approaching the Main Gate. "The board isn't going to like this."

Chase joined us. "What happened out here? Jessie, were you here when the knight came through?"

I explained everything I saw—including the threat to either me or Christine. Or both. "I don't know who it was, but I think he might have been after us. Maybe he was the killer."

"If you and Christine were together, it could've been either one of you."

"Or both of them," Merlin added. "Not that it matters. You have to get out there and do some damage control, Bailiff. I can't believe someone called an ambulance. How hurt could they be?"

It truly didn't look like anyone was badly hurt. But the arrival of an ambulance suggested someone was already thinking about suing the Village. Adventure Land handled dozens of lawsuits every year for everything from back injuries allegedly sustained while riding the camels to cuts and bruises suffered while navigating the climbing wall.

Merlin was done with the scene and moved off quickly so as not to be involved once the media got there. The security guards continued their cleanup efforts. No one wanted to spoil the Renaissance mood for longer than necessary. But a big emergency services vehicle with flashing lights right in the heart of the Village was enough to put anyone off.

"I'm sure the rider was after us," I repeated to Chase. "I don't know why. But it wasn't like any runaway horse I've ever seen. Maybe the killer wants me out of the way because he thinks I saw him, and he wants to kill Christine because he killed her husband. I don't know."

"But you're not hurt, right?" He put his arm around me.

"No. A little shaken up and a lot curious, but that's about it."

"Don't let your imagination work overtime. It was probably just one of the new knights who lost control of his horse. You know how easy it is to let the lance slip as you're riding. Let me check into it."

"Okay. I'm going to help with the Father Christmas photography again. Wait until I tell you about the new Father Christmas!"

"I have to go and deal with this. Promise you won't get in trouble trying to investigate anything by yourself."

I squinted up at him, the sun behind his head. "I don't know why you'd ask me to lie to you that way. I'll see you later."

Six

Christine and I worked the crowd waiting to have their pictures taken with Father Christmas. There were coloring pages to give out, pictures to take, and crying children to soothe. Christine was much better at that part than I was.

It wasn't long before the rest of the family had joined us. The parents and children, waiting sometimes for over an hour, enjoyed talking with Christine's kids, now dressed in their green elf outfits. The four young girls, Joy, Star, Faith, and Holly were very cute. They unwittingly did more to amuse the crowd than anyone else.

I watched Edgar, the new Father Christmas, while I worked. He wasn't as charming or genuine as Chris had been, but he had a certain flamboyant style that seemed to make everyone happy. I missed Chris and was sorry I couldn't have worked with him longer. I couldn't imagine how hard it must be for Christine and the children to carry on this way. Really, it was above and beyond what anyone could expect.

But I understood that there were bills to pay and contracts to fulfill. Christine had to do what was necessary to get by. She didn't have the luxury of breaking down.

Security guards for the Village came in at about five thirty to let everyone know that the Village was closing at six P.M. There were a lot of angry people even though they were given cards that would put them at the front of the line the next day. Adventure Land hadn't planned for people to wait in line so long, I guessed. These people should've been in and out more quickly, like at the games outside or the elephant rides. I wondered if there was a plan in place to make the wait shorter the next day.

Chase came by as we were sweeping up the gum wrappers and discarded coupons that littered the manor house floor. "I wanted to let you know what info I've gathered so far about the crazy rider who almost skewered you two this afternoon."

Christine stopped sweeping and shooed the children away to other tasks. "Please tell me Jessie was wrong and that the knight wasn't headed for either of us. I don't think I can handle anything else."

"There's no proof that it was anything more than a runaway. Some new knights have a hard time learning to control their horses. It happens."

"So we know who the rider was?" I asked him.

"No. Not yet. But we'll find out when he brings the horse back to the stables. There's a suit of armor missing, too." Chase shrugged. "I'm sorry. It gets out of hand sometimes. We took on a lot of new people for the holiday season. Training isn't always what I'd like it to be."

"That's all right. I'm glad no one was seriously hurt," Christine said. "I just hope you find out who it was."

I didn't say anything else. I knew Chase's visit was to make Christine feel better. He'd accomplished his task, but he'd left me with a lot of unanswered questions.

"Are you finished here, Jessie?" he asked with a smile.

"Of course she is," Christine said. "You two go on. We'll close up here. Thanks for all your help today, Jessie. I'll see you tomorrow."

I smiled, too, and said all the polite, pleasant things I should, but when I got outside with Chase, I let him know how I really felt. "I'm worried that someone is after Christine. We can't let those kids become orphans."

"I think your imagination is running overtime, my lady." Chase swept me a deep bow. "How do you know it wasn't someone after *you*? You were the one who might have seen the killer."

"You do that so well, Sir Bailiff." Betty from Bawdy Betty's Bagels winked and flirted as she passed us. "Would that I had a gallant like yourself to treat me so well."

Betty had always had eyes for Chase. She never minded letting him know about it.

"I would gladly acknowledge you as well, lady." Chase bowed to her, too. His gallant gesture set off a bout of giggles on her part. I was glad when she finally parted ways with us on the cobblestones.

"You weren't there," I reminded him, resuming our conversation. "I've worked the jousting ring. You know I don't panic because a runaway horse is coming my way. This was something else. We have to look into it."

"What do you suggest? I spoke with Sir Reginald, and he assured me that it was an accident and he would deal with the rider."

"When he gets back."

"What else can he do? He has a horse and armor that belongs to the Village. I don't think he'll want to keep them as a souvenir."

One of the security team members came running up to find Chase. "We have a problem at the elephant ride. One of the visitors is refusing to get off the elephant. He says he didn't get his full ride time because the animal trainers said the Village was closing."

Chase turned to me. "Hold that thought. I'll take care of this and we'll have dinner. Let's go to the Lady of the Lake. I'd like to eat there without being set upon by pirates for a change."

"They've started doing after-hour meals?"

"If you pay." He kissed me lightly, then followed security guards across the King's Highway toward the elephant and camel area.

I wasn't surprised to find that the Lady of the Lake Tavern was charging residents for meals. Usually residents received free meals after the Main Gate closed. These were leftovers, of course, but better than paying for dinner on the small salaries we made. I wondered if they at least offered reduced prices, like Polo's Pasta did.

I agreed with Chase about the constant pirate attacks on the tavern, which was located near the pirate ship's berth on Mirror Lake. It was all for the visitors, but after you'd been captured and taken to the ship a few dozen times, it got old. Not going along with the act, on the other hand, would ruin the experience for the visitors.

Based on the security guard's description of the incident unfolding at the elephant ride, I figured it would be a while before Chase could join me at the tavern for dinner. I decided to do a little snooping into Edgar Gaskin. Village records were kept at the castle, which was next door to the tavern. It wouldn't be difficult for me to pop in and take a look.

I cut across the King's Highway past Totally Toad Footstools and the Treasure Trove. Neither of these shops had actual crafts or artwork done on the premises. Not all of the shopkeepers were artisans. Some just brought in merchandise that looked like it could've come from the 1500s and peddled it to the visitors at a profit.

Not so Our Lady's Gemstones. I knew the owners actually cut and set their own jewelry. They were new arrivals at the Village—twins, like me and Tony. But no matter how hard I tried to feel differently, Rene and Renee still made me a little uneasy. They were spooky with their white hair, pale skin, and vampirelike habits. I'm not one to judge, but I skirted around their shop.

That brought me up by Polo's Pasta, which was closed for cleanup, and the Hanging Tree where they had mock pirate hangings from time to time. In between the two was the swinging wooden sign that marked the Lady of the Lake Tavern. The sign, with its half girl–half fish holding a sword in one hand and a tankard in the other, provided a colorful backdrop for visitors' photos.

There seemed to be no one at the castle gate farther up the hill from the lake, not even Master at Arms Gus Fletcher, who was a former professional wrestler. That was a good thing for me since his favorite pastime was pinching ladies' butts as they walked past him.

The record keeping and surveillance for the Village were computerized only two years ago. My friend Bart had done the job. Besides being a giant, he was also a whiz with computers. The first door to the right on entering the castle was his office. Most of the time, he wasn't there, unless there was a problem.

Of course, tonight, since I wanted to look through the records to see when Edgar had arrived at the Village, Bart was there to ask me questions.

"Hello, lady." He waved and smiled from his swivel chair at the corner of the cramped room. "What brings you up here?"

"I wanted to check someone's employment record." I was honest with him. "Is that okay?"

He frowned and shook his massive head. "You know I can't let you do that. Suppose everyone in the Village wanted to look at employment records. It wouldn't be fair, would it?"

"I suppose not." I sat beside him on a tall stool. "But suppose the person I'm looking for is a killer? That would be fair, right?"

He thought about it. "Is there a killer working in the Village right now? No one told me about it. What do you know?"

I told him about Chris's death. "His wife and I are investigating to help the police."

"Why?"

"Because the police can't be here all the time to do it." Even to my own ears, the explanation sounded lame. "And there are a lot of other reasons, too," I added hastily.

I wasn't really sure there were any other reasons besides my wanting to do it. And being curious, of course. Chase certainly wouldn't think there were.

Bart seemed to consider my reasoning (I hoped not so much that he could see the flaws in my logic) while he looked at the computers on the table in front of him. I couldn't tell what he was thinking, but when he turned and smiled at me, I thought that he'd decided in my favor.

"I think you should get permission from Adventure

Land to look at the employee records, lady. I think we might both get in trouble otherwise."

That wasn't the answer I wanted to hear. I thanked him and left him there fiddling with something I didn't understand—which was pretty much everything on a computer except how to go on the Internet.

As I was walking out of the tiny office, I saw Merlin approaching from the wide castle entrance. Maybe permission from a *part* of Adventure Land might be easier than I'd first thought.

"Lady Jessie." He greeted me with a respectful head bow that knocked his pointed hat off his scraggly white hair. "I hope I find you well."

"Better than this afternoon when that knight tried to kill me." I was formulating a plan to get the information I needed, which might or might not include a little blackmail.

"I'm sure no one was trying to kill you," he said. "Just a little mishap."

"That's not what I plan to tell the TV reporter who wants to interview me this evening. I think there's a killer on the loose in the Village. He killed Father Christmas, and now he wants to kill me. Or Christine."

Merlin shushed me and glanced around as though someone else might hear. "That could mean the Village being shut down, my lady. I know you wouldn't want that. We share a great love for this place, you and I. No matter how long you have to be away, you always come back."

"You're right," I agreed. "But something has to be done. If I can't at least try to find out who was behind that armor on the horse today, I'll have no choice but to talk to the press. I'm desperate, Merlin. No telling what I might do."

He looked around again—we were completely alone. Then he pulled me to the side of the entrance. "What do you want? I can't authorize any pay raises this year. I *can* get you free food vouchers from some of the shops."

Free food? I never knew that was possible. I was tempted, but I stayed on track. "I want to see the employee records."

He laughed. "Oh, is that all? Why didn't you just say so." He moved his star-crowned magic wand around in the air. "There you are. All taken care of."

"Merlin—"

"You can't look at employee records unless you work for Adventure Land."

"I work for Adventure Land," I reminded him.

"That's not what I mean. You have to be *authorized* to look at the employee records and work for Adventure Land. You don't have that clearance."

"Give it to me then," I persisted. "I'm going to meet that reporter in thirty minutes at the Pleasant Pheasant. I think I may have been injured trying to get away from that runaway knight this afternoon."

Merlin made a face like he'd been eating lemons, but finally nodded. "All right. You win. But someone will have to be there with you. We can't have you running through all the computer files willy-nilly."

"Bart's in there right now. All you have to do is tell him it's okay for me to look at those records."

"Done." He looked up at me with his keen eyes narrowed. "Would you *really* do something to close down the Village?"

Since I hadn't seen the files yet, I wasn't admitting to anything. "You'll never know. Let's go in."

Merlin gave Bart the okay for me to scan through the files. Bart shrugged and set up a monitor for me to look at. "This will only be employee files," Bart said. "You can't see the inner workings of the Village. Sorry."

I didn't care about that. I just wanted to see when Edgar was hired. I thanked Merlin and got to work.

What I hadn't considered was that thousands of people worked in the Village every year. They came and went like Christmas. Only a small group of permanent shopkeepers and characters kept it going year after year. The rest were like a cast for a major movie production. They were mostly extras who worked for a few days or a few weeks and moved on. Many of them were high school and college drama students, which had something to do with why the Village was so strange.

The files were set up by date on some pages and by name on others. They mostly went back ten years, though the Village had been open for twenty. No doubt most of the remaining files were in paper folders somewhere in the castle waiting for someone to put them into the computer.

"Who knew Robin Hood had so many Merry Men?" I said absently to Bart.

"I know, right? How many does he need? And how many are still out there in Sherwood Forest? They have five acres of trees. There could be a Merry Man behind each one of them."

There had also been ten Mother Gooses down through the years. They must have all looked exactly the same, because I'd never noticed the change.

The Village had employed hundreds of knights as well, for the joust and other promotional activities. Visitors loved the knights. I took a slight detour here and looked for the knights most recently hired. Of course, that section was set up alphabetically, so I had to trace down the hiring dates individually.

Ten new knights had been hired in the past week. I wrote down all of their names. They were from all over the

Southeast, from Virginia to Florida. Apparently, some people didn't mind traveling if it meant getting paid to wear a suit of armor.

I didn't know if the geographical information would help me find the knight who'd attacked me and Christine, but it couldn't hurt to know. I scribbled it down.

"There have been ten William Shakespeares and a dozen Galileos. You know, I thought the same two guys had always played those characters," I commented to Bart.

Bart kind of *humphed* but said nothing. He looked absorbed in his own work and didn't find my observation all that interesting.

It was fascinating reading about all the people who had worked here. I knew Roger Trent had been a bailiff for the Village before Chase. He now created glass art at the Glass Gryphon. He'd been a police officer before he'd come to work here. He'd been injured on the job and had taken early retirement from that life.

But what I didn't know was that there had been a bailiff *before* Roger. I laughed out loud when I read the name of the original peacekeeper here. Officer Donald Almond. Now Detective Almond. I would've given anything to see a picture of him in tights! Too bad these were only text records.

And all this time he'd called us freaks and weirdos. I couldn't wait to see him again.

The records listed three Robin Hoods and fourteen Lady Godivas, three of whom had filed sexual harassment charges against other characters in the Village. Of the twelve Green Men who'd come and gone over the years, three had broken their legs falling off of the stilts they used for the part and had collected workman's compensation as a result. The five Fred the Red Dragons and six blacksmiths, however, seemed to have enjoyed relatively drama-free employment here.

"There's no mention of the monks being hired," I told Bart.

He swiveled in his chair to look at me. "That's because they don't get paid to work here. Don't ask me. I guess it's some kind of religious calling."

That surprised me only a little. The monks from the Brotherhood of the Sheaf were a little stranger than even the strangest drama student. They'd evolved their own secret society with strict guidelines and ceremonies involving the making of bread.

I finally reached a page of recently hired side characters. Chris and Christine were there—and so was Edgar Gaskin. The new Father Christmas had been hired at the same time that Chris and Christine had been hired. He'd been given a room in the castle instead of normal Village housing.

In the "Hired by" field of Edgar's database file, Olivia's name appeared instead of the standard *Adventure Land*. The queen had hired a second Father Christmas before anything had happened to the first Father Christmas.

"It looks like Christine was right. Edgar was here before Chris was killed."

Bart grunted and ignored me.

Seven

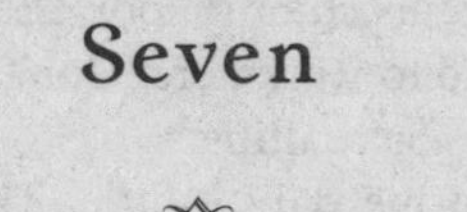

"Find what you're looking for?" Bart asked about an hour later, apparently having noticed my *ahas* even though he hadn't responded to any of the comments I'd directed at him earlier.

"I think so. Thanks."

"So now you can catch the killer?"

"Maybe. I'll let you know."

"Okay. Thanks."

I was about to get up when I noticed something else in the file. *Original king and queen of the Village, Chris and Alice Christmas.*

There had been another king and queen at the Village! Did anyone else know that? Probably the characters who had been at the Village since it first opened.

I looked at the dates. Chris and his ex-wife had worked as king and queen for only a few months before Livy and Harry jumped onboard.

My mind was racing with the implications of what I'd learned. I almost couldn't think coherently.

I already knew Livy'd had an affair with Chris and that Chris had been married before. Edgar had a grudge against Chris for turning him over to the Santa Fund for embezzlement. Livy had hired Edgar to take Chris's place *before* Chris was murdered. And Chris had been the first king of Renaissance Faire Village.

Did any of that have anything to do with Chris's death?

I thanked Bart for his help and went out the same way I'd come in.

Chase was waiting for me at the Lady of the Lake Tavern. "Where have you been?"

"Looking up employee records." I was almost bursting to tell him my news.

"Jessie—"

"What? Merlin told Bart it was okay." I didn't go into the circumstances involving that request.

"Why?"

"It's a long story."

We sat down at one of the wood tables made to resemble the no-frills furniture of the 1500s or 1600s. The wood was very distressed, unpainted, and heavily stained with food and beer. The workers at the tavern kept the tables clean and rubbed beeswax into the wood each day, resulting in an odd patina.

"Okay," Chase said. "It looks like we've got some time since you didn't come in and order for us. What's up?"

I told him about Harry and Livy hiring Edgar Gaskin before Chris had died. "Don't you think that's a little strange? It's not like you can have two Father Christmas figures in the Village at the same time. That would mess with all the little kids' fantasies."

We ordered from the menu, such as it was. Even though we'd be paying rather than getting the free after-hours left-overs typically doled out to employees, there wasn't a nor-mal selection. We had a choice of chicken or cheese with bread and beer.

"I know where you're going with this," Chase said when we were alone again. "You think Gaskin killed Chris to get his job."

"Not really. But that could be part of it." I leaned across the table closer to him, hoping to prevent anyone overhear-ing our conversation. "Livy had an affair with Chris. It was years ago."

"Father Christmas Chris?"

"Yep. Gaskin was directly hired by Livy, not Adventure Land. He's even staying at the castle. Chris didn't stand a chance. They were both out to get him."

Chase drank some beer and shook his head. "Okay, Sherlock. Why would Gaskin need to take Chris's job, espe-cially this time of year when there are thousands of Santa jobs out there?"

"Elementary, my dear bailiff." I told him about Chris catching Gaskin stealing money from the Santa Fund. I also explained my theory about Livy possibly wanting to kill Chris. "You know, the whole scorned woman thing. Of course, we'd have to find out if Chris was the one who broke up with Livy. So Livy and Edgar both could have had a motive to kill Chris. I think it's time to call in Detective Almond. Or should I say *Bailiff* Almond."

I couldn't resist telling Chase about Almond being the first bailiff.

"Please tell me there were pictures." He laughed.

"Nope. I wish. But I'll enjoy seeing his face when I tell him."

"You seem to have the Father Christmas case all sewn up," he said. "It sounds legitimate, although if your theory about Livy is correct, she'd have to spend the rest of her life killing off everyone she's ever been with. I'll give Detective Almond a call in the morning."

"There's something else." I told him about Chris and his first wife being the first king and queen. "Did you know that?"

"No. That was before my time. But Roger probably knows all about it."

"That's what I was thinking. I don't know if it has anything to do with Chris's death, but it's a good story. I'd like to hear the rest of it."

"Me, too. Just be careful how hard you push, Jessie. The person who killed Chris may still be here at the Village. Let's not get him riled up before we find out who he is."

The rest of the evening was filled with talking to old friends who stopped at our table. I was surprised that so many residents would pay to eat here when they could eat free at Peter's Pub or The Pleasant Pheasant. Maybe it was just a fad and would wear off quickly.

The Tornado Twins—Diego and Lorenzo—were kicked out of the tavern for bringing squirt guns in. Of course, that was their thing. Ginny Stewart, the owner, even spit on them as her wenches threw them out the door.

"Those two never learn." Ginny, always in the same green gown, bent close to Chase so he could have a good look at her enormous bosom. "Let me get you some cheesecake, dearie. I know you work hard out there for us. You deserve some cheesecake."

"Thanks," Chase said. "But maybe not tonight."

"I'll bring the girl some, too, if you like." Ginny sighed as though it was a difficult offer to make.

"That's okay," Chase insisted. "Next time."

"All right. But if you find yourself with a craving for . . . cheesecake, you know where to find me." She kissed his cheek and moved on.

"That woman," I muttered. "Someone needs to trim her sails."

From the table behind us came a voice I always hated to hear. "She pushes the whole meaning of *trollop* a bit to the edge, eh, Ducks?"

Wanda Le Fey was sitting close enough to touch me. A long shiver went down my spine when I realized she was there.

"Hello, Jessie, Chase." Master Archer Simmons nodded. "It's good to see you both."

"We need to get out of here," I whispered to Chase.

"The food isn't here yet," he reminded me.

"Wanda is almost sitting on top of me. You know what that means."

"You're paranoid, Jessie. You'll be fine."

"Then switch sides with me. She can't hurt me if she can't touch me." I couldn't believe he was accusing me of being paranoid about Wanda. Surely he remembered all the things she'd done to me over the years. It isn't paranoia when you *know* someone is out to get you.

"Let's just eat." The food had arrived, and Chase didn't want to move. "Eat fast and we'll leave before she can do anything too terrible."

I did exactly that. I was finished with my cheese and bread and had drunk the last of my beer long before Chase had finished his chicken. "Are you ready yet?" I asked him, mindful of the side of me near Wanda.

"I was hoping to have another beer. I'm not driving. I think it would be okay."

"If you hurry." I held up my hand to attract a serving wench to the table.

"Jessie, you make too much out of Wanda's sense of humor. It's a little odd sometimes, but she has a good heart. She's always there for anyone who gets injured."

Yeah, I agreed silently. *There to misdiagnose and mistreat.*

It took another five minutes for Chase to finish eating and drink most of his second beer. Already the big dinner crowd was dwindling, heading back to their homes around the Village. I kept hoping Wanda would leave, too. Each peal of her wacky laughter made me jump. I knew she was up to no good.

"Okay." Chase finally gave in. "I'm done. Let's go home."

He walked toward the door where Ginny was taking cash or Lady Visa. I started to follow him but couldn't get out of my chair. I tugged at my long skirt. It didn't appear to be stuck anywhere, but I couldn't stand up.

Chase came back after paying the bill. "I thought you were in such a big hurry to leave."

"I can't get up," I whispered to him. "Something's wrong."

"Aw, what's wrong, sweetie?" Wanda asked in a fake solicitous tone. "Cat got your tongue? Or does the chair have your butt?"

At that point, she let out a horrible laugh. Her cackles could be heard across the restaurant. I'd have bet even the pirates in the caves under the tavern could hear her.

And then I knew—I was the victim of one of the oldest pranks in the book. At some point, Wanda had glued my gown to the chair.

I've been through many embarrassing moments in the Village. But nothing compared to having to sit there while Chase and Wanda cut the skirt from my gown, exposing my chemise and loose-fitting bloomers (not so much Renaissance correct but necessary), while a tavern full of people watched.

I protested Wanda's aid since she was responsible for the prank, but Chase said he needed her help. What was I going to say?

After I was freed, I stormed out of the Lady of the Lake with one thing in mind—revenge. Residents of the Village loved to prank each other. I'd done my share of it, too. It's possible some of my pranks were worse than what Wanda had done. There *was* that time that I had the portable toilet dumpers collect one of their toilets with a pirate inside. That was a good one.

In all fairness, the pirate had already pranked me. He'd had it coming.

Not so, this case. I studiously avoided Wanda and would never have pranked her, mostly because I was afraid of her. But not anymore.

I wasn't sure what I was going to do to her in return for her prank, which would be all over the Village by morning, but it would be good. It would be something that would live in Village prankdom history for a long time.

"Wait up, Jessie." Chase ran out of the tavern after me. He was laughing. "Don't take it so hard. It could've been worse."

"I asked you to switch sides with me. She would never have pranked *you* that way."

"Probably not, but I've had my share of pranks. Everyone has. And you've pranked plenty of people, too."

"You're right," I agreed, walking as fast as I could across the King's Highway in my underwear. "And I'll make sure to get her back. But do you know what Portia is going to say when she sees this gown tomorrow? She's not going to care that I was pranked. They'll probably take the money for it out of my salary."

"I'm sorry. I'll pay for it."

I'd have found his offer more comforting if he hadn't been smiling when he said it. "This isn't funny, Chase."

"It is, you know. I'm sorry but it's funny." He tried to put his arm around me and I shrugged it off.

I noticed the light was still on in Christine's basement workshop. I needed some space, and I was pretty sure she wouldn't mind me stopping in to tell her my news—even if my bottom half was clad only in Renaissance underwear.

"I'm going to talk to Christine," I told him. "I'll see you later at the Dungeon."

"You're going in there like *that*?"

"I don't think she'll find it as funny as you do. See you later."

"Jessie. Come on. It's just a prank. It's funny."

"Later, Chase." I frowned at him as I opened the basement door. I wasn't sure if he could see me, but it felt like the right thing to do. I hated to be mad at him for what had happened, but he didn't have to be so cheerful about it. He could've immediately helped me come up with a suitable response.

Christine looked up from her work painting toys as I banged the door closed. "Jessie?"

"Sorry. I didn't mean to be so loud."

"It's late. Were you planning on working? What happened to your gown?"

I sat on one of the small wooden chairs across the worktable from her. She was wearing faded old jeans and a paint-spattered T-shirt that said Santa Rules! Her glasses had some paint flecks on them, and there was a blue streak on her cheek.

I explained what had happened to my gown. She shook her head but didn't smile. That made me feel better.

"Sometimes those pranks get out of hand. The members of the Santa Fund are always pranking each other, too. One time, Chris's beard was dyed pink through the whole Christmas season. One of the other Santas had rigged a balloon with pink dye in it and it burst in Chris's face when he was blowing it up for an event. He was lucky his eyes weren't affected. He lost three jobs because of that. It took a dozen washes, and then we still had to dye it white again."

I had to admit, that was a pretty good prank. I didn't laugh because she obviously took it as seriously as I took my recent run-in with Wanda. I realized I wouldn't have been as upset if one of the Tornado Twins or Friar Tuck had pranked me. Maybe this was a good time to get over my fear of Wanda once and for all.

"I found some interesting information from the Santa Fund," she told me. "It seems that I was right—Edgar was hired to be here at the same time as Chris. No one hires two Santas for the same gig. It's just not done."

I told her that I'd discovered the same thing in the Village records. "I know you said it had been a while since Chris and Olivia had . . . been involved, but Edgar was hired by the queen to be here. He's even living in the castle. There's something fishy about that."

Christine stopped painting a cute Ferris wheel. "Are you saying you think Olivia plotted with Edgar to kill my husband?"

"I don't know yet. We should go and talk to Livy first thing tomorrow morning. What do you know about Chris's ex-wife, Alice?"

She wiped her hands slowly on a towel. "I don't know. Not that much. She was long gone by the time I met him, and we were married for seventeen years. He only spoke of her briefly. Let's talk to her if you think it will help."

I knew I was holding back information, but I didn't know if Chris's being here twenty years ago meant anything yet.

"Chris was killed, Jessie. I want justice for him. It seems the only way that's going to happen is if you and I find that justice. I really appreciate your helping me."

We didn't say much after that, and I got the feeling that she wanted to be alone to sort through everything. So much had happened so quickly. She was handling all of it much better than I could have.

"I guess I better go home and change clothes," I said, getting up. "I'll be back tomorrow morning. Don't worry. We'll find a way to make all of this right."

She smiled but didn't speak. Tears were flowing down her cheeks, making the blue paint run down her neck. I didn't tell her. She could deal with it later.

The Village was dark and quiet when I stepped out of the lighted basement. It would be easy for me to get so caught up in trying to solve the mystery of Chris's murder that I'd lose sight of the emotional impact my efforts might have on Christine and the children.

He was gone and his family was left to fend for itself, no matter who had done the deed. Finding his killer wouldn't bring him back. But I hoped that by learning the truth and helping to put the killer away, I could bring some kind of peace to the family. Still, it was going to be a long, hard road for them either way.

Once the Village closed and the visitors went home, the area became like a small neighborhood of people who knew each other very well. True, there were the newbies who were lost for the first six months or so. But many of the residents were like family. They kept each other's secrets, fought, and pranked, but in the end, they belonged to the Village and this unique lifestyle.

The large stadium lights situated throughout the Village could essentially turn night into day, but they were only switched on in emergencies. That left the open parts of the Village between the residents' housing and the shops dark. But as I walked by the Village storefronts, lights still shone from some of the many windows. At Fractured Fairy Tales, assorted characters were rehearsing for the next day, and at the Monastery Bakery, the monks were making bread dough for the morning rush.

I waved to Mrs. Potts at the Honey and Herb Shoppe as I passed her window. She was busy baking her famous ginger cookies.

Some acrobats were practicing in the grassy area behind the Dutchman's Stage while a group of tiny terriers were learning their tricks for the show. The smell of roasting potatoes and grilling meats from the Three Pigs Barbecue wafted down the cobblestones.

The sights, smells, and sounds of the Village were as familiar to me as my own face. No matter how insecure I felt about the idea of living here full time, it was getting harder to leave and go back to that other life at the university.

Eight

When I arrived at the Dungeon, Chase apologized very nicely for laughing at me. There is no way to resist him when he works that hard.

The rest of the night was quiet in the Village. Chase and I slept through it without a single call about anything going wrong. The next morning, we went down to Fabulous Funnels for coffee and fruity funnel cakes.

"What's on the agenda for today?" he asked while we were having breakfast.

"Well, you're supposed to call Detective Almond for me. Then I'm going to get Christine, and we're going to question Livy."

"Okay. That wasn't something we'd talked about. I would've remembered."

"I know. But I think it might lead us to some other answers."

"I was worried that you might try to go alone and

question someone you thought had been responsible for the murder. That would be a mistake—even with Christine for backup."

"If I don't ask the questions, how will I know the answers?" I stabbed a strawberry with my plastic fork and plopped it into my mouth. Yum!

"Did you ever wonder why police officers travel in pairs?" he asked. "You watch a lot of police dramas on TV. Don't they usually have a group with them when they go in to snag the killer?"

I thought about it. "I don't know. I prefer the books and TV shows with the maverick cop who does it all by herself. Or a duo, like Cagney and Lacey."

"Give me some time to do my rounds and I'll go with you. If not, I'll send a security guard with you. I don't think you and Christine should wander into the castle and ask who killed Father Christmas."

"Okay." I shrugged. "I have to go and wrangle a new gown out of Portia this morning anyway. I can't walk around in my jeans all day."

"Just like that?" He eyed me suspiciously. "I say wait for me and you go along with it? That's not like you, Jessie. You wouldn't lie to me, would you?"

"Forsooth, good sir. I think you malign me. Your words wound my very spirit."

"Yeah. Whatever. There are no visitors to appreciate those pretty words, my lady. But if you don't wait after promising you would, I'll call for vegetable justice and clap you in irons."

"You don't have to threaten me. Not that I'm worried Livy will pull a gun and try to shoot us or anything."

Chase's radio went off, disturbing our breakfast. There

was a fire in a trash can near the blacksmith shop. Security was trying to put it out and wanted to keep him in the loop.

"I better go. I don't want the whole Village to go up in flames." He kissed me lightly. "I'll be at the workshop as soon as I can. Wait for me."

"I said I would. You don't have to keep saying it."

"With you, I can't say it often enough. Have you thought any more about staying with me in the Village?"

"Not really. I'm trying to find Santa's killer right now. But I'll get there."

A chorus of *oohs* arose when he kissed me again. Everyone loves a good Village romance. Chase and I were certainly that. I just wasn't sure if it was the kind of romance that lasts. Probably more to the point, I was afraid to find out.

I picked up my cloth bag filled with what remained of my gown from yesterday and trudged across the King's Highway where Bo Peep was herding her sheep for their early morning walk. Minstrels were set up at the Village Square, rehearsing their performance for the day. I noticed that Susan Halifax was playing the harp for that event. She'd injured her hand earlier in the year and had been unable to do anything but manage the Merry Mynstrel's Stage while it healed.

On the cobblestones ahead of me, the horse-drawn carriages were being readied for rides. Instead of the Cinderella blue and gold, the carriages, horses, and drivers were all wearing red velvet trimmed with white faux fur. The drivers' tiny little red hats sat cocked at a sassy angle on their heads, a large white feather tickling each of their noses.

At the castle, it looked as though some unseen workmen were experimenting with the snow, which was guaranteed to fall several times daily, according to the holiday brochure for the Village. Bart had been right. Rather than sprinkling down gracefully from above, the snow was shooting out of the castle, most of it ending up in Mirror Lake. The pirate ship, *Queen's Revenge*, was covered in it. I could hear the swearing and complaining from the pirates all the way from the costume shop near the Main Gate. They obviously needed to move the snowmaker to another location.

Portia was at her post, leaning her head against her hand in the open window. A few residents were in front of me, trading dirty costumes for clean ones. All of those costumes seemed to be in one piece, unlike mine. The trades went quickly, and I was soon confronted with Portia's pale, grimacing face.

"What is this?" she asked when she looked in my bag. "Is this one of the new Santa helper costumes? What happened to it?"

I explained that it wasn't my fault, that she should bill Wanda for the damages if she wanted to blame someone.

"Do you have any idea what these new costumes cost? And no one else had even worn this costume. Chase picked it up specially for you. I know Beth is going to have to get some money for this. This is damaged beyond repair."

Beth Daniels created all the costumes for the Village residents as well as rentals for visitors who wanted to look the part for a day. She also ran Stylish Frocks and made costumes for the royalty. She and I got along pretty well most of the time. I knew she hated to see her creations ripped apart like my gown had been.

"It wasn't my fault, Portia. It was a prank gone bad. I think you should garnish Wanda's wages for it."

"I'm not authorized to do that, Jennie."

"Jessie," I reminded her. "But you can take the money out of my paycheck, right?"

She frowned at me. "I'm certainly not taking it out of Chase's paycheck." She handed me a new green and white holiday gown. "Be careful with this one. You can't go around messing up all the costumes and get away with it."

"Don't worry. I'll stay away from Wanda." *Except for when I seriously prank her.*

"You'll get the bill for this with your next paycheck," she said.

"You'll have to take a number," I fired back even though I knew she wouldn't understand. "Thanks, Portia."

"You're welcome."

I took my new costume back to the Dungeon, plotting and scheming my revenge on Wanda the whole way. It wasn't going to be easy getting back at her. Since I always tried to stay as far away from her as I could, I knew nothing about her or her routines. I was going to have to remedy that without getting too close.

The green gown was pretty, and lighter than the one that Wanda had ruined. I knew the gown had cost hundreds of dollars. I shuddered even thinking about it. I made only five hundred dollars a month working at the Village. I hoped they'd take that into consideration.

I was finally dressed for the day—I didn't envy those poor, real-life Renaissance women who'd had to wear garments like these every day. Of course, ours were much simpler and didn't have the restrictions of that time. The costume gowns were made to look realistic but had modern conveniences, like hidden zippers.

I met William Shakespeare, who was on his way to his spot on the King's Highway where he would recite odes and poetry all day while flirting with the pretty girls who went by him.

He swept off his large, plumed hat and dropped into a

deep bow. "Good morning to you, Lady Jessie. I trust you are well this fine morning. You are looking particularly lovely. That green gown suits you well."

I curtsied to him and smiled. "My thanks, good sir. Your words are a soothing balm to my ears."

"May I escort you to your destination?" He held out his arm.

"If you have the time before the Main Gate opens, that would be wonderful. I love your new holiday brocade look. It's very colorful."

"There is always time to speak with a beautiful woman." He smiled and tucked my hand into the crook of his arm. "I hear you had an unfortunate run-in with Wanda last night."

Of course. Everyone knew by now. "Don't worry. I plan to seek revenge for the wrong."

He patted my hand as we began to walk down the cobblestones toward Squire's Lane. "Have I ever related the fact that Wanda and I had a short and ugly relationship once? Mayhap we might converse on ways to help you with that revenge—and seek my own at the same time."

Shakespeare and I parted company outside the manor houses at Squire's Lane. He had a few interesting ideas on how to get back at Wanda for her prank. It was going to take some time to decide on exactly the right course of action. I wanted it to be memorable.

It seemed odd that any of the Village attractions were in the brick manor houses. They'd stood empty for as long as I'd been coming here. I always wondered why they weren't used. Apparently, Adventure Land had been waiting for the right time.

The Main Gate wasn't open yet, but it would be any minute. I hurried across the damp, slightly snow-covered grass, anxious to reach the workshop before all the children came running in to see Father Christmas. I hoped Christine was up for a showdown with Edgar and Livy. If she opted out, I'd have to wait around for Chase, which would be rather deflating after my brave words to him earlier. But I wasn't sure if I should face my two chief suspects alone.

I opened the door to the workshop quietly. I knew Christine homeschooled the children first thing in the morning, and I didn't want to disrupt their lessons. But she was in the workshop, looking at a piece of paper, which she hastily shoved into one of the table drawers as I entered.

I said, "Hi, Christine. Something important?"

She jumped and almost lost her glasses. "Jessie. I wasn't expecting you this early." Her normally pink face turned a bright shade of red.

"We were going to the castle this morning, remember?"

She got to her feet quickly, not easy to do in her full, white gown. "That's right. What was I thinking?" She adjusted her glasses and the neckline of her bodice—Renaissance necklines can gape open very easily. Beth had probably changed her burgundy gown to match the new Santa's outfit.

I noticed that she'd made sure the drawer was closed. Whatever she'd put in the drawer wasn't something she wanted seen. "I hope I wasn't interrupting you," I said, hoping she'd tell me about the now-hidden paper.

"Oh no. Of course not. The children are finishing their reading. We have a little while before they want us at the manor house with Father Christmas. I'll just go and get my shawl and meet you outside." She smiled in a distracted way. I didn't say anything else about it.

Still, I couldn't help wondering what she'd been looking at.

The Main Gate had opened while I was waiting for Christine. Hoards of children poured in, thrusting and pushing their way toward the Father Christmas manor house. They looked clean and dressed up in their suits and ties, suits of armor, princess dresses, and Disney-character costumes. What pictures those were going to be!

"Do you think it's safe for us to just go up and accuse someone of killing Chris?" Christine asked as we walked past Eve's Garden to reach the castle.

"No. She doesn't." Chase was suddenly behind us. "That's why you two were waiting for me to finish my rounds before you came up here. Right, Jessie?"

"Of course," I lied with a smile. "We were going to wait for you at the entrance. I was about to mention that to Christine."

"Of course you were." He smiled back and put his arm around my shoulder.

"We're going to be diplomatic about this, right?" Christine looked at the two of us with a beginning-to-panic expression on her face.

"That's the plan," Chase assured her. "If we even have a hint that either Livy or Edgar—or anyone else, for that matter—could be involved in Chris's death, I'll call the police."

"Did you talk to Detective Almond this morning?" I asked him.

"He'll be here sometime today—unless we have to call him sooner."

Christine seemed satisfied that we weren't both completely crazy. I didn't bother mentioning *my* version of the plan—which didn't involve Chase, who could be a stickler for the rules, and which had *me* apprehending the killer myself, if I found him or her—since Christine seemed so relieved with Chase's version. Maybe Christine wasn't a maverick like me. She was probably a better-safe-than-sorry girl.

Gus Fletcher was at his post today in all his seasonal attire. He was a big man, broad shoulders and wide hips. He was wearing his usual helmet and armor, but he'd tucked a sprig of mistletoe into his breastplate. "Good morning to all of you." He swept a slight bow and kissed Christine's hand.

While I was watching him with Christine, he managed to tweak my butt. I yelped and slapped at his hand. "You need to lay off," I yelled at him. "I don't know why they haven't fired you for that."

"Because I'm too good-looking, and who else would want this job?" He laughed at his own joke and grasped Chase's hand and arm in a manly clasp. "Good morning to you, too, Bailiff. No offense to your lady."

Chase wasn't smiling when he said, "Good morning, Gus. You and I haven't sparred for a while, have we?"

Gus frowned. "No, we haven't. And I'm not partial to the idea either. The last time we sparred, I sustained a most delicate injury—for weeks. I had to have a pillow when I sat down. My apologies to you and your lady."

I would've liked to have seen the sparring, but Chase seemed satisfied with the apology. "Is the queen in?"

"Unless they brought in a chopper that picked her up from the roof. These days, anything is possible."

We left Gus at the entrance to the castle and walked past the Main Hall where the King's Feast was held every Sunday night. Visitors waited in line here to enter the arena where the jousting, eating, and other entertainment took place.

There was faux Renaissance art, tapestries, and suits of armor decorating the area. The visitors were not allowed past the entrance and into the private quarters of the king and queen unless they had a special invitation.

After walking through the heavy, stud-embossed door, we entered the residence area, where the art and tapestries were real and expensive. There was central air and heating in this part of the castle, with wide-screen TVs in every visitor's suite. The carpet was plush underfoot, and the accoutrements were fit for royalty.

I knew where everything was here. I began my career as a kitchen wench in the castle. I was glad to have escaped that drudgery soon after. Most people didn't linger long in those base jobs. Livy was an impossible employer with her daily tantrums and demands.

We passed Rita Martinez, who was the exception to the rule. She'd been head of the kitchen staff for as long as the Village had been open. She wasn't in the best of moods, which wasn't surprising.

Chase hailed her, and she gave him a quick nod of respect. "Is Livy up yet?"

"Don't mention her name to me," she spat back. "She was impossible before she was pregnant. There isn't a word to describe what she's become. But she's up and receiving visitors, Sir Bailiff. Good luck." She muttered a quick "Good to see you, Jessie," then was on her way.

"Maybe we should come back later," Christine said, starting back toward the door.

"It'll be fine," Chase said. "It's much better than it sounds."

That was only a moment before the door to Livy's bed chamber opened and a full serving tray complete with cups and plates was thrown into the hall. It just missed us.

"We refuse to eat this mush again. Take it and feed it to the pigs or the prisoners in the Dungeon."

Nine

A chambermaid and both of the ladies-in-waiting scurried out immediately after. The chambermaid was swearing under her breath. Lady Barbara, who'd been at the Village as long as I could recall, said, "I'm not getting paid enough to do this!"

But Chase was brave. He knocked at the door and peeked around the corner into Livy's chamber. "Your Majesty? I was wondering if I could have a moment."

Livy's face was red from crying. She smiled when she saw him. "Of course! Come in, dear boy. There's no one I would rather see."

She didn't look as enthusiastic about seeing Christine and me. "You, we know." She pointed to me, then turning to Christine, added, "You look familiar, but we don't know you."

"Could we sit down, Your Majesty?" Chase asked. "We have something important to discuss with you."

"That would be wonderful, Sir Bailiff. Come. Take a seat. Someone order tea for us."

All three of us quickly denied wanting any food or beverage. We'd all seen the tea set flung out of the door.

Olivia, wearing a flowered robe, flounced down on her velvet sofa and waited to hear what Chase (always one of her favorites) wanted to say.

"We have a problem, Queen Olivia." Chase's tone was respectful and never gave a hint that he might be about to accuse her of taking part in a murder. "We're trying to investigate what happened to Chris Christmas."

Olivia's fake eyelashes looked like spiders moving up and down as she rapidly blinked. "We are afraid you have wasted your journey here, Bailiff. We have no knowledge, beyond what we have read in the newspaper. We have heard gossip but pay no attention to such drivel."

"We believe the police may not know enough about this matter," Chase continued. "We believe Father Christmas may have been willfully murdered by someone in the Village."

Livy's head fell back against the sofa. Huge, gulping sobs shook her heavily pregnant form. "Are we never to lead a normal existence? When will the past ever stop knocking upon our chamber door? Oh! Nevermore."

With apologies to Edgar Allan Poe, it was a pretty good speech. I glanced at Christine, who appeared to be more amazed by Livy's words than Chase and I. But we had lived with the theatrics that went on in the Village—especially with the king and queen. After a while, you became immune to it.

"Does that mean she's guilty?" Christine whispered to me.

"Who knows?"

Chase was at the queen's side, trying to revive and console her. She cried pitifully into his jerkin. I didn't mind that so much. But when she started running her hands up and down his back, I knew things were getting out of control.

I pulled him away from her. I didn't know if he hadn't noticed her advances or what, but it was time for someone else to take over. "Queen Olivia, we know you had an affair with Chris."

She sniffled but seemed coherent. "It is true, but that was many years ago." Her tear-filled eyes gazed at Christine. "We know you now. You are Chris's wife. We are terribly sorry for cavorting with your husband."

In an unsettled voice, Christine said, "It was a long time ago, Your Majesty, long before Chris and I even met."

"We also know that you cavorted with the second Father Christmas." That was a long shot, but I had a hunch.

"It's true." Livy looked up at me and smiled. "We were unable to resist the outfit, you see. All that fur and jolly tidings. It quite affected our mind."

Chase shrugged, giving credence to my theory. "And you hired Edgar Gaskin to be at the Village at the same time as Chris and his family. Why was that, Your Majesty?"

Livy blew her nose on her lacy handkerchief. "He threatened to expose our affair to the king. Harry knew about Chris. He forgave us that years ago." She whispered, "He doesn't know about Edgar. We are in a delicate state for such information to become public knowledge. When Edgar asked to come here, we hired him and gave him a room in the castle."

Since Livy and Harry's bedroom exploits were legendary, none of us were too surprised by her confession. Hiring Edgar probably seemed the lesser of two evils. It hadn't been easy convincing the king that the baby she carried was his.

"What do you plan to do with this information?" she asked, her tone a little more regal.

"We are investigating who might be involved in killing Chris," I explained, keeping Chase an arm's length from her. The woman was insatiable. "We believe that Edgar could be involved in his death."

Queen Olivia sat up at that information, her rosy lips parting on a smile. "Well go forth then, my good people, and arrest the oaf. We would see him in the Dungeon before the end of day."

"We'll do our best, Your Majesty," Chase said. "We'll try not to involve you in what we learn, but we may have to."

"Do what you have to, my good Bailiff! We would appreciate if it were over before our baby is born." Livy went into a crying fit again. We left her chamber, reluctant ladies-in-waiting Barbara and Jane going to check on her.

"I guess you were right," Chase said. "It's not too much of a stretch to imagine Edgar killing Chris."

"It all fits together," I agreed. "But I don't know if we should clear Livy of this yet. Especially considering she was involved with both men."

Christine looked a little overwhelmed. I tried to comfort her—not only had she lost her husband, but she also had to endure our continued conversations about him. It couldn't be easy for her.

"I'll be fine," she said with only a hint of a sniffle. "I'm used to Chris's lady friends popping up now and again. But what in the world did he see in her? She's bordering on crazy."

"I guess that was before she was queen," Chase said.

"Not that she hasn't had plenty of action since she became queen," I reminded him. "Don't ever get that close to her again. She'd jump your bones right now, pregnant or not."

"What do we do now?" Christine asked as we emerged back in the watery sunlight.

I carefully avoided Gus as we walked by him. I didn't trust him even if he had apologized. "We talk to the police and tell them what we know."

Christine looked at the little Christmas watch pendant pinned to her bodice. "It's almost eleven. I have to get the children into the workshop for Father Christmas's tour. Then we'll be upstairs for the picture taking until lunch break."

"I'll give Detective Almond another call," Chase said. His radio went off—they needed him for the upcoming joust. The black knight had taken ill, and they had no one to fill in for him.

"I guess that will make us all free for lunch," I said. "Maybe Detective Almond would like to have lunch in the Village."

"We'll see." Chase smiled and kissed me before he headed down the cobblestones for the Field of Honor on the other side of the Village.

"Has Chase said if he's identified the runaway knight who came at us yesterday?" Christine asked as we headed toward Squire's Lane and the Christmas manor houses.

"No. I'm sure he's working on it, but he hasn't updated me on that yet. Whoever it was probably hasn't been at the Village for very long. The problem is that they've taken on so many new people for the season. When I looked at the employee records, I was surprised at how many there are. Adventure Land must expect a huge crowd."

Those words had barely left my lips when we caught sight of the line of visitors stretching from the manor houses all the way through the Main Gate. Bringing the holidays to the Village—along with Father Christmas—seemed to be a good idea.

Christine's blue eyes flew wide open. "I wish Chris could have been here. I'm sure it's the biggest crowd I've ever seen. I'll just go and get the children."

We walked through the mostly patient parents and children queued up to see Father Christmas. There were several residents giving out flyers for other areas of the Village, no doubt trying to piggyback on the success of the Christmas theme. Milton, a good-looking knight who was a regular from the University of Minnesota, was smiling and chatting with the ladies in the crowd.

Alex, one of the Merry Men from Sherwood Forest, was also trying to entice some visitors to head for the trees. Marcus Fleck, usually assigned as the Black Dwarf, was dressed in castle finery as he gave out invitations to the King's Feast on Sunday night.

Of course, the pesky fairies (in seasonal fairy colors) were out in force trying to move some of the crowd to events at the other end of the Village, such as the upcoming joust at the Field of Honor, the programs at the Stage Caravan, and the wild bird acts at the Hawk Stage.

"This has to be the most colorful place I've ever been," Christine said as we reached the basement workshop. "And that includes all the Santa Land parks, too."

I was about to answer as she opened the door. The sight that hit me was so unbelievable, it left me speechless. Whatever I'd been about to say flew completely out of my head.

Christine's expression was one of utter shock. She rushed in, crying, "Oh no! Oh no!"

All of the children surged to the center of the room. They, and the workshop, looked as though they'd indulged in a paint fight. Everything and everyone was covered in blue, red, yellow, and green paint. The smallest child, Faith, was crying as she lifted her arms to be picked up.

"What in the world is going on?" Christine sidestepped Faith's tearful entreaties and walked right up to Merry Beth and Jolly. Nick, who was somewhere between them in age, stayed away from that spot. "I can't believe you two let this go on. You know they expect us to be making toys down here when Father Christmas comes in a few minutes. What are we supposed to do now?"

Jolly stepped forward. "How about we don't act like nothing happened? Dad is dead. He was murdered. We don't want to be good little elves for everyone else's benefit anymore. Merry Beth and I are tired of wearing these stupid costumes and making toys all the time. Can't we just be a normal family for once?"

I could see Christine was taken aback by Jolly's complaints. She looked at Merry Beth. "You feel this way, too?"

The girl nodded. "We're supposed to be grieving, Mom. Not laughing and pretending we want to make toys. We're not *really* elves. We have feelings. Like when is Dad going to be buried? Are we having a day off for his funeral or what?"

I could see two bright red spots of color rising in Christine's otherwise pale face. She clenched her hands into fists. "We don't have the luxury of taking time off to mourn your father right now. And he can't be buried until the police release his body. We have to keep working or we won't eat. Adventure Land has let us stay on despite your father being gone. We have our parts to play."

The two kids standing close to her were still angry. I could see it in their mutinous faces. But they put it aside, and everyone worked together to clean up the mess.

I wasn't very surprised at Jolly and Merry Beth's outburst. The children were right—they'd lost their father and they needed time to grieve. But I understood Christine's concerns about trying to make ends meet, too. They were all probably still in shock from the events of the last few days.

We could hear the crowd coming down from the manor house, with Father Christmas and carolers in the lead. Most of the paint was gone from the walls and floor. Toys covered up some other spots. The remaining splotches looked like just another part of the workshop mess.

Christine told the children to go upstairs and get cleaned up. Joy and Star asked if they shouldn't stay and help make toys. Both of them had blue paint in their hair.

"Not right now," their mother said. "Jessie and I will handle this. You go upstairs with your brothers and sisters, take a shower, and change clothes. We all need to be at the photo shoot in thirty minutes. Help Merry Beth with Faith and Holly."

When the basement door opened, the kids were gone. Christine and I looked up and smiled at the crowd of visitors who'd flooded into the room. The carolers kept singing and by now had been joined by some of the Merry Mynstrels in their holiday gear.

"Welcome to my toy shop," Edgar Gaskin said to the group in his loud, dramatic Father Christmas voice. "As you can see, my elves are hard at work making toys for all the children of the world."

One little boy who was holding a candy apple looked around and said, "Are these *all* the elves you've got? I think you need to hire a few more if you want to make that many toys."

Father Christmas laughed it off, but I could see the irritation behind his happy smile. He continued leading the visitors around the workshop, but without all the children at their tables in various stages of toy making, it was a pretty quick tour.

When it was over, the crowd went back out the door, followed by the singers and music makers. Edgar stayed behind and closed the door.

"What was this supposed to be?" he demanded. "Where are the children? I felt like a complete fool. I thought you understood why you got to stay here, Christine. No kids, no contract. Adventure Land only kept you on because *I* felt sorry for you. Don't let this happen again."

Christine was angry, but she kept her mouth shut. I knew she had no choice with eight hungry mouths to feed.

Thankfully, I wasn't in that position. "Give her a break," I said. "All of them are doing the best they can in this situation. Act like Father Christmas and be a little forgiving."

He turned his evil eye on me. "You aren't one of the kids, are you?"

"No. I'm Lady Jessie Morton, apprentice toy maker."

"I thought not. You look a little old to be an elf. Don't be here when it's time for the next tour. Make your toys when everyone else is gone."

"Seriously? Do you think you're *really* Father Christmas or what? It would take only one word from me for you to lose your job. You don't know who you're talking to."

Mind you, it was all hot air. Even if I'd said something to Merlin, he'd probably throw a blue smoke pellet out and run away. I couldn't really think of anyone who'd care what Edgar did, except for me. But it couldn't hurt to threaten him a little.

He drew himself up to his full height—still a few inches short of my six feet. "I shall have words with whoever is in charge, young woman. You'd best pack your things and find other employment for the season. The queen personally hired me for this position. *You* don't know who *you're* talking to."

He swung his long robe elegantly around as he stormed out of the basement. I could almost see a cloud of steam accompanying him as he went outside.

"Oh, Jessie, what have you done now?" Christine asked in a less than confident voice.

Ten

"Don't worry. Everything will be fine." I wasn't completely sure about that, but what could the big blowhard do?

"I'm going to get the children and go over to the photo session," she said.

"I'll go with you."

"I don't think that's a good idea. Let's give Edgar a chance to cool off. If he sees you there, he might get me fired, too."

I didn't like her tone, but I understood her fears—even though I thought they were groundless. "Don't forget, Christine, we're going to get Edgar for murder. He's not going to get anyone fired."

She looked at me with worried eyes. "I know you mean well, but I can't afford to lose focus on what I have to do. I'm sorry. I hope you don't take it the wrong way. I appreciate all the help you've given us."

Her eyes were clouded, and her face seemed to have taken on new wrinkles overnight. She'd been through a lot. I was sorry that I had added to her problems, but I just couldn't stand to hear Edgar speak to her that way, not to mention talk about the kids like they were little slaves.

"That's okay. I'll talk to you later. And I'll stay away from Edgar for a while—unless Detective Almond wants to put him in jail."

She smiled a little, thanked me again, and disappeared upstairs.

I felt like I had ruined everything. The only way I could make it up to Christine was by convincing Detective Almond of our theory.

Chase had invited him to lunch. I met the two of them at Peter's Pub. It was early, so there was no crowd to vie with for a table. Most visitors tended to eat later in the day. Chase had already ordered me a tankard of ale. I sat beside him, across the rough wood table from Detective Almond.

"So what's this all about?" he asked, nursing a tankard of soda. "I have a lot on my plate right now. I hope this isn't a waste of time."

I looked at Chase and he nodded. "I think we have new evidence about Chris Christmas's death." That should have been blunt and short enough for him.

Detective Almond took a drink. "What's new? I haven't heard anything yet. I know you folks out here enjoy your drama, but this is police business. Why haven't you been down to the station for your interview, Jessie? Or are you confessing?"

I explained about Edgar and Olivia. "There's something there. First, someone was in the workshop and knocked me down when he escaped." I handed him the green felt that had been trapped in my earring. "And then there was the runaway knight who tried to kill me and Chris's wife."

I lost some of my momentum when Peter's sister, Maude, brought our lunch to the table. I could see Detective Almond was mulling over my words as he adjusted his cheeseburger on his plate so that it didn't touch his fries.

"And what do you think about all of this, Manhattan?" he asked. "Jessie isn't the new bailiff, right? That's still your job, isn't it?"

"Jessie put all of this together," Chase said with the patience of a saint (as far as I was concerned). "I went with her to interview Queen Olivia. No doubt she brought Edgar Gaskin here before Chris Christmas died. He's the new Father Christmas now."

"And this Gaskin had a beef with the old Santa." Detective Almond summed it up while he munched his fries—cheeseburger untouched until the fries were gone.

"Yes. Chris caught Gaskin stealing money from the Santa group they both belonged to. It's a national group that helps people who play Santa through job layoffs and that kind of thing," Chase explained.

"And you think Gaskin took advantage of the situation to kill Christmas?"

I glanced at Chase. It didn't sound like things were going well. I didn't know what else to say to convince Detective Almond that he should investigate Edgar.

Chase said, "I think it's worth looking into. There are a few things that seem to add up. I don't have experience with this kind of thing like you do. But it feels wrong. I'd hate to see someone still working here who's responsible for Chris's death."

Detective Almond smiled at him. "You mean you

wouldn't like the media to get wind of something like that, right? I understand that. But the Myrtle Beach Police Department doesn't have the money or the manpower to investigate every person who has some vague connection to the victim. I'm sure you can appreciate that."

In other words, he wasn't going to do anything about Edgar. There would be no justice for Christine. I'd made her life miserable for nothing.

"Cheer up, you two lovebirds." He wiped his mouth on his napkin. "I'll make you a deal. You do the legwork and if you find anything solid—I mean concrete—that isn't just how you feel or what you think might've happened, I'll take over."

I wasn't sure if that's what I'd had in mind, but it was probably as good as I was going to get. "You've got yourself a deal. What would you consider solid?"

He shrugged and started in on his cheeseburger. "A confession."

"Is that it?" Chase asked.

"I think so. You get me a confession from your so-called killer, and I'll bring the full weight of the Myrtle Beach Police down on him."

"Okay. We can do that." I glanced at Chase. He didn't seem too pleased with the idea.

"Good." Detective Almond took another bite. "This is a really good cheeseburger."

It was my turn to zing him a little. "Didn't you ever eat here when you were the Village bailiff?"

He almost choked on his burger. "How did you find out about that?"

"I was looking through the employee records. I didn't find any pictures of you in tights or anything, but I'm sure they're in the files somewhere. I'll have another look while we investigate. Maybe a nice group shot. Did you live in the Dungeon?"

"The Dungeon wasn't even built when I was here," he said. "I stayed in the castle, which wasn't as glamorous as it is now, I can tell you. And no, I didn't wear tights. I wore my uniform. I wasn't a detective yet. They needed somebody out here while the place was being set up. I'm just glad I got out before all the whack jobs moved in."

"How long were you here?" Chase asked.

"Only a few months before Roger Trent took over as bailiff. Technically, I never had that title. People started calling me that right as I was about to leave. I got my promotion because of that. I don't regret it."

It was hardly worthwhile bringing it up. I'd thought he'd be more defensive, maybe even wanting me to keep quiet about it. *Darn!* It would've been a nice diversion.

Then a thought occurred to me. "Were you here when Chris and Alice Christmas were king and queen of the village?"

"No. Not to my knowledge. Are you saying the deceased has lived here before?"

Too bad! I told him about the files. "This was before the new Mrs. Christmas came on the scene."

"And you think it might be important to the case?"

I shrugged. "I don't really know. I guess I was more curious than anything."

He kind of grunted. "If that's it, I'm going back to the office. Thanks for lunch." He pushed out of the booth and got to his feet. "Be sure to call me when you get that confession."

"Do you have the autopsy results yet?" I remembered to ask at the last minute. A few people around us in the pub looked up, probably surprised to hear someone in costume talking non-Ren speak.

"Not everything yet. I guess we all knew he died from that bullet wound to his neck. The medical examiner thinks he was sitting down, maybe making toys, and someone snuck up on him. He was dead before he knew it. Still had a paintbrush in his hand, poor devil."

"Okay. Thanks. Can he be buried now?" I pressed him for more information.

"Not until we get everything back from the ME's office. That could be a month or more. The widow has decided she wants him cremated when it's over. Probably for easy handling. They have no permanent address. Did you know that?" He put down a couple of dollars on the table. "Good burger. Thanks for the invitation."

I felt deflated by his information. How could I possibly get a confession from a killer? It seemed hopeless.

"Oh and by the way, if you're serious about finding a killer for this, you might want to talk to Santa's wife."

"Why?" Chase asked for me.

"She had a huge insurance policy on him. And we've heard rumors that she was fooling around. The older boy said she sent him out into the Village by himself when they got back from the store with the camera. She had a few minutes on her hands before *you* were in the wrong place, Jessie. Get it? That might be your soft spot here. Get *her* to confess. See you two later."

Eleven

I was devastated. I drank my ale and pushed my plate away. Who could eat at a time like this?

"Just because Almond said that doesn't mean Christine is guilty of anything," Chase said. "If I was the father of eight children and I made most of the money, I'd have some good life insurance, too. Come on, Jessie. You can't suspect her. What would she have to gain by killing Chris? She's alone with all those kids."

I thought about Christine carefully. "Of course not! There is no way Christine killed him. I just hate that she looks so guilty. It wouldn't be that way if they'd had a better marriage."

"Yeah. Sorry." He drank some of his ale. "Is that what's bothering you about the two of us being together permanently? Because you know I've been faithful to you."

"I know you have." I smiled and reached for his hand. "But you don't know how terrible it is for a family. I remember how devastated my mother was when my father left us. That's why I've never had a serious relationship, except for you. Robin Hood, the pirates, they were all summer flings that I knew I wouldn't come back to. I've always been careful that no one stood between me and being able to take care of myself."

"I understand." He squeezed my hand, his gaze steady on mine. "But I feel like we've reached a critical-mass situation, Jessie. I think you have to make a decision."

I didn't like the way that sounded and quickly changed the subject. I didn't want to be in an either-or position with Chase. I didn't want to lose him.

"Christine hasn't exactly been honest with me."

He sighed and sat back from the table, his dark eyes glancing around the crowded room. "Having an affair and buying a lot of life insurance for your husband aren't exactly topics for casual conversation with strangers," he said. "She's only known you for three days."

"Or she was afraid I wouldn't feel sorry for her anymore."

"Why not? She has years left of raising all those kids. It's going to cost a fortune to feed, clothe, and educate them. I'm sure that's why they got the big insurance policy on Chris. That's what those are for. It doesn't make her a killer. It still leaves her without a husband."

His tone had changed. I could tell he was suddenly out of this discussion. He was still thinking about us. The problem between us was becoming bigger. He felt like I didn't trust him. I had to think of some way to prove that I did—*while* I was getting the killer's confession.

Lucky for me, he was called away to an emergency at the Main Gate. He walked with me as far as the manor houses at Squire's Lane, but there was an awful silence between us. I hated it, but if nothing short of a Renaissance wedding would make him happy, I didn't know if I could go there.

I didn't mention to him the mysterious paper Christine had hidden, but when we parted a few minutes later, I headed toward the workshop. Christine and the children would be in the photo area for the rest of the afternoon. It was the perfect opportunity for me to check it out.

A parade was strolling through the Village—costumed camels, elephants, dogs, horses—even sheep and goats. They were all decked out in their holiday finery, like the rest of us, with sprigs of holly and ribbons around their necks. Even Tom's pig was dressed up.

Countless camera flashes went off as they walked along the cobblestones. Elegantly dressed fools, knaves, and varlets followed them with pooper scoopers (some very large) to make sure they left nothing behind but happy memories.

I slipped through the parade midway between the dancing poodles and baying hounds. I got a few dirty looks from the handlers, but that was all right. I didn't want to wait to get around the animals.

As I'd thought, the basement was empty. I went right over to the drawer in the table. Whatever had been in there was gone.

I didn't like Christine as a suspect. I felt sure Detective Almond was telling the truth about the insurance policy, but like Chase had said, it made sense. Without the money, what would she do to keep the family going?

I glanced up when I heard a noise at the door. A piece of paper was taped to the inside of it. Even though I was pretty sure someone was coming in, I ran over and grabbed it.

It was a threatening letter to Christine. Done in paint, it said, *You killed your husband. Now you pay the price.* There was nothing to indicate who'd written it.

The door opened slowly. I hid behind it. My heart was beating like crazy, but there was nowhere else to go at that point. If I was lucky, whoever it was would see the workshop was empty and leave again. If not, I might have to come up with a quick excuse.

It was King Harold, unusually alone. There were no courtiers, no fools or knaves to cater to his every whim. He was dressed in street clothes, no golden crown. I peeked through the crack between the door and the wall and saw him look around anxiously, his hands sliding in and out of his pockets.

He stayed in the doorway with the door open. Christine joined him.

She immediately put her arms around him, and they kissed passionately.

I didn't need to wonder anymore who she was having an affair with.

Twelve

"I'm so glad you could come," she said, smiling up into his face. "I'm so alone. I don't know what to do."

He soothed her, patting her back and holding her near. "Don't worry. Nothing is going to happen to you or the children. Edgar is just an employee. He doesn't make those kinds of decisions. Your place is safe here."

"Thank you so much." She wrapped her arms around him and kissed him for several more moments.

I stayed as still as I could, hoping they wouldn't notice me. Christine and Harry seemed pretty tight from my bird's-eye view. Their affair at least sounded serious. Had she been planning on leaving Chris? Or was this just pay-back for all his philandering?

A new thought hit me—maybe the two of them were responsible for Chris's death and Christine's grieving-widow act was just to throw everyone off.

I didn't like that idea at all. It squirmed inside of me but refused to go away.

I knew lots of people who'd had casual and not so casual affairs, but they didn't kill their mates. *Not even for a hefty insurance policy?*

"What about Jessie?" Christine asked. "Edgar threatened her, too."

"I'll take care of that. Are you sure you want Lady Jessie hanging around right now? She has an annoying habit of asking a lot of questions. I could get her reassigned."

"I like her, and she's good with the kids. That's all that matters. She's helping me try to figure out who killed Chris."

Harry seemed surprised (or guilty—those two expressions always look the same to me). "What do you mean? You should leave that to the police, my dear. They know how to get the job done."

Christine explained things the same way to him as I had to Detective Almond and Chase. "You know Edgar hated Chris. I wouldn't put it past him to kill him."

"Does she know about us?"

"No, of course not. But she knows that Chris had an affair with Livy. She could put two and two together."

"That sounds like her." He ran his hand through his thick, graying hair. "It would be uncomfortable for me if the police found out about us, Christine. Please don't encourage her. If anyone knew about us—how I got this job for Chris so you'd be closer—I could lose everything, especially with the baby due any time."

Christine rested her head against his chest. "I'll talk to her, tell her I don't want to pursue this anymore. I think she's only doing it for me anyway. Don't worry. If you can handle Edgar, I can take care of Jessie."

I didn't like the way she'd said that, even though she'd

been glowing with my praises earlier. I wasn't crazy about Harry making it sound like I was the Village busybody either. Between them, I seemed like someone I didn't want to know.

Christine and Harry embraced again, then separated. Harry went cautiously back out the basement door, putting on sunglasses as he went. How non-Ren could he get? Christine passed right by me and went up the stairs to the manor house.

I opened the door, my legs shaking from the effort it took to stand so still. I supposed I was also nervous about being caught there. Whoever said eavesdroppers never hear good about themselves was right. I looked at the threatening note again and stuffed it into the purse that hung at my waist.

I walked to the Village Square and sat beside the Good Luck Fountain, listening to the minstrels as they played on the green.

I wasn't sure why I'd felt like I knew Chris and Christine so well. We'd just met when Chris was killed. I really didn't know much about them at all. And what I did know—Chris sleeping around, Christine having an affair with Harry—I didn't like. How could I be so wrong about two people? I felt stupid and naïve.

Chase came and sat beside me. "I just came back from helping King Arthur find his missing sword. Phil at the Sword Spotte had hidden it because Arthur refused to do a commercial for Phil, who made the Excalibur sword. I've been looking for it all day. Visitors missed all those exciting moments with Arthur pulling the sword from the stone."

I sighed, glad he seemed to be over his funk. "That's great. Really great."

He put his arm around me along the back of the bench. "What's wrong? I take it no one has officially confessed to killing Father Christmas. You didn't work on it very long."

"It's far worse." I told him about Christine and Harry. "Detective Almond might be right. It doesn't look good for Christine."

Chase thought about it. "I don't believe it. If I had that much life insurance on you, I'd push you out of a tall window or drown you in a bathtub—something that *looked* like an accident. This is so obvious. They had to know there would be a big investigation."

Even though I'd thought the same thing, the way he'd phrased it made me even more depressed. "I don't think most people's minds work that way. Besides, they say most criminals aren't very smart. Maybe they were so much in love, they were willing to give up everything so they could be together."

"Harry will never leave Livy. He likes to fool around, but the two of them know what they're doing. Harry knows he'd have to give up his position if he left Livy. If Christine thinks he loves her enough to give up his life, she's got another thought coming."

"It doesn't make any sense," I protested. "How am I supposed to get a confession from a killer if I don't know who the killer is?"

"I'd say you need to clear your mind for a while," he suggested. "I could use your help with vegetable justice. What say you?"

"I'd say lead me hither, good sir. I shall do my best to aid you."

It seemed Adventure Land was worried about losing customers while Father Christmas took a break for lunch. That's why they'd ordered the parade of animals, put an extra dozen fairies out on the cobblestones, and asked Chase to do vegetable justice a few extra times each day.

The stocks by the Dungeon were ready, along with baskets of overripe tomatoes, old lettuce, and some squishy peppers. Nothing hard enough to hurt anyone—but just solid enough to put on a good show.

Sometimes, visitors asked that vegetable justice be administered to one or more of the people who came with them to the Village. When that didn't happen, Chase recruited Village residents to stage a performance of a grievance.

That was the case when I came down from the Dungeon in my old trousers and boy's shirt. I was the bailiff's errand boy who fetched and carried for him. I would help out with vegetable justice by putting the offender into the stocks and riling up the crowd so that (hopefully) everyone had a good time.

Because no visitor had asked for vegetable justice, Chase had recruited a few knights in training, a few of the Merry Men from Sherwood, and a few varlets and madmen who were wandering around.

Chase came out in his black robe and white wig. A pirate from the *Queen's Revenge* was brought forward in plastic chains. He'd been accused of stealing and causing mayhem in the Village. "How do you plead?" Chase asked the new pirate, Bucky. I didn't recognize him, so he had to be new.

"I plead innocent, though I don't give a rat's ass for your justice." He made the mistake of spitting on the ground. That led to a round of spitting from everyone else involved. Residents led the way, and visitors, thinking it was something interesting and fun, followed. I don't know why, but spitting had evolved into a popular sport at these events.

"Great," I whispered to Chase. "We could be here all day at this rate."

But as usual, a large crowd of visitors began to join the group to find out what was going on. They were soon booing the pirate and yelling "Huzzah!" when the knights in training stated their case against the pirate.

By the time Chase had passed sentence for the crime—vegetable justice to be administered at once—there were at least a hundred visitors who were ready to take up old vegetables to throw at the pirate.

I did my impression of a young helper and led the pirate to the stocks. There, his chains were removed and his neck and arms were locked into place. "Comfortable?" I asked him as the crowd began to fill their hands with vegetables.

"I guess. No one ever said anything about this. Should I expect to do this every day?"

"Probably not. Most of the time, the visitors want to be the ones in the stock."

"Really? Why would anyone *want* to do this?"

"Who knows? Just close your eyes tight and don't open your mouth. It'll be over quickly."

With vegetables in hand, everyone proceeded to throw them. Lucky for the pirate that they were soft and most of the throws missed him. He was still covered in tomato juice when it was over, but everyone had a good time. Several of the visitors suddenly remembered that they had disagreements with someone they were there with that day. Chase set up three more vegetable justice events with them.

"What ho, my good servant!" He hammed it up for the crowds. "Mind your manners or you'll be next in the stocks."

The visitors ate it up like bread bowls. The residents

faded back to their jobs since they weren't needed anymore. Everything was right on the cobblestones.

I spent most of the afternoon helping Chase before he had to abandon his part of the event. He was called away when a few girls got carried away by the excitement of the Village and took off their clothes to climb in the Good Luck Fountain.

"Maybe I should come with you on that," I offered, thinking the situation called for a woman's point of view. And I could protect Chase from any rowdy naked females.

"I'm just going to supervise," he said. "Two security guards are already there. I think we'll be fine. You could just walk around or go upstairs and get on the computer."

Since I was already in Renaissance garb, I decided to use my appearance to see if I could find out what had really happened when the knight came at me and Christine yesterday.

I looked like a squire, so I might as well hang around the jousting area and see what was going on. Maybe I'd pick up on something.

The Field of Honor was busy with knights practicing for the jousting event, which would take place an hour later. The knights were divided into groups based on experience. The queen's or king's champions were always set apart and practiced alone. The knights on the field were new or had never made it to that exalted status.

Usually one or two black knights were the terror of the jousting field. These knights were experienced and usually enjoyed the boos they received from the crowd.

I watched the horses go back and forth on the sawdust, working through the routines that would acclimate them to the sight of another horse and rider bearing down on them with a lance or sword. None of the jousts were real, just good theater. But injuries still occurred from time to time, mostly because of inadequate training.

"You there!" a young, blond knight shouted at me. "I need someone to fetch my lance. And be quick about it."

Well, I'd wanted to be at the field incognito. My plan seemed to be working. I found the staging area where the blond knight kept his effects and picked up his lance. I walked across the field, glad I'd changed my shoes for boots, and looked up in time to see a large horse and rider coming at me.

Maybe I'd already located the knight who'd tried to skewer Christine and me.

Thirteen

I dropped the lance and jumped the nearby fence to get away from the rider. Lucky for me, the blond knight took his position seriously. He rode up and hailed the helmeted knight who'd been charging toward me.

"Get your own squire. This one is mine!" he yelled at the attacking knight with all of the position and pomp of a more experienced rider.

I stood up, a little breathless. The knight pushed back his helmet. I'd never seen him before, but given all the new hires, that wasn't surprising.

"Sorry," he said, looking at me. "I guess the horse just got away from me. Are you hurt?"

"Of course he's not hurt," the blond knight told him. "Squires and lackeys don't get hurt. They get your lance if they know what's good for them."

I knew that was my cue to scramble. I jumped back over the fence and picked up the lance. I'd done my time at the jousts. I knew what was expected. "Sorry, sir. It won't happen again."

"Damn right it won't or you'll bloody be out on the cobblestones." The blond knight accepted the lance from me, then rode toward the center of the field.

The new knight climbed down from his horse and removed his helmet and gloves. He looked about sixteen, though I knew the Village never hired knights that young.

"Really, I hope you're okay. I like this job, but I'm not very good at it yet."

"That's okay. You'll get better. I guess you just started." I reached my hand out to him. "I'm Jessie."

"I'm Dennis Greene." He shook my hand. "You seem to have experience at this."

"Yeah. I've worked the joust several times. Not so much anymore. I do some apprenticeships with craftsmen."

"That sounds better than being out here in the smelly sawdust." He smiled and he looked like a nice person despite the grime. His blue eyes seemed friendly and open, not a bit like what I'd expected of the rider who'd rode toward Christine and me yesterday. Perhaps it was true that the incident had been an accident. Or maybe he wasn't the person who'd charged at us.

"It is sometimes. But you'll get the hang of it if you stick around."

He looked off in the distance at the Village behind me. "I don't know about that yet. I'm just checking it out right now. I guess I'll see how it works out. Maybe you could help me."

I wanted to know more about him, so I agreed to help. "We could meet up later and I could give you some pointers. It's not that hard once you know the basics."

"That would be great. Maybe around six after the Main Gate closes?"

"Great! See you later."

The blond knight was ready for his sword. He rode toward me and shouted, "I need my sword, squire. Stop dawdling and get it for me at once."

I made a face at him. "Get it yourself. I quit."

"You'll never work the joust again. By this, I do swear."

"Let's hope not," I muttered as I climbed the fence and got out of the Field of Honor. I noticed Jolly, Christine's oldest son, watching from the sidelines. He looked so wistful and sad that I had to go and say something to him. He might be the oldest, but that didn't make his father's death any easier for him.

"Would you like to give it a try?" I nodded toward the field and the knights still practicing. "It's not that hard."

"I won't be here long enough to do anything," he told me. "That's the way we live."

"Things may change now."

"You mean because my dad is dead?" He stared at me with a lot of built-up anger in his young face. "I don't see that happening. My mom will probably just hook up with some other guy who moves around. All I need is another year and I'll be eighteen. Then nobody can tell me what to do."

He pushed away from the fence and stomped back toward the main part of the Village. He was seventeen—of course he was angry. Even if his father had still been alive, he'd be angry. I wondered if Christine had given him that now-that-your-father-is-dead speech. I remembered my grandmother telling Tony that he was the man of the house after our parents died. It was a lot to take in at one time.

I walked around the Village saying hi to a few friends. Mrs. Potts gave me some honey cookies and a cup of tea at the Honey and Herb Shoppe. While I ate, she brought me up to speed on all the latest gossip. Mrs. Potts is a portly lady who always wears a blue dress with a white apron and a white mob cap. You can't let her friendly exterior fool you. She's one of the few people in the Village that Chase trusts with a two-way radio. That's why she knows all the good stuff.

"I think King Harold must be looking for a way out of this baby situation," she told me. "He took a bad tumble down the stone stairs in the castle a few minutes ago. Not looking where he's going, I suppose. He's got a lot on his mind. He wasn't hurt badly and swears someone pushed him."

Thinking about Livy's moods, I could understand that. "What do you know about the new Father Christmas, Edgar Gaskin? He seems to have some pull with Livy and Harry."

"I can't say that I know anything about him—except that he's already famous for his foul mood. The staff at the castle will walk around him rather than confront him."

"It seems odd, doesn't it, that Harry and Livy hired him even before the first Father Christmas was dead?" I wanted to see if she knew anything about that situation.

"I agree. It seems to me that he must have something over them. Esmeralda says that he gets whatever he wants, whenever he wants it. If she wasn't so far pregnant, I'd say he was Livy's new lover."

Mrs. Potts didn't really know much more than I did. I took some cookies for the road and set out on the cobblestones again.

The tableau of the Sheriff of Nottingham capturing Robin Hood was going on a few doors down. All the Merry

Men with their little green hats were on hand to help Robin free himself before they all took a bow and disappeared back into the forest. The crowds loved it.

Until the coming of the Knights Templar with their dashing black leather armor and fantastic, well-trained horses, Robin and his men were the most popular part of the Village. They got away with stealing trinkets—and toaster ovens—for years because of it. Chase had told me Village security had finally started cracking down on them.

Lucky for Robin Hood, the Templars, like the mermaids, were only a summer attraction. The forest bandits were enjoying their popularity again.

I knew the Templars would have their heyday, too. Then there would be someone else to take their place. It was the way it worked here. Keep it fresh. Keep it moving.

I saw Christine with all of the children except for Jolly in the Village Square watching an archery tournament. I wanted to talk to her, not necessarily confront her, about her relationship with Harry. Maybe this would be a good time.

I looked around for Edgar, but there was no sign of him. That was good for me, too. I didn't plan on apologizing to him. He was rude and threatening, especially for someone only visiting the Village. Even if he had slept with Livy and she didn't want Harry to find out, that didn't give him total power over the rest of us.

"It looks like the coast is clear," I said when I reached her.

"Jessie! I'm glad to see you. I'm sorry about the thing with Edgar. I hope I didn't hurt your feelings. I just can't afford to lose this job. I need time to figure out what I should do next."

I leaned my head close to hers. "Don't depend on Harry to save you."

She got all flustered and her face turned red. "I don't

know what you mean. Why would I depend on King Harold for anything?"

"I *know*."

Christine smiled. "I can't imagine what you're talking about."

"I was in the workshop today when you met him there. You should look around more carefully."

I probably shouldn't have said it. I was just surprised to learn that she was as unfaithful as her husband. It kind of blurted right out of me.

"Well, I guess you know then. I'd appreciate you keeping it to yourself." Her tone was curt and a little angry. "Nothing good comes from spying on people."

"I know. I didn't mean to be there. I certainly didn't want to know about you and Harry." I listened to the *oohs* and *aahs* from the crowd around us as the archer shot his arrow through a small pumpkin, splitting it perfectly in half. The archer's lovely assistant looked happy when it was over, too.

"What do you plan to do? Harry warned me about you. I guess you heard that, too."

"Listen, Christine, everybody sleeps with everybody else around here. Harry wasn't even sure Livy's baby was his, as pathetic as that sounds. I don't care if you two are hooking up. But Harry has done this over and over. He's not going to leave Livy for you. He's not going to help you raise your kids. I just want you to know that and not get your hopes up."

Her pretty blue eyes were wet with tears. "I feel like such a fool about this, Jessie. A woman my age should know better." She glanced at her children, but they were still watching the archery. "But Chris was always gone, and most of the time I think it was with some other woman. I was lonely and heartsick over our relationship. Then I met Harry at the summer Costume Characters Convention. He was representing the Village. Chris was busy, so I was standing in for the Santa Fund. We hit it off right away, and my life was so much better—*is* so much better. I don't want to think that I haven't meant that much to him."

I could understand her feelings, and I saw the emotion in her face. The man she'd loved had played her false through most of her life. He'd dangled his conquests in her face. This affair with Harry was her chance at happiness. Even though he was someone else's husband.

I put my arm around her shoulders. "I'm sorry, Christine. I hope I'm wrong about Harry. I just know what I've seen for the past few years."

"Thanks. I wish I'd never met him. I love him so much, but I know it's wrong. Now that Chris is gone, I'm so afraid. Harry has promised me and the kids a permanent toy-making shop here for as long as we want it. I think we could make a go of it, with his help. I don't know what else to do, whether he really loves me or not."

We finished watching the archery tournament together, then we took the kids to Fractured Fairy Tales where they were performing a hilarious version of *Snow White*. We all laughed together, then had pretzels with mustard at a traveling cart.

Christine was meeting with her lawyer outside the Village. She and the children returned to the manor house to change clothes. She said she wanted me to come back to the workshop the next day. She told me she wouldn't let Edgar's threats bother her again.

I'd wanted to ask her about the life insurance she had on Chris, but I couldn't find the words. And I respected her too much, as odd as it sounds, to think she'd be stupid enough to kill Chris in such a way that she wouldn't collect. If not for herself, then for the children. Christine might have been cheating on her husband, but I didn't believe she had anything to do with his death.

Now, Edgar and Harry were another story. I could see nasty old Edgar killing Chris. I wasn't so sure about Harry. That seemed like a lot of work for him to put into a relationship.

Finding myself at loose ends for a while, I thought I'd go back to the castle and see if anyone there had any information about Chris's death. Gossip traveled fast in those stone halls. At least fifty people worked there, and they were good at figuring out what was going on.

I reached the entrance just as Livy was making another practice run, preparing for her baby. It looked more like wrestling as Wanda, Ladies Jane and Barbara, and Esmeralda from the laundry room tried to wheel Livy out of the castle and down to the Main Gate.

"Don't just stand there, Jessie," Esmeralda said irritably. "Help us!"

Not seeing exactly how I could help and wary of getting too close to Wanda, I got saddled with Livy's three pieces of luggage. I looked around, but there was no sign of Harold.

"Shouldn't the father come, too?" I asked.

"He should," Lady Jane grunted. "But he's injured. He'll be no help to us when it happens."

Evidently, Mrs. Potts had underestimated the extent of Harry's injuries. If he was too badly injured to work on the practice birthing team, he was in bad shape. Everyone had gone on about how devoted he'd been to Livy the last two months.

Of course, they didn't know that he was sleeping with

Christine. I guessed his devotion didn't extend to monogamy.

Livy was crying loudly as the two ladies-in-waiting and Esmeralda pushed her wheelchair past the pirate ship and a group of gawking visitors who readily snapped pictures of the sight.

"Were there wheelchairs during the Renaissance?" one man with thick, black-framed glasses asked as I struggled to keep up while holding Livy's heavy bags of necessities.

"I'm sure there were," I replied. "Now get out of the way."

By the time we reached the Main Gate, we were all breathless and ready to cry. Livy was shaking back and forth in her chair, her pretty plump face covered in runny mascara.

Wanda snapped her stopwatch closed. "It took longer this time. We'll have to improve on that."

"For heaven's sake!" Lady Jane panted. "Either put her up in a hotel room near the hospital or get a helicopter. I can't take much more of this."

Esmeralda, who was used to telling laundry wenches what to do all day, collapsed on the cobblestones. "Find someone else. I'm not doing this again. Where's Gus? He should be doing this."

"I am your queen," Livy sobbed. "I am with child. You have to take care of me. What is wrong with all of you?"

Visitors were passing on their way out of the Village, watching the event with interested eyes, some holding up their cell phones to get pictures. This wasn't the kind of publicity the Village normally wanted. But the king and queen were important to everyday life here. The birth of Queen Olivia's baby was important, too—and would bring a fair amount of publicity, the kind the Village liked.

I had dropped Livy's luggage on the ground when we'd

stopped at the gate. I wasn't sure if they would call some varlet over to haul the bags back to the castle. The three pieces felt like they had rocks in them. How much did Livy need for a short stay at the hospital?

Lucky for all of us, Chase, Gus, and Merlin showed up, wondering if they could lend a hand. Merlin was no help at all, casting colored smoke bombs left and right that smelled like rotten eggs.

Chase and Gus were a different story. Chase lifted Livy from the wheelchair and started walking back to the castle with her. She put her arms around his neck and smiled up into his face. I ground my teeth a little but knew there was nothing she could do with all of us watching her.

Gus picked up the luggage as though the bags weighed nothing, which left Esmeralda pushing the empty wheelchair back up past the *Queen's Revenge*. The ladies-in-waiting had quickly retreated back to the castle when they'd seen everything was taken care of.

I followed them back, still hoping to do a little investigating into Chris's death. I knew Esmeralda had been at the castle for a long time, so I asked her about the first king and queen.

"Why are you asking me that at a time like this?" she impatiently demanded. "Isn't it bad enough we are all out here like idiots? Have you become the Village historian or something?"

Hmm—not a bad idea. Maybe something I could suggest to Merlin.

But I kept my focus on my question. "I know that Chris Christmas was the Village king when it first opened. I was just wondering what happened to his wife, Alice. Did she leave the Village, or is she still here?"

She stopped walking. "Jessie, there have been so many

ladies-in-waiting, knights, lords, and madmen that I just can't keep up with it anymore. I recall someone was king and queen before Olivia and Harold, but I don't know what happened to either of them. I'm sorry."

"Chris was killed here," I reminded her. "He was remarried. I was hoping to notify his ex-wife. I thought she might want to know."

"I'm sorry," she said again. "I just don't know. Maybe Merlin or Roger Trent could help you. They were around then, too."

I crossed her off of my list of people to talk to who might remember Chris and Alice. I didn't like the idea of talking to Roger about anything. We got along only so well. But if it meant understanding what had gone on in the first few months after the Village opened, I was willing to do it. I didn't know if locating Alice would bring me any closer to a confession, but it seemed worth a shot.

And who knew? Maybe Chris's ex-wife had killed him. Stranger things had happened.

Fourteen

I walked on to the castle anyway with the idea that I could walk back with Chase. I wondered if Rita Martinez had also been at the castle when Chris was king. She might remember something.

But everyone from the lowest chambermaid to Princess Isabel was trying to get Livy settled in her chambers. I walked in just as Wanda was telling her that she wasn't having a heart attack and could bloody well handle having a baby. Livy still had her arms locked around Chase, refusing to let him put her down on the chaise.

I stood in the doorway, not wanting to be drawn into the theatrics but hardly able to look away from them. I didn't realize King Harold had joined me until he said, "Livy has always been sensitive."

I looked at him, seeing the man behind the costume. Harold was pretty ordinary. I never understood what women saw in him—same with Livy. There were people out there who *weren't* middle-aged and slightly frumpy who couldn't get dates like those two did. Livy and Harry could hardly keep the opposite sex away. Maybe it was the royalty bit. Look at Henry the Eighth.

Of course, Harry had been injured. It didn't help that his arm was in a sling and he had bruises on the side of his face. It must've been a nasty fall.

"Your Majesty." I nodded respectfully but didn't curtsy. My feelings were still a little hurt from his description of me to Christine. Not to mention his offer to get rid of me. I didn't even want to know what he thought he could do.

"Lady Jessie. It's good to see you. You're looking tolerably well."

"Thank you." Should I bring up knowing about his affair with Christine? What would be the point? He'd either deny it or worse, act like he was in love with her, ready to leave Livy when the baby was born.

"I've spoken with Christine. I *know*." The words were out before I could stop them. I needed to see his reaction, I told myself. But it was really more that I had to say it.

Talk about theatrics. If Livy was the queen of melodrama, Harry was the king. He said, "I know, too." Like he'd rehearsed it for weeks. There was an important lift to his brow to underscore his words. He said it in such a way that it was almost poignant.

"I'm glad." I faced him, enjoying looking down at him. "This way we can talk about it."

He sniffed royally and attempted to return my stare, though his eyes didn't get further than my bosom. "This is not the kind of thing one stands in the corridor and talks about. Come with me, lady. We must speak in private."

I thought it couldn't hurt. I knew he was leading me to his personal chambers, but I wasn't worried about being seduced, and I had enough on him that he wouldn't want to fire me.

I wasn't worried about it at all. Nothing he could say would convince me he was right in sleeping with Christine while Livy was carrying his child. How could it get lower than that?

Harry actually let me walk in his chamber first. He had to be nervous to do that. Royalty always went first. "Would you like a drink? I have some excellent peach brandy."

"No thanks." I sat down on one of the uncomfortable chairs that looked like a wooden scoop with a little cushion on it. Everyone who served in the castle hated them. I felt safe in this one. It was as far away from the sofa as possible.

Harry poured himself some brandy, then sat opposite me. "The future of Renaissance Village is at stake, Lady Jessie. Without a king and queen, what would become of this place we all love so well?"

Oh, the drama. "First of all, I think you and Livy could be replaced. Honestly, it's not like you're the first royalty of the Village, right?"

He took a swallow of his drink and glared at me. "You've done your homework. You're correct. Chris and Alice were the first. Olivia and I were asked first by Adventure Land, but we weren't sure about doing it. We were making good money selling advertising for the company. Why give it up?"

I waited as he stood up and paced the wood floor. "But Chris wanted to make the Village too much like Santa Land for the higher-ups. He decided to leave. Alice wanted to stay on as queen, but Adventure Land wanted a married couple. They made it very attractive for me and Livy. We decided to take them up on it. We've made the Village what it is today."

"I think that's questionable. But thanks for telling me

the story. How would losing you and Livy take down the Village?"

"We are the goodwill ambassadors, Lady Jessie. We personify the Village. We hold it together. And marketing says that our child will grow revenue shares at least forty percent in the next two years."

I understood *that.* It was always about the money and the shareholders. "Okay. Why do you think your affair with Christine would change that? Everyone knows you and Livy get around. I can't imagine anyone being surprised by this."

I couldn't help remembering what Livy had said about Harry finding out about her affair with Edgar. It seemed to me that both of them were skating at the edge of the limits their marriage would allow.

"That would have been true before the baby," Harry said. "Women hate men who cheat on their pregnant wives. It wouldn't market well. Besides, you know me. I don't plan to make my relationship with Christine permanent. It was just something fun to do. And it relieved my stress—and it was ironic in a way because Livy slept with Chris."

I got to my feet, a little sick and disgusted. I knew how Christine felt about him. She was stupid for getting involved with a married man in the first place, but hearing his callous remarks made me think even less of him than I already did.

"You don't have to worry. I'm not going to tell anyone, except Christine, unless you break it off with her. Did you ever think this"—I poked my finger into his injured arm—"could be the result of playing fast and loose with people's emotions?"

He looked at the sling. "I thought I felt someone shove me down the basement stairs. It was dark and I couldn't see anything. Was it you?"

I laughed. "Not me. I was too smart to fall for your BS when you hit on me the first day I worked here. You probably don't even remember."

"But *you* do." He looked at me through half-closed eyes and parted his lips. "There may be a reason for that."

Ugh! That really turned my stomach. "Okay. Enough of that or I *will* push you off of something. Either tell Christine it's over, or I'll tell her what you said, and then I'll go to Livy with the information. That's your choice." I curtseyed to him. "Good afternoon, Your Majesty."

I got out of his chambers as quickly as I could. Harry had some nerve trying to hit on me during that conversation. The man was no better than a stray cat. Maybe I could find some way to pin Chris's murder on him. The Village might lose some market shares if Harry and Livy split up and took their child away. But we might all be the better for it.

Chase was waiting at the castle gate for me. I had planned to wait there for him if he hadn't been finished with Livy. I just couldn't go back in there again. At least, not then. I needed some fresh air.

"There you are," he said when he saw me. "Where'd you get off to?"

I explained about my tête-à-tête with Harry. "I think he'll tell her. It's stupid to keep leading her on that way. What a jerk!"

I was moving really fast down the hill, frustration and anger adding speed to my feet. Chase kept up with me. "Will that help? Did he know anything about Chris's death?"

"I don't know. I asked him about Chris being king. He remembered it, at least, which is more than I can say for Detective Almond or Esmeralda. He knew Chris had been here."

"So you think Harry had something to do with Chris's death?"

"I don't think so. It would take some passion for him to care enough to want Christine for himself. I don't believe he has that in him. You were right. I hope Christine can handle it. She really cares about him."

"She's better off forgetting him," he said. "Cut it off fast. That's the best way."

I smiled at him. He looked so handsome walking beside me, the wind blowing his hair. "Is that what I can expect if we break up? A sharp cut?"

He smiled back and put his arm around me. "That's not going to happen. I never want to live without you. I thought you knew that."

I felt all warm inside and changed the subject. "That leaves me back with Edgar as my suspect."

"Or Christine. When Detective Almond finds out she was having an affair with Harry, she'll be suspect number one. If she isn't already."

"I thought that was me because I found the body."

"Maybe. He did mention something about keeping an eye on you. I told him I had that covered."

"Anyway, I don't think Christine is guilty."

"Because you feel sorry for her?"

"No, because raising eight kids alone isn't going to be any fun—even with the insurance money. Besides, there's the threatening note." I told him about the crude note I'd found on the workshop door.

He shrugged. "I agree, but she could have done the note herself. And the police could argue that she doesn't realize she and Harry won't be together. She might think she'll get the money, have Harry, and live a good life."

"I thought you didn't think she was guilty?"

"Not me. I'm just playing devil's advocate here. And I've worked with the police enough times to know how they think. Edgar is a long shot. Christine is a bird in hand."

I had to laugh at that. "Please, stop mangling all those metaphors. It's giving me a headache."

He stopped walking. "We should immediately return to the Dungeon for emergency first aid."

I had to stop walking, too. It struck me that there were some things I needed to say to this man who was so important to me. "I love you. You know that, right? I know I'm being stupid and stubborn over this thing with staying in the Village. I'm just scared. I wish I wasn't, because you're the most awesome person I've ever known."

"I know." He smiled and kissed me. "But you'll come around. I'll be here to soften you up until you do."

As we were romantically standing in each other's arms, gazing lovingly into each other's eyes, a short man dressed in elf green and peasant brown made a loud coughing sound. "Excuse me," he said finally after we'd ignored him for a few seconds.

"Sorry." I glared at him for interrupting the moment. "Do you want something?"

"I'm Officer Paul Miller from the Myrtle Beach Police Department. Detective Almond told me to contact you right away, Ms. Morton. I'm supposed to arrange a time here, at your convenience, to take your statement about the recent character death here in Renaissance Village. He said, and I quote, 'It might be faster than waiting for her to come to the station.' End quote. You can call him if you like."

Chase smiled and held out his hand to the other man. "He might be right. I'm Chase Manhattan, Village bailiff.

You must be one of the undercover officers Detective Almond is assigning here until we crack this case."

Paul shook Chase's hand with plenty of gusto. "It's very nice to meet you. Detective Almond always has good things to say about you."

"Really?" Chase raised one brow as he looked down at the officer. "That's good to know."

"Oh yes. He's always talking about what a good police officer you'd make in the real world because you do such a good job in what he calls the *squirrel factory*. I think he's referring to the Village. Although I don't know why. It seems very pleasant here."

"I see." Chase laughed. "I'll have to remember to thank him for that, Officer Miller."

"Please call me Paul. I'll just be one of the crew now, Mr. Bailiff. I understand that I'll report to you while I'm here. I don't know if knaves have names or not."

"I'm not sure either about the names, Paul. Where would you like to take Jessie's statement?"

"Where's good?" We all looked down from our vantage point at the Village stretched below us. "Where would you go?" Paul asked.

"The Dungeon," I answered. After all, he was there to talk to me. "I'll lead the way."

Chase's radio went off—something about a lost child. "I'll see you later," he said. "Let me know how it goes."

Paul was full of pleasant conversation, asking curious questions about the Village as we walked down the cobblestones to the Dungeon. It was the only place I could think of where there wouldn't be tourist cameras or listening ears as he asked me questions about what had happened the day Chris was killed.

I took him upstairs to our apartment, and he raved about how quaint and interesting it must be to live over the Dungeon. I agreed with him, even got him a bottle of water. Everything seemed to be going just fine.

He took out his tape recorder as well as a notebook and pen. We both sat down, and I was fooled into thinking this would be a continuance of our conversation on the way here.

But the first question out of his mouth was, "Do you have any verification of your whereabouts at the actual time Mr. Christmas was killed?"

Fifteen

"What do you mean?" I demanded. "You sound like I'm a suspect."

He smiled politely. "You *were* first on the scene, Ms. Morton. Were you having an affair with Mr. Christmas? There had to be some reason you were there to see him even though everyone else was gone."

"Are you insane?" I bounced out of my chair. "I barely knew him. We'd just met a few hours before. I hadn't slept with him and had no plans to do so. I'm shocked that you'd even ask. And I was going to make toys. That's what my job is."

"Sorry. These are the questions Detective Almond told me to ask. I'm just doing my job. You want to see the killer caught, don't you?"

"Whatever." I didn't believe Detective Almond had told him to ask those questions. I stalked around the apartment—

it was too small to stalk far. I fingered the swords in Chase's collection, wishing I could use one on Paul.

"And your location during the approximate commission of the crime, sometime between noon and two P.M.?"

"I was on my way to meet Chris at the workshop. Or I was eating at the Pleasant Pheasant, buying a turkey leg for Chris, or getting out of bed with Chase. Take your pick."

"How long after the crime took place would you say you were at the scene?"

My temper was about to get the better of me. This wasn't what I'd expected. "Very soon. So soon, I think the killer was still there." I showed him my bruises. "I got these from him as he left the scene."

"So you're convinced it was a man? Why not a woman?"

"You mean Christine, don't you? You think his wife killed him."

"Maybe." He smiled again. I wanted to hit him. "Do you think his wife killed him?"

"No! I know she has a big insurance policy on him—"

"And she was having an affair with another man, isn't that correct?"

I *really* didn't like him anymore. He was worse than Detective Almond. I wouldn't have thought that was possible. "I don't know that for sure," I lied. "I'm guessing you don't know either."

"We know she was having an affair, Ms. Morton. She's still seeing Harold Martin. I think they call him the king, is that right? Do you think her lover helped her kill her husband?"

"No," I responded fiercely. "Because I don't think Christine killed anyone."

"You've spent a lot of time with her since the death of her husband, haven't you?"

"Yes."

"Has she told you where she was when her husband was killed?"

"Yes." What was he getting at?

"Has she told you where she was when he died?"

"I know where she was. She was with her son purchasing a new camera for their work."

His eyes narrowed as he leaned closer to me. "Would it surprise you to learn that she was back in the Village for an hour, without her children? Where was she during that hour, Jessie? Has she confided in you? Holding back won't help, you know."

"She hasn't said where she was, but I know she wasn't far from her children. She's a good mother."

"That may be true. However, that left her with plenty of time to kill her husband, leave the workshop, probably knocking you down as she ran out, then return after Bailiff Manhattan arrived."

"That sounds like a stretch to me." But there was a cold sensation in my chest. The police had obviously thought this through. The way Detective Almond had thrown out the idea—I hadn't thought he was serious.

"Has she ever shown you a gun, Ms. Morton?"

"No! Guns aren't allowed in the Village. As far as I know, she doesn't have a gun."

"You know there was no murder weapon found at the scene, don't you? We believe she still has it. Probably hidden somewhere in her apartment."

"I don't believe it. She didn't kill him. Everything you've said is circumstantial."

"We'll see." He turned off the tape recorder and put down his pen.

I glanced at all the scribbling in his notebook before he

put it away. I couldn't tell what he'd written, but I was pretty sure it wasn't good. I felt like I'd been mauled by a pit bull.

"Thank you for your cooperation. That's all I'll need from you—at least for now."

I couldn't believe he could look and sound so harmless while we'd been out in the Village, then turn so vicious once we got inside. I really believed he tried to make me feel threatened so I'd reveal something about Christine that would help the cops make their case against her. What a weasel!

"Where would you recommend eating here at the Village?" He was back to the sweet weasel part of his character. "I'm starved!"

"Get out of my apartment," I said through my teeth. "Don't ever talk to me again."

He made a placating face. "Please don't take this personally. May I call you Jessie?"

I marched the few feet it took to reach the door and opened it for him. "No, you can't call me Jessie. And get out now before I call security."

He persisted. "Let's let bygones be bygones. I'll buy you a drink. You can tell me exactly what a knave is expected to do in the Village."

"I don't think so. You'll have to find someone else to interrogate about that. Good-bye."

He shrugged and looked a little mystified that I was throwing him out. But he left. I slammed the door closed after him. I wasn't sure if he was trying to be a tough guy or what. I didn't care. I didn't plan on answering any more of his questions or helping him out in any way. He was on his own.

I sat down on the bed and thought about the case he'd

just laid out for me. It sounded bad for Christine. It would be a terrible tragedy if they arrested her. They still needed a better case against her but that could be possible.

I'd been wishy-washy, too. Hadn't I felt the same about her for a short time? She *did* appear to be guilty of something. I could even see the cops' point about Harry looking guilty. I didn't know how much the large insurance policy was for, but it sounded a lot like motive when it was paired with the fact that she'd been cheating.

Maybe I'd cut my own throat by kicking Paul out. If I'd kept calm, I could've floated the idea that Edgar could be guilty. That way, Paul wouldn't pay much attention to me.

I couldn't have helped it anyway. He'd tricked me into trusting him, then attacked me when we got here. I was going to have to find out about Edgar on my own.

In the meantime, I thought I should warn Christine about the police making a case against her. Maybe she had a friend or family member who could take care of her children if something happened to her. Otherwise they'd probably go to Social Services. I wasn't sure exactly what that system was like, but I remembered my grandmother always saying how happy she was not to have lost me and Tony to them. It sounded bad anyway.

Chase still hadn't returned, so I decided to see if Christine was back from meeting with her lawyer. I was on my way to the manor houses when I spotted Roger Trent. He was beginning the trek to the castle to set up for the King's Feast. The Village was closed for a few hours and would reopen later for the event.

All of the craft people brought their wares to the castle on feast nights to sell to the large crowds who came for the dinner and show. It was a sales highlight for most of them. Everyone did well at the King's Feast.

"Hi, Roger." I smiled at him, hoping he was in a good mood. "I wanted to ask you a few questions, if you don't mind."

"Hi, Jessie. I don't mind, if you carry half of this stuff for me. What's up?"

Roger could be curt, part of his background as a police officer, I supposed. He was still in good shape, too. His shoulders and chest were wide, narrowing down to his hips and muscular legs. He kept his head shaved, and he was almost as tan as his brown jerkin and trousers.

I explained the basic situation to him. He'd given me mostly baskets from his wife, Gullah weaver Mary Shift, to carry. I'd apprenticed with both of them and had learned a lot from them. I was also instrumental in bringing them together. It was satisfying to see that their relationship was still working.

"So, do you remember Chris and Alice Christmas being here as king and queen?"

"Sure. I had dinner with them many times at the castle. They were good people. I was sorry to hear Chris had been killed."

"Do you know if anyone who was here at that time had any kind of problem with him? Could he or she still be here?"

Roger shifted his heavy load of glass items. "There aren't a lot of us still here. Me. Livy and Harry. They came in right as Chris and Alice were leaving. I made sure that was a smooth transition. Some of the castle staff were here. A few of the original craft people are still here. Does Chase think the killer is hanging out waiting to be caught?"

"I don't know. It's just a theory of mine. Do you know what happened to Alice after she broke up with Chris? Did she stay on?"

"Alice?" He thought about it as we passed the Sherwood Forest entrance. A series of whistles and strange cries accompanied our passage. We both glanced that way, then shrugged and moved on. "I'm not sure. They left the Village together, if I remember correctly. There was a lot going on here at that time. Not to mention that I was in the middle of a life crisis. I'd given up my job with the police. My wife had left me and was suing for sole custody of our son. I had a lot on my plate."

"And Alice?" I prompted. Sometimes Roger got caught up in his own life's story to the exclusion of everything else.

"Oh yeah. I don't know for sure what happened to them after that. I heard they'd gotten divorced. I didn't see Chris again until he came back here."

"What about Edgar Gaskin? Have you ever met him before?"

"I haven't met him at all. I've never heard the name. Is he someone here at the Village?"

"He's the new Father Christmas. He was here before Chris was killed and then stepped right into his job."

He made a *humphing* sound. "Sounds like someone did some good planning for a change. Bringing in a feature Christmas character looks like a real ticket seller. That means more people and more sales for me. Is he going to be at the feast tonight?"

"Don't you think that seems a little suspicious? It's like someone was expecting Chris to fail—or worse."

"Not really. You have to protect your investment, Jessie. The Village can't run on *huzzahs* and turkey legs, you know. Adventure Land needs to update their plan for us every couple of years. Things have to run on schedule. You're a tight ship or you sink."

He talked on, but all I heard after that last part was *blah-blah-blah.*

I agreed with him—halfheartedly. I knew the Village would cease to exist if it didn't turn a profit. Taxes had to be paid, and people liked to get their paychecks, no matter how small, at least once in a while.

Roger and I reached the castle, joined by other residents who were setting up shop. Only the food vendors weren't allowed to sell their wares on this night because it created a conflict with the castle kitchen. But all vendors and characters were commanded to attend. Failing to show up at the King's Feast each week was grounds for dismissal.

I couldn't remember anyone ever actually being fired for not coming. Certainly there were some characters who didn't make it every week. It was probably not enough to bother with for whoever kept track of those things.

So far, I didn't have much on Edgar, and despite my best effort, I had even less on Alice. It was time to take the investigation to the next level—in this case, searching Edgar's room at the castle. I'd learned that I wouldn't get much from him by being friendly or confronting him directly.

Tonight's festivities, however, would be built around Father Christmas. Or so I'd heard. It seemed like the perfect opportunity to search through his things. Maybe I'd find something incriminating there. My plan, such as it was, was to leave the feast as he was introduced. There was bound to be some showy production to bring him out. I'd go to his room, take a look around, then head back to the feast. I was a very minor character. I felt sure no one would miss me.

The King's Feast was always a dazzling sight to behold. Every jester, knight, lady, and lord was in his or her finest as hundreds of visitors packed into the Great Hall. Once there, they would dine on small chickens, bread, vegetables, and dessert, washed down with plenty of ale, soda, or iced tea. The king and queen with all of their court presided over the affair in regal splendor.

For entertainment, the residents of the Village paraded their wares. There were jousts in the arena, displays of bravery, swordsmanship, and other heroic feats. There were also magicians, jugglers, acrobats, and everything one could imagine possible at a Renaissance feast.

It was a lot of work for everyone, but the big event brought in more first-timers who everyone hoped would return for a full day sometime later. With Father Christmas on the menu, it was bound to be even more impressive.

I started back to the Dungeon so I could change clothes. I saw Christine and the kids walking up from the parking lot through the Main Gate as I reached the cobblestones. I waved and waited for them.

This didn't seem to be the appropriate time to reiterate that Harry didn't love her and wouldn't leave Livy. And maybe that wasn't my job. Maybe Harry would do the right thing.

"Did your meeting go well?" I asked when they got close.

"I don't know. There's some holdup in collecting the insurance for Chris's death." She sent the children to play while we talked.

There it was—one of her motives, according to the police. Would it be impolite to ask how much of a motivator it was?

"It looks like the police have put some kind of block on me getting the money," she said. "The insurance company said they won't pay until they clear the case. I don't know what to do, Jessie. I don't have the money to bury him. I don't even have the money to cremate him and put him in a jar."

At that last part, she broke down into huge, gulping sobs. I put my arms around her and tried to comfort her. But what could I say to her? I didn't have any money either. For her, I'd be willing to ask Chase.

On the other hand, it could be a while before Chris's body was released by the ME's office. It probably wouldn't be until the murder was solved.

"I'm so sorry," I finally said. "I'll see what I can do to help. But you won't need it right away. The police won't let you do anything with him until they're done."

"What do you mean?" She moved away and pushed at the tears streaming down her face.

How could I put it delicately? "The medical examiner does tests, but they have to be sent somewhere else for the results. That can take a while. They won't release the body until all the tests are back—or they close the case."

"I see." She scanned the area for the children. Seeing them, she looked back at me. "This is never going to end, is it? It feels like a nightmare I just can't wake up from."

Again, I didn't know what to say. I hugged her again and asked if she was going to the King's Feast. It sounded kind of lame, but I needed something normal, at least for me, to hold on to.

"Yes. I believe we are. Edgar sent us a command that we'd better be there. So we will." She smiled a little. "Father Christmas doesn't want to be seen without his family, even if we aren't really his family."

"It will be a big spectacle tonight. Be prepared."

"I'll be as prepared as I can be. I just received a text from Harry. He said our relationship is over. He asked me not to contact him in any way. That has made everything even worse. At least when I believed he loved me, it all made sense somehow."

That was fast work. Leave it to Harry to text someone that they were breaking up. All those feelings of dislike I had for him became even stronger. But at least he'd responded appropriately to my threat and *I* didn't have to tell Christine.

"I tried to explain earlier. Harry is only in it for himself. Nothing else matters. But I'm sorry anyway."

"Well, it goes along with the rest of this week, doesn't it? I guess I'd better round everyone up and get them changed for the feast."

"Can I give you a hand?"

"No. Thanks anyway. I've got this under control—if nothing else. But you've been a great help to me, Jessie. I'll never be able to repay you."

I saw Detective Almond with two officers in uniform out of the corner of my eye. They were coming through the Main Gate. Chase was with them, already in his feast finery. He had a look on his face that made me quake in dread.

Christine and I turned to face them as they came closer, obviously on their way to speak to one of us.

"Mrs. Christine Christmas," Detective Almond said in a flat monotone. "We are here to arrest you for the murder of your husband, Christopher Christmas. These officers will read you your rights."

Sixteen

"Why?" I demanded. "What's changed?"

Detective Almond scowled at me while the officers put handcuffs on Christine.

"They found the murder weapon in her apartment," Chase whispered, coming close to me and holding my hand. "That's it. They have everything they need."

"But what about the kids?" I asked him. "What will happen to them?"

"Social Services is on the way," Chase explained. "I'm sorry, Jessie. This is the way it works."

"No!" I said it to him in a whisper, then shouted it at Detective Almond. "No! Don't take the kids. Let me take care of them, at least for now. We can look for someone else later if this isn't rectified. Don't just put them out there. You know they'll have to split them up. They'll be miserable."

"Jessie!" Chase muttered. "There are *eight* kids. You know that, right?"

Detective Almond actually smiled. "How about it, Manhattan? I can leave them with you and Miss Jessie for tonight. Are you up for that?"

Chase didn't look as certain as I did, but he confidently responded, "Sure. We can handle it."

I loved him even more for that.

"Thank you, Jessie—Chase," Christine said. "Bless you both. Merry Beth will help you. Let her take the lead. The kids are used to her telling them what to do."

"We'll have to revisit this tomorrow," Detective Almond promised. "Have a good night, Mom and Dad." He went away chuckling.

"I'm sorry," I told Chase when they were gone. "I know this will be hard. But I couldn't let them go like that. Everyone needs someone who can save them."

"It's okay," he said, putting his arm around me. "I suppose we should look for them."

I looked up, prepared to search the area around us under the quickly darkening sky. But they were all standing together at the foot of the stairs that led to their apartment in the manor house. They were staring silently, not moving as the police led their mother away.

Chase and I had just started toward them when Jolly seemed to realize what was happening. He gave a loud cry that sounded like it'd been ripped from his soul and ran after his mother.

Chase caught him and talked to him alone for a while. I continued on until I'd reached the rest of the children—then explained what had happened.

"That's stupid!" Practical, mature Merry Beth let out a stream of language I felt sure her mother wouldn't have approved of. "My mom would never kill my dad. And she doesn't even own a gun. Somebody made a mistake."

"If the police found a gun, someone must've planted it on her," Garland said. "Like on TV. Someone is trying to frame her."

I agreed with him but didn't say so. Those poor kids needed protection. They needed some normality. I couldn't do anything about their mother being arrested, but I could help with that.

"Are you sure this is the right thing to do?" Chase asked thirty minutes later when all of the kids, except Jolly, were dressed in their green elf costumes.

"This is what they know," I explained. "And everything going on at the feast will distract them, at least for a while. If they were any other group of kids, it would seem weird. But this is part of their lives."

"A life I hate!" Jolly yelled. "I don't want to be part of this anymore. It's stupid and lame. And all of you are stupid for going along with it." He slammed into his bedroom. The rest of the kids were silent after he left, clearly frightened by their brother's outburst.

"Well, all right. I guess we all know that Jolly is in a bad mood right now. That's okay. Everyone has the right to be in a bad mood occasionally. The rest of us are going up to the castle for the feast. I'm sure you're going to love it."

Chase volunteered to escort them to the castle while I ran back to the Dungeon to change clothes. I tried not to think about what I'd just volunteered us to do. If I had thought about it, I might have run away screaming. What did either of us know about taking care of kids?

But I managed to block it out as I changed into my bright red gown for the evening. It was pretty but very modest compared to what most women would be wearing. Let's face it—women bared their chests during the Renaissance. I had always conjectured it was to make up for the rest of their bodies being heavily covered all the time. They needed something to attract a man.

I'd found out early on in my Ren Faire career that having a neckline that barely covered you made it hard to do anything useful. Sort of like two-inch fingernails. So my gowns were always a little on the modest side—most of the time.

I kind of fluffed up my short hair a little and slipped my feet into half boots that almost matched the gown. That was going to have to do. I didn't want to leave Chase alone too long with all that responsibility.

And I was still considering how I could get into Edgar's room without him knowing.

I joined the rest of the latecomers on their way to the castle. The Main Gate was open. Security and barricades would keep the visitors from going out into the rest of the Village. They were sent on a path that edged along Mirror Lake. It gave the pirates a chance to show off and let the visitors see some of the Village without venturing down the dark cobblestones.

"You are looking particularly lovely tonight, Lady Jessie."

I barely recognized the voice and was surprised to see the young knight I'd met, Dennis Greene, walking beside me. He'd cleaned up well—young, tall, and handsome in his bits of shining armor. The only knights who wore full armor to the feast would be jousting. Dennis was too new for that.

"Hello. It's good to see you." I was surprised and embarrassed. I'd totally forgotten I was supposed to have met him after closing.

He laughed. "You forgot about me, didn't you? I checked up on you. You were incognito at the field. Were you spying on someone—or looking for a secret lover?"

Obviously this wasn't the conversation I'd wanted to have with him. Yes, he reminded me of Chase when I'd first met him, in some ways. But that was a long time ago. I wasn't that same kitchen wench either.

"Neither. I was looking for the horse that went missing when the knight rode it out of the Village yesterday. He almost skewered me and my friend. I wanted to know who he was."

"Why didn't you say so?" He took my hand and drew it on his arm between us as we walked. "I happen to know exactly who that was. I saw him bring the horse and armor back last night."

"Who was it?" I decided to leave my hand on his forearm, at least until I had an answer. "Do you know his name?"

"I don't know his name, my lady. I've seen him since standing at the fence watching us practice. I don't believe he works here, but he appears to like the idea of doing so."

Rats! "Would you know him, good sir, if you were to see him again?"

"Of course. And I would be happy to point him out if you would consider supping with me one night. I believe even the moonlight would pale compared to your beauty."

The visitors around us were eating up our conversation, savoring every morsel like coffee and cinnamon rolls. But I was used to this. Visitors always enjoyed hearing costumed residents speak in romantic prose. Three older ladies were giggling and encouraging Dennis as we reached the castle gate.

"Give her a little kiss to break the ice, sonny." One of them nudged him with her elbow.

"I do not know this young man well enough to allow him to be so bold." I glared at him in what I hoped was a significant manner.

"My lady is shy." He smiled at me warmly before he lifted my hand and planted a kiss on it. "I would woo her in such a manner as she finds comfortable."

"My lady is with *me*, young sir." Chase stepped out of the shadows created by the torches near the entrance. "My gratitude to you for seeing her safely to the castle."

Of course all the ladies started giggling again. Dennis gave Chase a formal bow of deep respect but didn't say anything else. He walked in before us to the Great Hall.

"I'm up here with the kids *you* volunteered us to take care of and you're flirting with that—other kid," Chase whispered as we walked in together.

He rarely got angry, but I realized this was one of those times.

"I'm sorry. He had information for me about the rogue knight that came after me and Christine. I still think that incident could be important to the case. And where are the kids?"

"A few of the PR ladies from Adventure Land took them so they could get ready for their entrance with Father Christmas," he explained. "I hope you're ready for this. There's a big sleigh that's going to drop down from the ceiling. The kids and Edgar will throw out candy, and flower petals will rain down from the ceiling."

"Flower petals? In winter?"

"It was supposed to be glitter, but they nixed that idea—they didn't want to take the visitors out of the Renaissance theme."

"I can see that. Hothouses but no tiny metal flakes. They could have used kernels of corn or maybe seeds from fruits or vegetables."

He pulled me into a shadowed corner of the entryway as visitors streamed in. "Seriously? You're flirting with that kid-knight wannabe on the way up here and you want to think about what kind of natural foods they could drop from the ceiling?"

"That's what *you* were talking about. I thought we were having a conversation about the sleigh event."

"That's not what I really want to talk about. I just didn't want to get into it where everyone was listening and taking notes."

"You never get jealous," I reminded him, poking my finger into his chest. "Why are you so insecure all of a sudden? You know no one can hold a candle to you."

"Except that you won't stay here with me."

"This isn't the time for that argument, Chase. I have something I have to do."

"Such as?" He circled me in his arms, my back to the fake stone wall. "What's so important, Jessie?"

I couldn't tell him that I planned to visit Edgar's room. In his present state of mind, he'd think I was hooking up with Edgar, too. *Ugh!* But whether I was going there to be with Edgar or to search through his belongings wouldn't matter. Chase would go ballistic. It wouldn't help my case after that stupid flirty conversation with Dennis on the way in.

"You're right." I hoped to disarm him, throw him off the scent. "It's not more important than you. Nothing is. And I won't ever forget how you backed me on keeping the kids. I love you, Chase." I put my arms around his neck and kissed him until I was seeing stars.

"I believe you," he said quietly when I'd pulled away. "I'm sorry I was jealous. I was wrong to let that kid bother me."

"Thanks. Shall we go? Are you sitting with the king and queen tonight?"

"Yes. How about you?"

"Probably not."

"You're a member of the royal court now, Jessie. You have a right to be there."

And be watched constantly, making it impossible for me to sneak away. "I don't know. Normally I would've sat with Chris and Christine, being their apprentice. At least I won't be in the sleigh. That would be awful."

I bantered. I flattered. I sweet-talked, as my grandma used to call it. I didn't want Chase to get suspicious.

We parted at the landing that separates the royal family, their friends, and servants from the visitors seated on the top floor above the arena. Already I could see the knights below in the sawdust with their magnificent horses, getting ready for the show.

"I'll see you later," Chase whispered with a kiss.

"Love you," I answered and wasted no time making my way to the long line of Village residents with no particular place to sit during the event.

It didn't matter. I felt reasonably sure the sleigh full of kids and Father Christmas would be the first event. That meant I wouldn't be at the table for long. I could slip in and out of the Great Hall without anyone noticing.

Fortunately, I was near one of the serving doors. The kitchen wenches brought out the big platters of food through here. It would be easy to get to Edgar's room from the kitchen since I knew my way around the castle. My time on the computer wasn't wasted. I knew which room he was staying in.

I waited long enough for the holiday music to begin playing. Lord Dunstable, master of ceremonies, was talking about Christmas during the time of the Renaissance. I knew Father Christmas was about to make his entrance.

I shifted my bulky skirt, got up, and headed for the door.

"You're going to miss everything if you leave now," Sam Da Vinci whispered, garbed in his gold and purple finery. "I helped design the sleigh, you know."

"That's great." I smiled encouragingly. "But I have to go—lady's room, you know."

I swung the door open to the kitchen and walked right into Chase.

"Where are you going?" He put his hands on my forearms to steady me. His tone told me I'd overdone it. I'd made him suspicious.

"The bathroom. I thought this might be the fastest way around."

"Where are you *really* going? You know the castle well enough to know the bathrooms are the other way. What do you have in mind, Jessie?"

"You're not going to like it." I sighed, knowing I was caught. I could either admit that I was going to search Edgar's room or tell him that I was going to meet Dennis. Out of the two, I thought the truth was the better option.

I explained my plan to take a look through Edgar's stuff. "There might be something incriminating that would give him away."

I could hear the sounds of the event getting started. Queen Olivia and King Harold were welcoming the visitors. If I didn't go soon, Edgar's part in the festivities would be over.

"You can't just go around searching people's rooms, Jessie," Chase said. "Nothing you find would be admissible in court. That wouldn't help Christine or the police."

"But it might make Edgar confess, if it's the right thing."

"How are you going to get in without being seen? There are castle staff everywhere."

"There could be an emergency," I suggested, still not sure where Chase was on this.

"There could be," he agreed. "I think Edgar will join the royal court when his part is over. But I'm not sure. We'd better get moving."

"Have I mentioned how much I love you?"

"Maybe." He smiled and took my hand. "But feel free to say it anytime. You know how insecure I am."

Seventeen

I felt bad walking out right as the kids were about to have their big moment. On the other hand, bringing their mother home from jail would be the best Christmas present I could give them. Finding the real killer would also bring them closure.

I wasn't sure what kind of emergency we could come up with on such short notice. As usual, I had an idea that seemed like it would work but no real plan to implement it. Lucky for me, Chase could be cleverly devious when he wanted to be. And he was one step ahead of me.

Although the entire kitchen staff was involved in the King's Feast, the household staff wasn't really part of it. We went to Edgar's suite of rooms and asked the first staff member we saw to help us with his room. It was simple for Chase to tell a chambermaid that Edgar had requested clean sheets for his bed. The bailiff was like the king and queen—no one questioned him.

While we waited for the chambermaid to return, we heard shouts of "Huzzah!" coming from the Great Hall.

"I hope the kids will be all right," I worried out loud.

"They'll be fine," he assured me. "You should've seen everyone with them. They all know about their parents. I'm sure the royal family will take great care of them."

"Why doesn't that reassure me?"

The one thing we didn't count on was Esmeralda. Instead of the chambermaid, Esmeralda arrived with the clean sheets. Anger flashed from her dark eyes as she faced us down at Edgar's door.

"We just changed these sheets this morning," she raged. "I don't know who he thinks he is, but we can't do this two or three times every day."

Chase smiled, after she'd turned her back to open the door. He'd come up with an idea that fit right in with what was already going on in the castle. It's great when a plan comes together.

We followed her into the room. Esmeralda glared at us. "What? Edgar needs someone to watch while we change the sheets? Come on, Chase. Do I tell you how to do vegetable justice?"

"No. But you're welcome to," he said. "Really, I was just wondering if you have any other problems in the castle. I thought this might be a good time to ask. I'm working on the annual security report for Adventure Land."

"And Jessie's here because she's always with you." She smiled. "Smart girl. Never take a man for granted, especially one who looks like you."

I didn't want to get into that. Obviously, Chase knew how to get information without seeming to ask for it. Besides, this seemed like a good time for me to slip away and look around.

"I'm just going to use the bathroom," I said.

"Clean it up when you're done," Esmeralda scolded.

I could hear Chase and her talking as I left them in the bedroom. That would've been my first choice of areas to look through, but the bathroom and living room would have to do.

I searched through drawers and cabinets, under the sofa, in the medicine chest and the closet, anywhere one could potentially hide damning information or evidence. I didn't find anything that would help confirm my belief that Edgar had killed Chris. I wasn't really sure what I was looking for—which might've been part of the problem.

The murder weapon had already been discovered in Christine's possession. Nothing I found here would be as incriminating as that. Edgar must have put the gun in the manor house. What other evidence could there be?

I found his cell phone and looked through his calls. There were plenty of calls to one number, which turned out to be Livy's cell phone. I stayed away from that. If Livy was involved in Chris's murder, there had been no suspicious activity or evidence to back that up. I was probably better off concentrating on Edgar as my suspect.

He'd left his laptop on. I could hear Esmeralda still venting to Chase about everything she considered of importance at the castle. I took the few minutes to scroll through the files I could access. There were pictures, a few e-mails. Nothing that seemed to have anything to do with Chris's death.

A few of the e-mails made me go back and look at the cell phone again. He and Livy were definitely chatting a lot. The tone of the words between them wasn't friendly at all. In fact, it had me wondering if Edgar was blackmailing

Livy for something besides a stint playing Father Christmas at the Village.

Livy was obviously frantic for Harry not to find out that she and Edgar had been a couple for a short while. I was surprised to learn that their affair had taken place only a few months before Livy found out she was pregnant. It made me think again about Harry's demanding a paternity test when he'd first learned of the pregnancy.

On the other hand, Harry was sleeping with Christine up until today, as far as I knew. I should never be surprised by anything either of them did.

I sat on the sofa and looked around the expensively decorated room. Everything was in high Renaissance fashion but with all of the modern conveniences. Not a thing was out of place. It didn't even look like anyone was staying there.

I was disappointed. Had I missed the big score by not being able to search the bedroom? I wandered back that way and saw Chase helping Esmeralda make the bed. He probably felt guilty about putting her through that extra work.

"And talk about security," she was saying. "What about someone pushing the king down the stairs into the basement? I know people get angry at him, but shouldn't there be some safeguards against things like that happening?"

"Absolutely." Chase sounded as though he'd agreed to too many things already. "Do you have any idea how that happened? Harry seems unwilling to talk about it."

"I don't know," she admitted. "Maybe we need security cameras in here. I can't keep my eyes on everything all the time. I heard that someone saw a kid come up the stairs after Harry went down them. I don't know who said it or who the kid was. It might not be true. Maybe Harry was just clumsy and wanted to blame it on someone else."

"It was a kid who came after me and Christine the other day, too," I added to the conversation.

"Christine?" Esmeralda glanced at me as she stuffed pillows into fresh cases. "Who's that? Is that the new Lady Godiva?"

"I thought news traveled faster than that." I explained that Christine was Chris's wife. "She was arrested for his murder tonight."

"I guess we aren't as screwed up as that," she said. "But maybe we can put out a Village APB on this unknown kid, huh, Chase? I don't like the idea of some young punk hanging around waiting to push one of my girls around."

"I'll get right on it." Chase stood up after giving the bedspread one last pat. "Thanks for all your input, Esmeralda. If anyone knows this place from ground to ceiling, it's you."

"Next time, ask me about new rules we need for castle guests," she said. "But you better have a few hours to listen."

She ushered us out of Edgar's rooms and locked the door behind her. Chase gave her a formal bow and kissed her hand. She giggled like a schoolgirl.

"Well that was a waste of time," I remarked as we went back to the feast.

"Not really," he said. "She actually had some good ideas on castle security. Most of them would cost more money than Adventure Land would be willing to spend on the problems, but now I know about them. Maybe I can find some creative solutions."

"But we aren't any closer to helping Christine get out of jail."

He put his arm around me. "We're going to have to deal with that in the morning, Jessie. Maybe we can find some new ideas for that, too."

A few people remarked on our being gone for part of the feast. Most of them did a lot of smiling and winking—they thought we'd been sharing a private moment in some secret corner of the castle.

Chase and I laughed but didn't say where we'd been, which made us look even guiltier. Livy had a few angry words about it, but she was probably just envious because no one had invited *her* to sneak out.

Chase had been right about the kids. They'd been having a great time tossing little chicken bones down at the jesters in the arena, yelling "Huzzah!" and cheering on their favorite knights. They hadn't even missed us.

It seemed as though I'd been right about taking them to the castle to help them forget, if only for a little while, what was happening in their lives. Their little faces were red and excited, eyes shining as they told us about everything we had missed.

Edgar was seated with the royal party, too, of course. He was his usual nasty self for the remainder of the feast. I heard him say several times that the children weren't going to be part of the show again. They'd upstaged him with their infectious enthusiasm.

Livy winced every time Edgar spoke to her. I thought about their e-mails and phone calls. He was definitely using what he knew to his advantage. It made me feel protective toward Livy—a strange and unaccustomed experience. It wasn't necessarily a feeling I enjoyed. But I couldn't think of any way to help her out either.

She'd literally made her own bed, et cetera. Still, Edgar was taking full advantage of her at a time when she couldn't defend herself and couldn't ask anyone for help without giving away her secret. It seemed to me there should be some way to make this backfire on him.

When the feast was over, Livy was immediately escorted to her chambers by her unhappy ladies-in-waiting. Jane's mouth was pursed like she'd eaten a lemon. Chase asked me to wait a few minutes while he took the kids down to meet the knights in the arena.

Harry hung back and touched my arm. "I know about Christine," he whispered as the royal box emptied. "If there's anything I can do to help—"

"Find Chris's real killer," I suggested. "We both know she didn't kill him."

"I wish I could help." He dusted an imaginary crumb from his regal red and black costume. "If any of my royal spies hear anything, I'll be sure to let you know."

His attitude of being above it all grated on my nerves. He was as dirty in the trenches as Christine was—there just wasn't anyone to harass him about it.

Except me. "Have the police called you yet?"

He looked a little worried. "No. Should they?"

"The police know Christine was having an affair. It's one of the reasons they charged her with Chris's murder. I'm sure they'll be curious to know who she was having an affair with. It seems to me that person could be considered an accomplice. Or possibly even the killer, for that matter. You didn't kill Chris, did you, Your Majesty?"

Harry was seriously agitated by then. He was a little pale and breathing fast. "How now, Lady Jessie? What matter of question is that?"

Chase joined us. That meant an extra seven pairs of eyes looking at Harry, as the children had come along.

"It's a legitimate question, King Harold," Chase said. "Did you or didn't you kill him?"

The king seemed acutely aware of his interested audience. "Of course I didn't kill anyone. What possible reason would I have to kill—that person." He apparently didn't want to say the name with the children present.

"I can think of one or two reasons," I added. "To have *that person's* wife all to yourself. And there's the little matter of *that person* having an affair with your wife. Both of those could be considered motive."

I was pretty sure we weren't fooling the kids at all, especially since none of us were skilled in hiding things from children.

Harry drew himself up to his full, less than regal, height. "We shall consult our royal attorney on this matter this very night. I thank you both for your valuable information. But know that I am not involved in what happened to that person. However, I shall do everything in my power to help Christine."

He left with his courtiers, no doubt royally rattled. *Good.* Christine was spending the night in jail because of their affair. I hoped Harry didn't get a good night's sleep either.

Chase and I took the kids back to the manor house. If they'd caught on to our conversation with Harry, they didn't give anything away. They were tired but excited by the event. None of them could stop talking about it. They all enjoyed the funny parts of the show, but the girls liked the elegant gowns and the horses best. Garland and Nick favored the swords and jousts.

We walked in a group through the darkened Village. The candles throughout the shops and residences made the whole place glow. The kids screeched and ran around through the snow, except for Hope who was asleep on Chase's shoulder.

Snow was shooting from the castle. The effect was enchanting. The little crystals of frozen water caught the light as they cascaded down on us and covered most of the Village in white.

"It was fun messing with Harry," I said as we watched all the kids—even the staid and responsible Merry Beth—run and play in the frozen white stuff.

"It gave him something to think about anyway," Chase replied. "Royal spies. What a joke."

"I thought maybe he was talking about you."

He brushed some snow from my hair. "Yeah. Right."

"Not that it really makes any difference. I still don't think Harry had anything to do with Chris's murder."

"Maybe not." Chase stooped down and picked up some snow. He made a perfect round ball out of it. "But somebody had to do it, Jessie. I agree with the police. Christine is a perfect suspect. But Harry could have been involved."

I watched as he threw the snowball at Nick. "What about Edgar? He's definitely blackmailing Livy. And his personality sucks. Why couldn't Chris's murder be a crime of opportunity? He was here and needed the job so he killed Chris."

"Not very compelling," he said. "Especially in comparison to his wife and his wife's lover."

That was about all the rational conversation we got to have for a while. Nick returned Chase's snowball and before I knew it, all of us were involved in a snow-battle free-for-all. I'm sorry to say that I had to declare Team Christmas the winners. They pelted Chase and me with so much snow that we looked like we'd been through a blizzard.

Lucky for us, the snow melted right away. It was embarrassing to be beaten down by little kids. We were going to have to pick something we were better at to get our revenge.

It was late when we finally got back to the manor house. Merry Beth supervised as the kids got ready for bed. There was a mad rush to the bathrooms and out again to change into pajamas. Then everyone ran back to the bathrooms to brush their teeth.

They were all a little rowdy after all the excitement and began using their toothbrushes as lances and swords. Either Joy or Star (I couldn't tell them apart) sat on Garland's back and began riding him like a horse. We had to put a stop to that right away.

"I guess this is what it would be like if we were an old married couple with kids," I said to Chase with a smile as we passed each other in the hall between bedrooms.

"But not in the Dungeon," he replied. "We'd have to pick up a craft and get a house with a shop underneath."

"You've always loved the idea of making swords," I reminded him, liking his train of thought.

"Have you seen Jolly in all of this?" he asked.

"I don't think so, but there are a lot of them."

We got everybody settled into their beds, and I read Christmas stories to the youngest ones while Chase looked around the house for Jolly.

"No sign of him," he told me after all of the kids were finally down for the night.

"He's older," I said. "Maybe he wanders around on his own. Tony and I did when we were his age. We used to sneak out a lot."

"Ever get in any trouble?"

I thought back to all the trouble we did get into. "Oh my God—we already lost one of them and it's only the first night."

"I already called security. We'll go out and look for him. You stay here with the other kids and the phone. I'll call if I see him."

I waited with phone in hand after Chase left. All the

time, I was thinking about the rogue knight and what had happened to Harry on the castle stairs. Both times there was a young man involved in the incidents.

Could Jolly have a part in all of this? He was angry at his parents and bitter about his life. Not that his attitude was unusual for his age. But maybe he'd decided to do something about it. Maybe he knew about Harry and Christine, too. He might have attacked Harry.

I hated myself for even thinking it was possible. He was just a kid with problems. Where was my sympathy for the angst of youth?

A minute later, Jolly walked in the front door. He was dirty. His clothes were messy and torn, and he was covered with blood.

He'd come back on his own—I hadn't heard anything from Chase. Maybe that was a good sign.

"We were worried about you, Jolly," I told him. "Are you hurt?"

"I just fell down." He looked at his hands, which were also dirty and covered in blood. "I was out at the jousting field. Can I get washed up now?"

My cell phone rang. It was Chase. "No sign of Jolly," he said in a terse voice. "But I was called to the castle. Someone stabbed Harry."

Eighteen

I looked at Jolly—covered in blood that I sincerely hoped was his. "Thanks, Chase. Jolly is here now. Keep me posted."

"Okay. I'll get back when I can. Are you all right there by yourself?"

"Fine. Don't worry. Everything is fine."

My brain was frantically trying to process everything as I slowly closed my cell phone. I wasn't sure what to do or say. Maybe all of this was coincidence—I prayed it was just coincidence.

But what if it wasn't? How would we know unless Jolly confessed?

"What happened to you?" I couldn't hold back. I knew I should probably wait for his mother, but I had to know.

"I got hurt a little. You don't have to make a big deal out of it."

"A little? You're covered in blood. Where did you get hurt?"

"I don't know. Out in the Village. You're not the police or my mother. You don't get to ask me personal questions."

I could remember myself being this way when I was his age. I gave my grandmother so much grief. I wished I could take it all back.

"You're right," I finally said. "I'm not your mother. She loves you, and you're making her life miserable. I'm glad you're not my responsibility. But someday, you're going to look back on this and want to kick yourself for being such a jerk."

"So can I get cleaned up or what?" Jolly asked again.

"Of course. Sure. Go right ahead." I was still steaming and scared at the same time. I didn't want to think how terrible it would be for Christine if Jolly was also in serious trouble.

"What's going on with Chase?"

"He's looking into some things. He'll be back later."

He nodded and passed by me going toward the bathroom. "Is there anything to eat? I'm starving."

"I'm sure we can find something. Get washed up and we'll look."

I wished there was someone to call in times like this. I didn't want to accuse Jolly of anything. On the other hand, if he knew something that could help Christine, he should come forward.

I waited in the kitchen with a jar of peanut butter, a jar of grape jelly, and an almost empty gallon of milk. If we were going to continue to take care of Christine's children, Chase and I would have to go shopping. How much food could eight children consume in a day?

Jolly joined me, showered and changed. "Any word about my mom?"

"No. I'm sorry. There's nothing yet."

He sat down at the wood table and made two sandwiches, both with holes in them from pulling too hard on the bread. I kept reaching out to help him, then pulling back. He wasn't a baby.

He didn't seem to mind about the holes, bolting the sandwiches down, then swallowing them with the last of the milk.

"You don't have to stand here and watch me," he said. "I'm old enough to take care of myself and everyone else. You don't have to put yourself out for us. We've lived without real parents for a long time."

It sounded like he might want someone to talk to—despite his bitter words. The fact that he'd said anything besides the traditional teenage pity-party refrain was promising.

"I think your parents love you. Maybe they haven't done everything you thought they should. But they seem to care about you. All of you look healthy, you have clothes to wear. They do what they can."

I wasn't prepared for his angry outburst—or the empty milk jug being tossed across the room.

"Oh, sure. They *really* care about us. Especially when the new Santa gig wants children dressed as elves. They've dragged us around, paraded us as part of the act all of our lives." He laughed, but it wasn't a pleasant sound. "They named us after Christmas things. I've never even been in a real school. That's love."

"I'm sorry." I could see he had some legitimate grievances even though there were probably many children who would have enjoyed living their lives. That seemed to be the way it always was when people were growing up. Everyone wanted something different than what they had.

"Me, too. I'm tired of it. I want a real home, not one we have to leave every other week. I want to go to college and be a veterinarian. And when I'm an adult, I'm never celebrating Christmas."

I almost laughed at that. It was said in such a childlike manner. But I knew laughing at his heartfelt confession would only make things worse.

"My parents died when my brother and I were just kids," I told him. "My grandmother raised us. Before that, we had to go through my parent's divorce. I don't know which part was worse. My grandmother loved us, but she was really old. She hadn't expected to have to take on two kids. She made that clear to us."

"That's bad, too," he agreed. "Is she still alive?"

"No. She died years ago. At least my brother and I were out on our own when that happened. What will you do now that your dad is gone?"

He shrugged. "I don't know yet. I guess it all depends what happens to Mom. Do you think they'll put her in prison?"

"I hope not. I don't think she killed your dad. Do you?" I kind of held my breath in case Christine's troubled son was against her, too.

"No! Mom would never hurt anyone. Not that Dad didn't deserve to have his butt kicked." Jolly got up and put the milk jug in the trash. "I knew about him messing around. We all did. He was a good guy except for that. Even so, I don't think Mom would hurt him. And I know she didn't have a gun. Can you imagine Mom shooting a gun at someone?"

Obviously *he* couldn't. That's what mattered, and it was a good thing. I thought Christine seemed like the kind of person who could do whatever she felt needed to be done.

"I think it was the guy who took Dad's place," Jolly said. "He threatened Dad once. It was a long time ago, but still."

Since we seemed to have established a good rapport, I took the next step. "Were you so angry at your mom that you dressed up like a knight and came after her? I saw you at the field, you know."

"Not me. If anything, I'd be angry at Dad. He brought this on himself. All he had to do was look the other way when he found out that guy was stealing. Since when did he care so much about right and wrong? Maybe he should've thought more about the consequences, something he never did. I don't blame Mom for any of it. She just loved him and was ready to do whatever he wanted, you know?"

Was he telling the truth? I wasn't sure. He looked and sounded sincere. There was one more thing—probably the most important.

"I guess we should get some sleep," I said. "Are you okay? I mean, that looked like a lot of blood when you came in."

"It isn't too bad." He got up and showed me his lacerated hands and cut on his forehead. "I got a cut on my knee, too. It's okay. Just messy, I guess."

Jolly seemed much calmer when he told me good night. I sat on the uncomfortable sofa after he'd gone to bed and looked around the pretty but impersonal room. The orange light from the electric fireplace made it seem a little homier, but it still felt like a hotel. I could see why Jolly would promise himself a real home in the future.

Maybe the rogue knight, Harry's injuries, and Chris's death had nothing to do with each other. Maybe Jolly was just a scared, unhappy teenager who'd lost his father. All of it could make sense that way, too. It would certainly be better for this family if that were the case.

Chase got back a little before two A.M. He looked exhausted as he closed and locked the front door.

"How's Harry?" I asked.

"He had to do Livy's run to the hospital instead of her," he said. "But he's doing okay. The knife didn't hit anything vital. It wasn't even that deep. He'll probably be home tomorrow. Unless Livy decides to add to the chaos by having her baby in the next few hours."

"Is she at the hospital with him?"

"No. She fainted when she saw him being taken out. Wanda said she'd be better staying at the castle. She can always go to the hospital tomorrow if he's going to stay longer than that. Sir Reginald went with Harry, along with a full retinue of courtiers. They should keep the hospital staff working while they're there."

Chase sat on the sofa beside me. "Lots of teenage angst when Jolly came back?"

I told him about my talk with the boy—and the blood on him and his clothes. "I don't think he was involved in what happened to Harry, despite the way it might look."

"But you thought so to begin with?"

I shrugged. "Maybe. I don't know. He was gone. He came back covered in blood. Harry was stabbed. Esmeralda said people thought they saw a young boy at the castle when Harry fell down the stairs. I guess I have a suspicious nature. I felt bad about it, though."

"I suppose it might make sense if Jolly knows about Christine and Harry. He could have worked himself up to do something he might not have done otherwise. Not that Harry didn't deserve it. But that would be a serious charge against Jolly, if that were the case."

"We don't know that it is. And I'm too tired to think about it anymore tonight. Let's go to bed, huh?"

He stood up and helped me to my feet. "Sounds good to me. I'll be glad to see the back end of this day."

The Christmas family's morning routine was similar to their evening routine. Everyone got up, showered, dressed, ate Pop Tarts, and drank a gallon of juice. There were long lines at the bathrooms, but eventually everyone was ready to go.

Chase had a plan to keep all the kids busy for the day while we tried to find out what would happen with regard to their custody. We adapted a few costumes destined for the scrap heap into clothes they could wear working at various places around the Village.

It was doubtful Christine would make bail, but even if she did, her hearing wasn't until late in the afternoon. If she didn't come home and there wasn't a willing next of kin to take the kids, they would be split up and sent to foster care. There wouldn't be anything else we could do about it.

At least working with the animals in the petting zoo, helping out with the carriage rides, and doing the other jobs Chase had found for them, they would all be too busy to worry about it. Mother Goose and Bo Peep had graciously agreed to keep an eye on them when we couldn't.

Except for Jolly. Chase and I had discussed what to do with him. Chase didn't want to let him loose in the Village. He was worried about what he might do next, including running away. So Jolly was spending the day working with Chase.

I knew I had done what I could to help. I wished I could do more, but Detective Almond was willing to stretch protocol only so far. I hoped Christine came home before day's end, but I knew the chances were small that would happen.

I gave each of the kids five dollars for drinks and snacks. The adults who'd agreed to let the kids work with them would give them lunch. It seemed we were set up for the day.

At least everyone else was set up. I wished someone had set something up for me. I had a long day with nothing much to do looming in front of me.

I picked up the mess left behind by the rapidly departing family, cleaned the kitchen, and put the dishes in the dishwasher. I didn't know what to do after that.

I didn't technically have a job anymore. I sure didn't want to work with Edgar. I couldn't make toys without Christine. I was at a loss.

To make matters worse, my investigation seemed to be at a dead end. I knew Detective Almond wouldn't be interested in pursuing any other suspect—even if I had one—since he had Christine in custody.

I had to find a way to earn my keep. I might be able to float for a day or two, but it was a long way until Christmas. I had to find some job, even if it was menial. I'd waited tables and mucked out stalls before.

Too bad everyone had taken on extra help for the season. It seemed that every job was already filled in anticipation of the holiday crowd.

Master Archer Simmons, my mentor during one of my first apprenticeships and a good friend, told me to try the castle. He had three apprentices and two assistants. There wasn't enough room for anyone else at the Feathered Shaft.

The castle.

I sighed, staring up at it just as I had the first time I'd seen it. It was where I'd worked my first job at the Faire, when I'd come here that fateful summer. I would never forget that time. I'd met Chase right after I'd been hired.

The structure itself looks like it's three stories, but the top story is a façade with turrets and towers. Most of the main living space is on the ground floor, along with the kitchen. The laundry and storage areas are in the basement. The second floor has suites for VIPs, but it's rarely used.

When the castle was built, someone had planned big. The structure was erected around the old traffic control tower for the Air Force base, most of it with concrete. Stone work was added later, creating the illusion of a real castle—although one with every modern convenience.

The Great Hall is attached to the side of the castle, and holds the large arena, the seating area for visitors, and a short passageway to the castle kitchen. It is an impressive structure, and at least fifty people work here at any given time. Employees range from maids and wenches to royal attendants and even a few footmen. Most of them don't live in the castle. They spend their nights in Village housing. Only a handful of people actually live in the castle full-time.

I stood there thinking about my time spent here during that first summer. I had peeled potatoes until my fingers ached, made beds, scrubbed floors, and taken late-night snacks to royalty and their guests.

Looking back on it was almost as terrible as living through it. At times, I couldn't believe I'd been willing to do some of those jobs. But there had been a spark that had brought me back the following summer and the one after that as things got better. It was that same spark that had made me walk toward the castle entrance from the Feathered Shaft.

Chase would find me something to do, I reminded myself as I came closer to the entrance. He didn't have three or four helpers working with him for the season. I didn't have to take a job here as a servant or some other less than desirable helper again.

Yet as I continued to stand at the entrance, trying to decide what to do, it came to me. If I was working at the castle, I could keep an eye on all the goings-on within its walls. I could also watch Edgar and try to figure out what he was up to.

It made sense. I certainly didn't want to believe that Jolly was responsible for the attacks on Harry or Chris's murder—Christine either. Taking a job in the castle might give me a chance to prove their innocence.

"Lady Jessie." Gus nodded briefly in respect and didn't try to pinch my butt. That was a novelty. "How goes it?"

"Not too bad. Looking for a job."

"The Christmas gig let you down, huh? I might know someone in the castle who could use an extra hand."

"Thanks. Has Harry come back from the hospital yet?"

"Not yet." He pointed toward the entrance. "But one of Livy's ladies finally couldn't take it anymore. Livy's hysteria after Harry was stabbed must have put her over the edge. She ran out of here screaming this morning and hasn't come back again."

"Sounds like the job for me." I smiled but kept a safe distance between us. "Thanks."

"My pleasure. Tell Chase I said hello when you see him."

"I will."

I passed Detective Almond, who was flanked by two officers, as I was entering the castle. He was on his way out. He nodded but didn't speak. I'd seen thunderclouds less angry looking than him.

Of course there had to be an investigation. Harry had been attacked. Did the police have any suspects? No doubt Detective Almond would meet with Chase before he left the Village. Chase might have some news to share when I met him later for lunch.

I knew Chase wouldn't give Jolly up to the police. But what if someone had seen him wandering around, covered in blood?

I walked quickly to Livy's chamber and rapped hard on the door. The sooner I got to work, the sooner I might have some answers.

Nineteen

"Oh, Lady Jessie, we would be so happy to have you here with us during the last of our confinement." Livy was teary eyed as she absently rubbed her baby bump. "There is so much going on right now. It will be wonderful to have a true confidant at my side."

I curtsied, as was appropriate. "It will be my honor to serve you, Your Majesty. Have you heard anything of the king as yet?"

"No. And I am beginning to get worried. They said he would be home this morning. Could you ask someone—perhaps the bailiff—if there is news?"

I was more than happy to go along with that request since I had some questions of my own to ask the good bailiff. But first, I wondered if I could get the scoop on what had happened to Harry.

Livy blew her nose on an elegant lace hankie when I asked her about the incident. "I don't know. He was in his chambers at the time. It seems someone stabbed him in the back upon entering the room. The doctor has told us that the wound, though painful, did little damage. I am only happy to have my darling lord still with me."

"He didn't see anything unusual?"

"You mean the young man so many workers have seen in the castle the last few days? I know the story about such a man pushing the king down the stairs. But I tell you, Lady Jessie, that this young man means no harm to anyone. He is not the person who attacked your king."

"You mean you know who it is?" I braced for something I might not want to hear. But if Livy knew Jolly was walking around in here, why didn't she suspect him?

"I have seen him myself at times, when the night is long and the shadows lengthen in the hallway."

What the—?

She smiled and clutched her hankie to her ample bosom. "He is the ghost of a young soldier who died here before the Village came. He walks these lonely halls, looking for his lost love."

I glanced at Lady Barbara, who stood behind the sofa. She shrugged and rolled her eyes.

Both she and Lady Jane were always appropriate, always well dressed. Their hair was covered by scarves that matched their gowns—usually matching as well. They rarely spoke out of turn or expressed dismay at the things they saw in their service to Livy.

I was continually amazed that both of them were still with her. They had to be the most tolerant women in the world!

Apparently Barbara hadn't seen the ghost the queen was describing. That didn't relieve my fear that the alleged ghost could be Jolly.

"Your Majesty, I don't believe a ghost injured the king either. But someone has tried to harm him twice, the last time most grievously. Did you or the king see anything else out of the ordinary?"

"No. We have the police to look into these things." She smiled and pushed herself up and off the sofa, no mean feat. "I do believe you were about to talk with the bailiff about the king, Lady Jessie. Hurry back when you have answers for us."

Livy was acting weirder than usual. I thought I might as well blame it on her pregnancy. I didn't want to think what kind of mother she would be once the baby arrived. Maybe the poor little thing would have a very competent nanny.

I nodded and started to leave her chamber. It had been easier than I'd expected to join Livy's staff. With another lady-in-waiting quitting just before I'd arrived—usually there were four in attendance—it had been a snap. I knew the woman's departure was because of Livy's tantrums, not to mention her quick mood swings. But I could ignore all of it to ensure my access to the castle.

Before I could leave the room and ask Chase anything, Edgar burst in, demanding to know why the children weren't making toys at the workshop.

Livy's face paled, and she sat back on the sofa again. "I'm not sure, my lord. I am not privy to such information."

"You can't just hang me out to dry on this," he said accusingly. "People want to see those kids, for whatever reason. It's part of the show. Part of what you promised me. I suggest you take care of it right away."

I put myself, all six feet of me in a gown at least three feet wide, between him and Livy. It was that feeling of protection again. Not sure what was wrong with me. I saw recognition in his eyes when I faced him down. "Mayhap my lord should find a way to be more entertaining on his own instead of depending on young children. These children have been through enough. They may not even be here by the end of the Village day."

"You!" His face turned a mottled shade of red, and his hands clenched in fists as he stared at me. "What are you doing here? Olivia, I must insist that you get rid of this woman. Or—"

"Or what?" I stood as close to him as I could given the depth of my skirt. "My Lord Gaskin makes a bad habit out of bullying Village women. Mayhap a turn in the stocks might help his attitude."

"In *what*?" He began shouting for real. "You *dare* suggest that?"

"Please calm yourself, Edgar," Livy entreated. "And keep your voice down."

"Why?" He strutted through the room, then returned to his spot before the door. "You mean you don't want everyone to know that we had an affair, Your Majesty? If that's the case, and you still want to keep this from your husband, get rid of this woman now."

I glared at Edgar, daring him to make another move toward Livy. I saw the door to the chamber open behind him as he shouted his dirty little secret. I heard Livy begin sobbing as we both saw Harry, held erect by two of his courtiers, come to stand in the doorway.

At least Edgar's hold on Livy was over. With the secret out, he had nothing left to threaten her with.

Edgar finally calmed down enough to notice that we were all looking at something behind him. "King Harold," he said in a much lower voice as he turned.

Harry didn't say anything. He just stood there, glowering at Edgar.

Edgar grabbed his chest and made a few choking sounds, then crashed sideways to the heavily carpeted floor.

No one moved for a brief instant. Then I grabbed the two-way radio Livy always kept on her side table and called for help. Chase responded, and I told him what had happened.

Livy had fainted and was being attended by her stalwart ladies, Barbara and Jane. How those two managed to stay here and not run out screaming as their coworker had done was beyond me sometimes.

Harry, still not saying a word, nodded to his gentlemen, and they escorted him from the room.

As much as I disliked Edgar, I crushed my gown so I could get on the floor beside him. I flipped him over and began CPR. He had no pulse. His lips were faintly blue and cold to the touch. A few of the household staff took turns relieving me, but it was too late.

Edgar was pronounced dead at the castle when the paramedics arrived a short time later. Chase got there, accompanied by Detective Almond and his officers.

"What a surprise," Detective Almond said when he saw me. "If I ever need to know where the trouble is, I can always look for you. You're usually in the thick of things, aren't you?"

I didn't bother responding to that, but I did accept Chase's help getting to my feet. You can crush those skirts, but don't try to get up in them—too stiff and thick. No wonder women spent so much time doing needlepoint and had to ride sidesaddle.

"Does she need an ambulance?" Detective Almond asked, nodding at Livy.

"I don't think so. She fainted," I answered. "A paramedic is checking her out."

"So what happened this time?" he asked me, glancing at Edgar as they put him on the stretcher.

"I think he had a heart attack." I shrugged, wishing someone else would speak up. I certainly wasn't an authority on the subject. "I don't know for sure. One minute he was yelling at us—the next he was on the floor. It happened really quickly."

The last paramedic agreed with my diagnosis before he left the room.

"What were all of you arguing about before the man fell over?" Detective Almond glanced at the other ladies in the room. They didn't speak.

I looked over at Livy, who was still out of it on the sofa. No help there. My protective instincts took over again. "I think Mr. Gaskin was upset about Christine's kids not working today. He wanted them to make toys for the workshop tour that Father Christmas is supposed to do every hour or so."

"And that's why he was dressed that way," Detective Almond said. "He thought she could fix that? Is she head of the Christmas show or something?"

I glanced at Chase. He nodded. We both knew I might as well tell him the whole story. "He was blackmailing the queen. They'd had an affair, about a year ago, I think. He threatened her if she didn't invite him to the Village to play Father Christmas even though Chris and Christine were already here."

Almond frowned. "This is the man you suspected of killing Mr. Christmas, right?"

"I'm afraid so." I couldn't help but feel a little let down by the recent event.

"Why so glum? He's out of the way now."

"Because now I can't get him to confess and we'll never

know if he killed Chris. Christine—or some other innocent person—will be blamed for it. Edgar gets away free."

"Not exactly free," he reminded me. "He won't threaten anyone else again. Do you think he could be the one who stabbed the king last night, too? Might as well pin as much as we can on him since he's gone."

I realized he was making fun of me. I didn't return his banter. Maybe he didn't consider Edgar a suspect in Chris's death, but I did. I *had* anyway.

While everyone else in the room was being questioned by Detective Almond and his officers, Chase escorted me out into the hall. Maids, kitchen workers, and a few jesters were out there rehashing everything that had just happened. Sir Reginald, Lord Dunstable, and Esmeralda stood nearby, too. Everyone was curious. Most of them thought Livy had killed Edgar.

"No jury would have convicted her either," Esmeralda said. "The man was a curse upon this castle. He deserved to die."

At first everyone looked surprised at her words, but seconds later they started agreeing with her. It seemed I wasn't the only one who didn't like Edgar.

"But what will Adventure Land do without a Father Christmas for the season?" Sir Reginald asked. "I doubt we can get another one this late in the year."

"Especially since two of them have died here," a chubby chambermaid added.

"They'll think of something," Chase assured them. "Someone will turn up."

Most of the action was over, and people started moving off to wherever they should have been. I was a little worried, despite Chase's words, that the Village would have to shut down the holiday event. No doubt that would mean a large dip in profits. No one likes that.

"What do we do now?" I asked Chase.

"I'm thinking about questioning Harry about the attack. Want to come with me?"

Of course I wanted to. I just wasn't sure if Harry would say anything after our previous conversation. I didn't want to hamper the investigation.

"Maybe I'll just hang around out here. Harry might be more willing to talk to you alone—man to man—that kind of stuff."

"All right. I'll meet you here in a half hour or so. What were you doing with Livy anyway—questioning her?"

There wasn't really time to explain. "I'll tell you over coffee when you get done."

He kissed me and walked toward Harry's chambers.

I thought about Harry's first accident and went to the stairs where he'd fallen. It was dark on that side of the hall. Someone needed to install more lighting over here. I went slowly down the faux stone steps, amazed that Harry had only injured his arm in the fall.

The stairs led to the basement, which was divided into several sections. In one area was the laundry room, crowded with huge washers and dryers, steam presses, and ironing boards.

I remembered that it was always cool down here, even in the deep heat of summer. It was also surprisingly dry considering the concrete construction and the humidity everywhere else. That made it a perfect place for storage, too.

The storage room housed what seemed like every item that had ever been used and then taken out of service in the Village. There were parts of the original *Queen's Revenge*, set ablaze by accident on her maiden voyage. (She'd been rebuilt, and the crew now took more stringent fire precautions when they used the cannons.) Worn-out signs and remnants from long-gone shops cluttered the area as well.

I walked through the aisles of shelves stacked with memorabilia, admiring items I'd never seen before and smiling at those I remembered from previous seasons at the Village. I really missed the curly-cheese-fry vendor who had once walked the cobblestones. He'd had images of a Rapunzel-type character on his cart (long curly hair, long curly fries). He'd been closed down for health reasons, and an obvious lack of common sense. Who wanted to think about hair and food at the same time?

It was a trip down memory lane for me. Old costumes, like the king and queen's coronation outfits, were there. I laughed at the huge crowns first created for each of them. Neither one of them could even hold their heads up under them.

And that's when it hit me. There must be something here that had belonged to the first king and queen. I remembered when they'd brought in an artist to paint a portrait of Harry and Livy, which now hung in the royal hall.

Maybe Chris and Alice had their portraits painted, too.

I knew Chase would be waiting for me soon, so I hurried to the farthest corner of the storage room. The light was very dim, no windows to the outside for natural light. I was going to need a flashlight if I was going to search for anything in here.

Costumes were heaped in piles and laid across old broken chairs. Pieces of furniture and elegant lamp shades mingled with paste diamonds and other fake jewelry. Many of Andre Hariot's grandest hats lay atop one another, gathering dust. This corner of the storage room was like the cave in Aladdin except that none of the treasures were what they seemed to be. They were only imitations of the real thing.

"Is someone back here?" Esmeralda's voice reached me in the tangled recesses of the dark room.

"It's me," I called back. "Just looking around."

"Jessie? I thought we had a mouse again. The last time, a pack of mice did a lot of damage to the old costumes. I don't know why they don't box up all this stuff and start a Village museum. Or better yet, burn all of it. Maybe we'd have room for more important things that we really need."

"It would be terrible to get rid of all of this. But I like the idea of the museum. I take it the deeper you go into the storage room, the older the stuff gets."

"I don't know. It's such a mess in there. What are you looking for?"

"I was hoping to find some of the stuff that had belonged to the original king and queen."

"You're wasting your time," she said. "My time, too. I've got to get back to work."

"Don't you think it's kind of sad and romantic that the first king and queen have been forgotten? We should have their portrait up with Livy and Harry's, don't you think?"

"They didn't have a portrait. Things weren't so elaborate back then."

Aha! She knew something.

I pushed through all of the garments and other items to reach the door to the storage area. Esmeralda was gone already, but I tracked her down to her domain—the laundry room.

She was getting ready to steam press some of the ladies'

clothing hanging on large racks. "I'm busy, Jessie. I don't have time to think about the past. Why don't you find something else to do?"

"You knew Chris and Alice, the first king and queen, didn't you?"

"I haven't been here that long."

"Then how do you know there isn't a portrait of them?"

She sighed and put down her steamer. Her face looked tired, but I knew she had the stamina that kept this whole place going. If it wasn't for her and Rita, the castle would've collapsed years ago.

"Okay. What do you want to know?"

"Everything! How long were they king and queen? Roger says Alice and Chris left the Village together and got divorced later. Is there a photo of them?"

"You're like a dog with a bone." She took a deep breath and leaned back against the washer. "They weren't king and queen for long. Their relationship changed as the Village got started. I don't know if they left together or not. And if there's a picture, I've never seen it. Satisfied?"

"What was it like back then?"

"Less dramatic, I can tell you that."

"But was it still as much fun? What was Alice like? Did Chris look like Santa back then?"

"I suppose it was more fun, in its way. Things were smaller. People were friendlier. There weren't so many lords and ladies. It was more like a fairy tale. Not so corporate. I don't remember what Alice looked like. Chris looked like a young Santa. I guess that was what was always in his heart. He didn't really want to be king. They found out too late that it wasn't right for them."

There were so many questions I wanted to ask her, but Chase came down the stairs looking for me. Esmeralda smiled. "Thank God you've come for her! How do you stay sane with her asking questions all the time?"

"I don't ask questions *all* the time," I said defensively. "I don't know why everyone doesn't find this fascinating."

Chase laughed. "She's right. She doesn't ask questions all the time. Just most of it. But speaking of questions, have you noticed anything unusual going on in the castle?"

Esmeralda shook her head. "Unusual? Could you give me some idea of what that would be, Bailiff? Because I think I've forgotten what's normal for most people."

"Unless a castle resident pushed Harry down the stairs and then stabbed him, someone is sneaking in and out of the castle. I thought you or Rita might have noticed. You notice everything."

"Maybe you should talk to Livy's ghost," she said. "She swears the place is haunted by a dead soldier. I haven't seen it, but it wouldn't surprise me. If you ask me, Livy probably pushed Harry and stabbed him. I'm sure if it hasn't happened already, it will soon."

It wasn't much of an answer. Chase thanked her, and we went back upstairs. I confirmed the ghost story on our way down into the Village for coffee at the Monastery Bakery.

"Maybe she's been seeing someone real and just thinks he's a ghost because of her raging hormones," I suggested.

"Maybe. But I don't understand why anyone besides Livy would want to hurt Harry in the first place, and do such a bad job of it in the second."

I gave him my knowing look. "Can't you?"

We ordered coffee and sat at one of the rustic tables outside.

"Are you saying Jolly did this and he's the ghost Livy's been seeing?" Chase asked.

"He has good reason. He probably knows his mother

was sleeping with Harry. Add that to the rest of his teenage dynamic and he could be volatile."

"That would make sense, I suppose. But I hope that's not what happened."

I agreed, sipping my coffee. I glanced toward the Main Gate where a pretty young flower girl was playing the lute, and saw a welcome sight.

"Christine! Over here! I'm so glad to see you."

Twenty

When you're taking care of someone else's children, plants, or pets, there's nothing like that magic moment when they come home. All of the worries you might have about these people and things that don't belong to you are magically lifted from your shoulders.

"Jessie! Chase!" She ran to us, dressed in street clothes, and we all hugged. "Where are the children? Are they all right? I hope they've been good for you. Jolly can be a little hardheaded."

"They've been fine," I assured her. "They're all out working and playing at various sites around the Village." I explained what had happened to Edgar and how we'd wanted to keep them out of his way. "We've been waiting all day to hear something about you."

"It sounds like you've been busy anyway." She smiled, tears misting her blue eyes. "I'm back—for now at least. Harry posted bail for me. Wasn't that wonderful, especially after someone attacked him? I know he really loves me. I understand that he can't leave his wife, but I know he cares."

I couldn't argue with that, certainly didn't want to. What Harry felt or didn't feel seemed like the least of her problems.

Chase and I filled her in on everything, and she told us that her court date would be after the first of the year. But Christine's mind was more focused on Harry and Edgar.

"I hope Harry will be all right" she said. "I'm not sorry to see Edgar go, though I wouldn't have wished it on him. But now we'll never know what happened to Chris. I still feel sure Edgar killed him. I don't know how I'll clear my name."

"I think we should go and find the kids." Chase diverted her from that topic. "I know they'll want to see you right away."

We started down the cobblestones, mindful of some droppings from a reindeer that had recently passed by. The street cleaners were right behind us. It was just another day for them.

I hadn't realized how far Chase had scattered the kids around the Village until we started picking them up. They had started in a few places then gravitated around the Village. Nick was helping out at the Hat House. Merry Beth was at the Romeo and Juliet Pavilion working as a stagehand. Garland was helping the clockmaker at the Hands of Time clock shop, and the four youngest were all at the Mother Goose Pavilion.

The only one missing was Jolly. Chase had left him at the blacksmith's shop, helping with the horses that needed to be shoed. I saw him standing by the fence at the Field of Honor again and volunteered to go and get him.

I'd also noticed Dennis Greene on the field working on

his routine. This seemed like a perfect time to ask him if he recognized Jolly as the rogue knight.

I dreaded the answer, but we had to know. Jolly had been through a lot in the past few days. If he was responsible for some of the mayhem that had gone on, he probably needed help to get past the anger that was feeding those destructive actions. It didn't have to ruin the rest of his life.

I was glad Christine was there, no matter how hard this would be on her. Jolly needed her. All the kids did.

I hailed Dennis, who smiled and rode up to me on his dashing white gelding—a hero if ever there was one. He wore only his breastplate armor over faded trousers and a plain white shirt.

"Lady Jessie! It's good to see you. No repercussions with the bailiff from the King's Feast, I trust, since he hasn't tried to take my head off. I meant no disrespect."

"Thanks. It's good to be seen. And no problems with Chase. You don't have to worry."

"You're not dressed for the field," he said.

"That's for sure." I stepped carefully on the patches of thick hay, avoiding the brown places on the field. There was no one to sweep the droppings away here, as on the cobblestones. The squires raked the field several times a day and threw down more hay, which was promptly trampled by the horses.

"Have you come alone?" He grinned at me, the breeze catching his short brown hair. "I wouldn't like to cross swords with the bailiff—I've heard he's quite good—on the field and off. Though I'd take him on, if it would win your hand."

His handsome face was so young, so vibrant. It was hard to ignore him, even knowing his intentions. But I thought about Chase and straightened my spine. I hadn't spent *that* much time in the castle. I remembered who I'd come to the dance with.

"I need your help, Sir Knight. Do you see that boy at the fence over there? Do you recognize him?"

Dennis looked at Jolly, who was entranced as he watched the other knights put their horses through their paces. "I do not recognize him, lady. Should I?"

My heart leapt even as my mind wondered—*if not Jolly, then who?* But I wanted to make sure. "You said you saw the young man who brought back the stolen horse and armor. Is he the young man?"

"No. But now that you mention it." He pointed behind me. "There he is now."

I turned and saw that Chase, Christine, and the rest of the children had decided to come up to the field. "That's the bailiff, Sir Knight. I know you aren't identifying him as the rogue knight."

He laughed. "No, my lady. The tallest in that group of children. He looks to be thirteen or fourteen, I think. That's why I knew he was too young for the job."

I looked again. He was talking about Nick.

I wanted to ask him one more time if he was absolutely sure, but by that time Christine was hugging Jolly and Chase was staring at me, probably wondering why I was talking to Dennis again.

I excused myself from the knight and walked carefully back to the fence.

I would've ducked between the rails as I had before, but Chase lifted me over with his hands on my waist. "Is that the same knight you were with outside the castle before the feast?"

"I told you he had information," I muttered, wishing he'd get over it. "He just identified Nick as the rogue knight."

That took his mind off Dennis. "Maybe he needs glasses. Nick is just a kid. Jolly, I could believe. He's got to be lying."

"There's only one way to find out."

I decided that confronting Nick would best be done in more pleasant surroundings. I offered to buy everyone fudge at Frenchy's, which was only a short walk from the field. The little sweet shop also had outside tables where we could discuss what was going on with a little privacy.

The kids were all for it. They raced each other away from the field. Christine wasn't sure. She had so much to do and needed time to talk with her children about what might happen next.

"The only thing I can think to do is to send them to my sister in Des Moines. She and her husband have two children of their own. It would be hard for them, but I've spoken to her and she'll take them if I have to go back to jail. Better a crowded house with family than a foster home."

I agreed. "But maybe you won't need that plan. I'm still hoping we can figure out who really killed Chris."

"Without Edgar's confession, I feel like my goose is cooked. I don't see how we can prove that he did it now that he's gone."

There was no doubt that it would be much harder. "It's not impossible. We just have to figure out how all the pieces fit together."

Chase didn't look very convinced either. I knew how he felt about all the evidence adding up against Christine. I hoped he wouldn't say it out loud.

"Anyway, we've got time before your trial," I continued. "We have time."

"Except that I'm going to have to leave the Village," she said. "I can't leave Myrtle Beach, but Adventure Land doesn't like the idea of someone charged with murder being onsite making toys. Really, I think the whole Christmas theme is a bust for the Village. You'll never get another Santa this late in the season."

"I've heard a few rumors about that," Chase said. "Adventure Land isn't giving up on the project just yet."

"But we still have the problem with them wanting to evict Christine," I reminded him. "You could talk to Merlin. He could change that edict."

"That's true. I could ask him about that. Or you could ask him. He likes you, Jessie."

Christine smiled between us. "You're both so good. I wouldn't dream of asking either one of you to put yourselves out that way. The kids and I will manage. We always have."

"But, in this case, we need you here to help solve the murder." I hoped Chase wouldn't say anything about us not looking for Chris's killer.

"I'll talk to Merlin," he said. "I don't like getting in the middle of things like this, but someone needs to do it."

I hugged him. "Thanks."

He whispered close to my ear, "But the first time you go off without me to interrogate someone you think might be the killer, the deal is off. I'm the bailiff. You can snoop around, but when it comes to closing the deal, I want to be there. Right?"

"Absolutely," I quietly agreed. If I wanted to see this through, it seemed I had no choice.

We had finally reached the fudge shop. I felt a little guilty to have raised Christine's spirits and expectations only to get ready to accuse Nick of something terrible. But I felt it would be better to clear the air. We could go on from there.

True to my word, I picked out several different kinds of fudge, but before I could pay, Chase stepped in with Lady Visa. "I'll take care of this. You get ready for the bad news."

Christine had waited at one of the picnic tables outside under a makeshift umbrella designed to look as though it could've been used during the Renaissance. During the hot summers, people needed someplace to sit where they could escape the sun. It was the best the Village could do, historically speaking.

We took the fudge outside and divided it up among the group. As the children ate happily, I struggled to find the right moment to ask Nick about his part in the events of the past few days. A juggler came along with a distraction, and it looked like perfect timing to me.

"Nick, a friend of mine saw you return the horse and armor you borrowed from the Field of Honor," I said between bites of fudge. I needed chocolate, too.

"What are you saying, Jessie?" Christine stopped watching the juggler and turned toward me.

"Do you want to tell her, Nick?" I asked. He looked guilty enough without saying a word.

"It wasn't him." Jolly stepped in. "It was me. I did it."

I was surprised. Jolly didn't seem to be much of a family person. Of course, in a crunch, even Tony would come down on my side.

"Did what?" Christine stood up and folded her arms across her chest. "Somebody better tell me what's going on."

All the kids started talking at once. Apparently, they all knew about Nick's outing on the horse. I should've known they'd cover for him.

"I took the horse," Nick finally admitted, his voice rising above the others and silencing them. "I borrowed the armor and lance. I knew what was happening, Mom. I knew you were seeing that other guy, the king. I saw you with him the first night we got here."

Now it was Christine's turn to look guilty. "You should've said something. We could've talked about it."

"I thought you probably killed Dad so you could be with the other guy," Nick said. "That's why I was so angry. I didn't really mean to hurt anyone with the horse. I just wanted to do *something*."

Christine sat back down. "I had no idea. I'm so sorry. You should know I would never have hurt your father. I loved him. I was just lonely. If you know about me, you must know about him, too."

Eight solemn faces nodded (though I was pretty sure the younger kids didn't know what she was talking about).

"I'm sorry." Nick put his arms around his mother and cried. "I thought it was you I saw in the workshop when Dad was killed."

That made all of us sit up a little straighter and pay more attention. Chase started to speak, but Christine frowned at him. She tugged the teenager on her lap and held him.

"Explain what you mean, Nick. What do you mean you saw someone in the workshop when Dad was killed?"

I could tell it was hard for Nick to explain his actions through the grief of losing his father. "I went down from the house to get my MP3 player. Dad was in the workshop, waiting for Jessie. He was setting up to make some toys."

"What did you see?" Chase asked impatiently.

I tugged at his arm and shook my head. It wouldn't do any good to push Nick right now. He needed to tell the story in his own way.

"He was sitting at a worktable when the woman came into the shop. I couldn't see what she looked like—she was wearing one of those big scarf things across her head and face. She was dressed all in black. I thought it was you, Mom. I waited by the stairs to listen to what you were talking about."

Nick wiped his eyes and his voice steadied. "She didn't say anything. Dad didn't move. He kept right on working on the toys. She walked up behind him. That's when I heard the loud popping sound. Dad fell on the table, then on the floor. I couldn't move. I'm sorry. I should've done something. I let him die. I'm sorry."

He broke down completely after his recollection of his father's death. He sobbed into Christine's arms like a baby. I wondered how he'd managed to keep it inside and quiet for the past few days. Then I realized he'd been protecting his mother.

"It's okay, Nicky," Christine said, tears sliding down her face. "You couldn't have known what was going to happen. There was nothing you could do. You did the best thing by staying hidden. Who knows what would've happened if she'd seen you."

"What happened next?" Chase looked at me and shrugged. I guess he couldn't help himself.

Nick wiped his nose and face on his shirt. *Eww.*

"The woman looked at Dad for a minute, then threw the gun on the floor. She walked back outside. I didn't know what to do. I went and got the gun and took it upstairs. I didn't want the police to find it and blame you, Mom."

"That's why the police found the gun in the house," I said. "There has to be some way to prove that to Detective Almond. Maybe if Nick told the police what happened, they'd drop the charges against Christine."

"Not necessarily *drop* the charges," Chase said. "But maybe it would give them something else to think about. That's one less strike against her."

"But how in the world would we prove that what Nick described even happened? I don't think they'll take the word of a fourteen-year-old boy," Christine said.

"I'm sorry, Jessie," Nick continued. "I thought it might be that woman again when you walked in. I got on a chair behind one of the wooden posts and whacked you as hard as I could with a piece of wood. It was too late once I realized who you were, so I ran out."

How could I not forgive him? Nick had been through a horrible experience. He'd been scared out of his mind. "You did what you thought you had to do. I'm not mad at you."

"Thanks." He smiled at me.

"Okay, I understand about the horse, trying to show your mother how angry you were," Chase continued. "But what about the king? Did you push him down the stairs in the castle?"

As Nick shook his head, he looked at Jolly.

"He didn't do that," Jolly said. "I did."

Twenty-one

"We know you want to take up for your brother, Jolly," Chase said. "But we need to know who's really responsible."

"I'm not taking up for anyone," Jolly snarled. "I went to the castle to have a talk with that guy and tell him to stay away from Mom. I saw him walking around, so I followed him. I watched him go to the stairs, and I was so angry. Nick told me that he thought Mom had killed Dad, and I blamed the king for it. When he started down the stairs, I pushed him. I know I shouldn't have, but I just did. Maybe they should put me in jail, too."

I could tell Chase was choosing his words carefully before he asked the next big question. It was one thing to push someone down the stairs, but stabbing them? That was something else entirely. Jolly was looking guilty of both attacks.

"The king was stabbed, Jolly," Chase said finally. "Were you responsible for that, too?"

I half expected Merry Beth to admit to stabbing the king. There seemed to be a network among the children for finding things out, getting things done, and keeping secrets.

But no one said anything until Jolly spoke up. "No, sir. I didn't do that. I pushed him. That was all."

"You came back to the house late," I added. "You were covered in blood, Jolly. Are you sure you weren't involved? It's better to admit it now."

"No! I didn't do it. I'd tell you if I did. I don't think anyone would blame me even if I killed the bastard."

"Jolly!" Christine tried to rein in his language. "There's no reason to get vulgar about it."

"Sorry," he said, although he didn't sound sincere.

Chase took a deep breath. "I think we're going to have to talk with Detective Almond about this. I'm sorry. Jolly, you might get in some trouble for what you did. But in the long run, this could help your mother. I think we all want that, right? All of you understand that your mother wasn't responsible for your father's death."

They all nodded.

"Is there anything else you recall about the woman who shot your father, Nick?" Chase asked. "I'm sorry to take you through it again, but the police will want to ask you the same question. It's better for you to have a chance to think about your answer."

Nick sniffed and wiped his eyes. He got up from Christine's lap and sat down next to Merry Beth. "She was dressed like all the other ladies here—in a big, old dress. Everything was black. I can't think of anything else."

"But you're sure she didn't speak to your father? And he didn't see her at all?" Chase continued.

"No. She didn't say anything. If he saw her, he didn't act like it. That was another reason I thought it was Mom. You know how people act around each other when they're used to someone being there? They kind of ignore the other person sometimes. Dad did that a lot with Mom."

"I know what you mean," Chase said. "You know what to tell the police then. They might ask you to help them make a sketch of the woman."

"What about the note that was left at the workshop?" I asked the group in general. "Did any of you see the threatening note to your mother?"

"I saw it," Garland said. "But I didn't write it." He looked at his brothers and sisters for confirmation. All of them shook their heads. None of the others had even seen the note.

"So the woman who killed Chris might have left that note, too," I said.

"*If* it was a woman," Chase replied. "Just because the killer was wearing a dress, doesn't mean it was a woman. A man can wear a dress, too. Maybe that was why he or she used the heavy black veil. There might be a way we can pick up some other details about her from Nick."

"How?" Christine asked.

"We'll have to go back into the old workshop where Chris was killed. We might be able to get a general idea as to how tall the killer was if there's some object Nick can compare the woman's height to. Maybe the chair Chris was sitting in or the door where she came in."

"Kind of like the height chart they use at fast-food places to help ID robbers?" I guessed.

"Exactly. We might be able to determine a few other things, too." Chase smiled at Nick. "Are you up for it?"

Nick nodded. "Anything to help Mom."

Christine agreed, reluctantly, to take the other children back to the apartment in the manor house where they were staying. We all knew it would be easier for Nick to concentrate on trying to come up with more details about the killer if the other kids weren't there.

Maybe I should've volunteered to take them so she could go with Nick and Chase, but I felt that the kids needed to be with her. I knew she felt the same way. She was worried about Nick, but she also knew he was in good hands.

I was relieved that Nick and Jolly hadn't done anything worse than move some evidence and push Harry down the stairs. That was bad enough, but at least it wasn't the next step up—which was how I viewed Harry getting stabbed.

"If Jolly and Nick aren't responsible for what happened to Harry last night," I asked Chase, "who do you think is? What did he say to you when you talked to him?"

"Not much. He was kind of fuzzy about the whole thing. He didn't see anything, didn't hear anything. The next thing he knew, there was a paring knife in his back."

We were standing outside the door to the workshop where Chris had been killed, waiting for Paul Miller to join us. The police had padlocked the door to be sure no one went inside. He had the key.

Chase had already called Detective Almond. He couldn't be there until later that day. It wasn't going to be any fun for the kids or the rest of us when he talked to Nick and Jolly. There would definitely be consequences for their actions. I just hoped he wasn't too hard on them, considering all they'd been through.

It started raining as Paul Miller arrived. He was in a red

vendor's costume and was pushing a pretzel cart. He smiled and shook Chase's hand. I ignored him when he tried to be friendly with me. I didn't trust him.

"So you say this young man has some information pertaining to the case?" He ignored me in return and talked to Chase, ruffling Nick's dark hair with his hand. "How will it benefit us to go in and disturb the crime scene?"

Chase explained that Nick had seen the killer. "I thought if he went back inside we might be able to pick up on more details. If we know the killer's height, at least, that would give us something more to go on."

Miller shrugged. The rain had begun falling harder, chasing visitors and residents into shops and restaurants. Most visitors would wait to see if the sun would come back out. Tickets weren't refundable because of bad weather. No one wanted to go halfway through the Village and have to leave. It was too expensive and annoying.

"I think that's possible," he finally said. "Detective Almond called me. He said to let you have some leeway on this."

"Thanks," Chase said. "Can we get out of the rain now?"

Miller opened the door with the key on his rope belt. I was surprised to see that he was carrying a small gun in his costume, too. I would've thought, since there were a lot of children and other people who could get hurt, that a gun wouldn't be allowed.

"Looking at my gun, Jessie?" he asked. "It's loaded, too. I won't give the killer a chance when I finally meet him."

"It's possible the killer is a woman," Chase said.

"That doesn't matter." Miller smiled at me. "The female of the species is more deadly than the male. Ever heard that, Jessie?"

I didn't answer—but I did wonder why he was so weird.

As soon as the door was open, I followed Chase inside as quickly as I could. I didn't want to be alone with Miller any longer than I had to be.

"Try not to touch anything," Miller said. "And be careful you don't walk on the chalk outline where the dead man was lying."

I saw Nick wince at his words and I turned on the man despite my best efforts not to talk to him. "This is traumatic enough for this boy. A little tact would be nice. Or don't they teach basic humanity in police school?"

Miller kind of chuckled, but he also stood by the door and didn't say anything else stupid, at least for a few minutes.

Chase put his arm around Nick's shoulders. "Show me exactly what happened and where you were."

I stayed off to one side, not wanting to get in the way. Nick showed Chase where he'd stood at the bottom of the stairs when he'd first come down.

"I was right here the whole time. I think she couldn't see me because the big lights in the ceiling weren't on. Dad liked to work with just a lamp on near the toy. He didn't like bright lights. He said they hurt his eyes."

"Okay, Nick," Chase said. "I'm going to come over here and sit where your father was sitting. Jessie is going to come in the door and be the woman you saw. Okay? You're doing great so far."

"Okay," Nick agreed.

"You tell us if we do something different than what you saw," Chase told him. "Don't be afraid to speak up. This could be very important."

I went to the door while Chase went and sat down at the table beside the chalk mark on the floor. Chase picked up a toy and turned on the lamp beside him. He looked down at the toy as though he were trying to work on it.

I walked in as I thought the killer might have done. I didn't act out holding a gun or anything since Nick hadn't described her doing that. I approached Chase slowly from behind and then used my fingers to pretend to shoot him in the back of the head.

The whole time, Nick hadn't said a word. I looked at him and tears were streaming down his face. Despite my role as the killer, I rushed over to him and hugged him. "It's okay. It's not for real."

"I know." He sniffed. "But it was a lot like the real time."

"How was Jessie's height compared to what you saw?" Chase asked despite Nick's tears. "Do you need her to stand near me again?"

"Chase!" I hissed. "He's very upset. I think this could wait."

"He'll feel better when we catch the killer," Miller joined in. "Was she about Jessie's height?"

"No. She was much shorter. And even in the big dress, Jessie is skinnier," Nick said. "She was wearing black gloves, too. And I think I was wrong. I think she put her head by Dad's and said something before she shot him. I couldn't hear what she said. I guess she was whispering."

"Let's try it that way," Chase said.

It seemed a little relentless to me to put Nick through that again. I knew we needed to find the killer, but he was just a boy who'd been in the wrong place at the wrong time.

"Maybe we should wait." I tried to give Chase a look that might help explain my reasoning. Maybe it was the shadows in the room, but he didn't seem to get my message. In his way, he was as relentless as Miller.

"There won't be a better time," Chase said. "The longer we wait, the less he'll remember. He'd already almost forgotten that the killer talked to Chris before she killed him."

I had to agree with that, though looking at Nick's face made me sorry Christine hadn't come instead of me. I left my arms around Nick and asked, "Are you okay with this? If not, I don't care what those bullies say, we'll quit."

"It's okay, Jessie." He wiped his eyes. "I want to help. I'm the only one who knows what happened."

Except the killer. "Okay. Let's try it one more time."

This time, as Chase pretended to work, I came up behind him and lowered my head to his, whispering, "How can you be so mean to this poor boy? I didn't know you were that kind of person."

And I got a strange satisfaction from pretend-shooting him again, even adding a gunfire sound effect, like one from a cartoon.

Chase looked at Nick. "Was it like that?"

"Yes. Except she didn't have to lean down as far. And she moved her head away before she shot him."

"So he knew the killer," Chase surmised. "She spoke to him. He was familiar enough with her not to get up right away or turn around."

"He should've," I muttered. "Maybe he'd still be alive."

"Good exercise, people," Miller said. "We might have to go through this again for Detective Almond. But I think we've learned something here. Good job."

Miller unlocked the door that led from the workshop to the upper floors of the manor house, and Chase, Nick, and I went upstairs to the apartment where Christine and the kids were staying. Miller left through the outside door, locking it behind him.

A strong rumble of thunder shook the house around us. It looked as though the bad weather was settling in for the remainder of the day. Rain pounded on the rooftop and blew against the windows. Most visitors weren't going to wait this out.

We walked into the living room, surprised to find Detective Almond already with the rest of the family. They were all eating Christmas cookies and drinking eggnog.

"I thought he couldn't make it until later," I whispered to Chase.

"He knew this was an important development," he said. "And I'm sorry if I seemed heartless downstairs. But what we found out could be really important. Just think—if we clear Christine's name, she's out of jail and gets the money from the insurance policy. That seemed worth a little discomfort for Nick. Don't you think?"

A knock on the front door had Merry Beth scrambling to answer it. It was Miller again. It would've been nice not to see him for a while.

"Great! Cookies and nog. Just what we need on a stormy day like this."

Twenty-two

An almost festive air permeated the discussion that followed even though it was about Chris's death. Christine had sent the children, including Nick, to their rooms. I felt sure they were listening anyway. That was why they were so well-informed.

"Tell me how the role-playing went." Detective Almond sat next to the Christmas tree, which was covered with twinkling lights and shiny ornaments. "Find out anything we could use?"

Chase didn't say anything. He let Miller take the credit for the idea and act as if he'd actually participated in some way other than being mean to Nick.

"Sounds promising," Detective Almond commented as he ate a cookie. "Any thoughts, Manhattan? This is your show after all."

I was surprised that he was perceptive enough to realize that Chase had been taking the backseat.

"One thing we discussed before our reenactment with Nick downstairs is that there's no way of knowing for sure if the killer was a man or a woman." Chase reiterated what we'd talked about earlier. Miller hadn't thought of that. "Everyone here is good at role-playing. Any one of them could've dressed up like a man or a woman."

"I get it," Detective Almond said. "But did we get an approximate height and weight?"

"Maybe between five-six and five-nine. Thicker in the waist than Jessie," Chase said.

"How did you come up with that, the part about the waist?" Miller asked.

"The only place you can really tell a body-size difference is in the waist," I explained. "The rest of it is hidden by the big skirt. And don't forget, the killer was wearing a large black veil."

"But the part about her putting her head near his and whispering something," Miller interjected. "That sounds like something a girl would do."

A girl? The man was a complete loser.

"It does seem like a feminine gesture," Detective Almond agreed as he wrote in his stained notebook. "Any ideas about a woman who could have a grudge against your husband and lives close by, Mrs. Christmas?"

Christine got to her feet. "I don't know. I've already told you that Chris was indiscreet. I know I was, too, but only on this one occasion. There have been women in the past who were angry when I had him break it off. He always left them when I told him to. He didn't want us to break up, you know. He just got . . . bored sometimes."

"What about the guy in the castle who was your lover?" Miller asked. "Any chance he has a nice black dress and wanted you for himself?"

"He's got an alibi for our time frame," Detective Almond said. "Otherwise I'd like him for this, too. If he'd wear that silly outfit as king, he'd certainly wear a dress to disguise himself."

"What about Chris's first wife, Alice?" I asked.

"What about her?" Detective Almond faced me. "Any idea where she is? Do we know if she's in the Village?"

"No. But she could still be here, or she could've come back after they split up."

Chase shook his head. "I checked when you mentioned her, Jessie. There's no one named Alice working here."

"She could be using another name."

"Would that be on the off chance that her ex-husband would show up so she could kill him?" Detective Almond sounded dubious. "That seems like a long shot after all this time."

"What about Queen Olivia?" Christine wondered aloud. "She was here when Chris and Alice left the Village. She had an affair with him. And we came at her personal invitation. If I had known that she and Chris had an affair, I would never have come. But he didn't tell me until we got here. He didn't think it was important."

"She's a little pregnant to be going around shooting people, isn't she?" I pointed out.

But Detective Almond seemed to like Olivia as a suspect. "Maybe that explains what happened to the king, too," he said. "Maybe she just got fed up with everyone fooling around."

"That could explain why Harry wasn't very forthcoming about who stabbed him," Chase suggested. "But I can't imagine Livy shooting or stabbing anyone without fainting when it was over."

"I've heard there's some talk that her baby isn't her husband's," Miller added. "Is it possible the dead man is the father?"

Everyone looked at Christine, who sniffed and wiped her eyes. "I don't know. Your guess is as good as mine."

"Have a talk with her anyway, Manhattan," Detective Almond said. "God knows I'm putting it off on you—I never want to discuss anything with that woman again."

He told Christine to come up with a list of all the women she knew of who'd dated her husband. Christine agreed, but I could tell from her face that she was embarrassed and heartsick at the thought of doing it. It was one thing to know your husband was sleeping around, but quite another to have to parade that fact in front of everyone.

Chase didn't mention anything about Jolly and Nick and their modest thirst for vengeance. I was glad he'd gone that route. The boys didn't deserve to be punished. I hoped they could be kept out of it altogether.

"What about Christine?" I asked. "Now that you know that Nick found the gun after seeing his father killed, will you drop the charges against her?"

Detective Almond shrugged. "Who knows? For now, nothing changes. We'll compare the boy's fingerprints to the one's we found on the murder weapon. But let's face it—he could've come into contact with the gun here after she tried to hide it. Until we know better, nothing changes. Sorry."

At least he looked apologetic, as if he wished there was something else he could do for Christine. He didn't say anything else, just left with Miller and a pocketful of Christmas cookies.

Christine sat down hard on the sofa. "I wish we hadn't told him about Nick. What if he tries to make it all his fault?"

"I don't think that will happen," Chase said. "Despite appearances, Detective Almond is a fair man. At least he was open to the idea that you aren't guilty."

"So what do we do now?" I asked him.

"You go and see Livy—I agree with Detective Almond right now. You seem like you can handle her."

"Okay. I guess I'm working as her lady-in-waiting anyway. I can talk to her as easy as anyone else. But what else can we do?"

Chase's two-way radio went off. A coolant line under the ice skating rink had ruptured, and they couldn't get in touch with the repair person who'd installed it.

"I'm on my way," he said, then turned to me and Christine. "Let's try to come up with some real suspects for the police. Anyone you think might have wanted to hurt Chris. Let's get the police talking to them, especially if they're living within fifty miles or so of the Village."

He kissed me and was gone. I comforted Christine as best I could. I knew Livy was waiting for my report from Chase—if she was up and around after Edgar's sudden death in her parlor.

"There's still hope," I told Christine. "Christmas isn't here yet. Maybe something wonderful will happen."

"I hope so. Do you think Chase will be able to convince Merlin to let me stay in the Village?"

"I'm sure he will. I'm sorry, but I have to go. Don't do any packing until we know something for sure. Take the kids out for supper."

I was about to open the front door when it suddenly burst open, slamming against the wall behind it.

"Ho ho ho! I'm Father Christmas. I hope there is someone ready to make some toys for me. Well, really, I hope someone here can tell me exactly what Father Christmas is supposed to do."

Christine jumped to her feet, and all the kids came running out of their rooms, bearing out my theory that they were all listening anyway.

I laughed. "Bart, you make a great Father Christmas. The kids are going to love you."

"I hope so, because Daisy isn't in love with me doing this. The only reason she let me go was because Merlin promised her something. I don't know what I'm supposed to get out of it."

"A lot of enjoyment and satisfaction," Christine said as she took his arm and smiled up at him. "My, you're a big one. I thought my Chris was big. Children, let's go and help Father Christmas."

To my surprise, even Jolly agreed to go with them. I left as they were explaining everything to Bart. Maybe it wasn't too late to get a new Father Christmas after all.

I walked to the castle with a borrowed umbrella. The worst storm clouds were moving quickly toward the ocean. There were still a few visitors left in the Village. They looked a little wet but seemed to be having a good time at the climbing wall and the hatchet-throw area. The well-dressed lords and ladies—and anyone else with expensive costumes—hadn't emerged from their shelters yet. The heavy rain might have signaled the end of the day for them.

Gus was gone from his post at the castle gate. That was good news for me. I walked in and checked to see how Livy was doing. Lady Jane and Lady Barbara looked relieved when they told me that Wanda had given Livy an herbal sleeping tonic to relax. She was still sleeping off the trauma of Edgar's death.

I certainly didn't want to be the one to wake her much less ask questions about where she was when Chris was killed.

It was stupid anyway, thinking she had actually taken a gun and killed her former lover. Her affair with Chris had been a long time ago. I felt sure Harry either knew about it or no longer cared. It was water under a very wide bridge for both of them. Edgar was a different story, though, not only because he had been involved with Livy so recently but also because their affair had taken place very near the time Livy had gotten pregnant. If it turned out that Edgar had been murdered, well, I might have to rethink Livy's innocence on that score. But as Chris's killer? No way.

And I believed even Nick would've noticed if the killer's stomach had stretched out two feet in front of her—no matter the wide base of the gown. Livy's pregnancy was very obvious.

Of course, I might be biased. I just felt sure Alice was involved in some way. Maybe she hadn't actually pulled the trigger, although it seemed to be established that it was a woman who'd done it. She could've hired someone. Nick's story strengthened my theory. Who would hate Chris more than his first wife? Sure, the divorce happened a long time ago, but bitterly divorced couples had been known to feud for longer than twenty years, in my experience.

Alice was our best suspect. Maybe she was one of the group who'd been at the Village almost since its opening. Or maybe she was a recent hire. I hadn't considered that idea. Maybe she came back because she knew Chris would be here. There had been plenty of advertising about the Father Christmas event. I'd even seen a commercial with him in it when I was in Columbia. Maybe his killer had seen the ads, too.

With that in mind, and since I was already at the castle

and the rain had started again, I decided to go back and take another look at the computer.

I might've been wasting my time trying to figure out what Alice had once looked like from pictures or paintings. Maybe she was right under my nose. The chances were good that I might not even recognize her from an old photo. It had been a long time. People changed. I needed to know what she looked like now.

Had Chris known who she was when she whispered to him before she shot him? Had he thought she was just fooling around, or had he felt that he deserved to die for what he'd done to her? It wasn't normal for someone to sit still and let himself be shot. Maybe she'd whispered something romantic and he'd had no idea she meant to kill him. Maybe he'd thought she wanted to be with him despite all their years apart.

It was a good time to look through the computer files for another reason—Bart was busy trying to get his Father Christmas act together. It would be good not to have him looking over my shoulder and asking me questions I'd rather not answer. Not yet anyway.

I hurried down the empty hall and entered the small room near the castle gate. I was surprised to find that I wasn't alone after all. Esmeralda was there, too.

"We keep running into each other," she said. "You must be working at the castle again."

"Livy's new lady-in-waiting," I explained. "My toymaking apprenticeship kind of went south and I had to find something else to do. Livy's going through more ladies-in-waiting right now than usual."

"Not surprising. She's not easy to get along with when she's not pregnant. You know how they say some women glow when they're pregnant? Livy just screams louder."

We both laughed at that. I'd known Esmeralda since my first summer here. She was tough about getting things done at the castle, but I'd always liked her.

She nodded at the computer. "They want me to start using this thing to order what I need for the laundry. Like I know how to do that. We live and work in the 1500s here. What's wrong with paper? Even paper is a modern-day device for that age. I don't think we should progress further than that right now."

I agreed with her and sat in one of the other chairs facing a monitor and keyboard "I'm still trying to find out what happened to Queen Alice. I know if I keep looking, I'll find out."

"You're still stuck on that? Jessie, that was twenty years ago. I don't think they even had a computer here then. What difference does it make now?"

Maybe it was the wrong thing to do, but I decided to lie to her. I thought I might be able to get her to help me if my reasoning sounded inoffensive. Not everyone wants to help with a murder investigation.

"I'm putting together a history project for the Village. I'm hoping they'll hire me to keep up with it once they see it. There have to be some records from the beginning of the Village. I'd like to know what she looked like and what happened to her. The answers are here somewhere."

She smiled and stood up. She was wearing street clothes, jeans and a sweater, so I knew she was on her way out. "Well, I wish you luck. I can't get this thing to make a list of supplies. Every time I try, I get an error message. I think I may have to give my usual paper list to Bart and he can do the rest."

"I know what you mean."

Esmeralda left me there, closing the door behind her as

she went. I found the files I'd been looking through before pretty quickly and started searching through them again.

But this time, Alice's employee records were gone, erased. There was no mention of the first queen. Only Chris was listed as the first king of Renaissance Faire Village.

I typed her name in the search box—nothing came back. It was as though she'd never worked here.

I knew it. Not that it was hard to get in here and mess around with the computers—I'd just done it. If Alice was in the Village, she might've done the same thing.

Bart was going to be furious.

Twenty-three

Maybe, if Alice *was* here, she was a new hire. At least I thought I would test that assumption. Chase had already confirmed that there was no Alice currently working at the Village. But she could be working under a different name.

I wasn't sure how I'd find her. My only option was to search through all of the new-hire records using certain parameters. She had to be at least forty. That narrowed the field. Chris and Christine were in their early fifties. Alice had to be somewhere between forty and fifty. How many women had been hired in that age group recently?

I restarted my search. I was amazed at all the women over the age of forty who'd been hired recently. There were even two over the age of seventy. Seventeen women fit the age bracket I'd specified. Their assignments ranged from castle help to carriage driver and goat herder.

That gave me seventeen women in the Village to check

on using absolutely no criteria other than height and body build—were they shorter than me, with a thicker waist? It seemed pretty hopeless. What were the chances that any of them *weren't* shorter than me?

I went ahead and made a list of all the people in the Village who'd worked there since it first opened. That was twenty-five people, most of them men. I separated the men from women and ended up with six women.

Rita Martinez and Esmeralda had both been here that long, as had Ginny Stewart at the Lady of the Lake Tavern. Bawdy Betty of Bawdy Betty's Bagels and Mrs. Potts at the Honey and Herb Shoppe were on the list, too.

I printed the list, wishing I had my flash drive with me instead. I had just taken the pages from the printer when King Harold joined me in the computer room.

"Jessie." He looked surprised and unhappy to see me there. He shifted his arm, still in the sling, as though it pained him. I thought he might turn around and leave, so I said, "I'm leaving, Your Majesty. You can stay."

"I, uh, wasn't leaving. I have a few things to do. Adventure Land wants to computerize us, you know. I need a laptop in my chamber, but until then—" He looked embarrassed to have explained himself.

"I'm sorry we had that argument." I needed to mend some fences if I was going to be at the castle full-time until Christmas. "I hope we can be friends again."

To my surprise, he sat down in one of the chairs and put his head in his good hand. "I'm sorry, too. Everything is in a bad place right now. I know it shouldn't be this way with the baby coming and all. This should be a joyous time for everyone in the Village."

He had spoken like a king for so long, occasionally that regal phrasing crept into his normal conversation. It happened to everyone who lived here—spontaneous bouts of old English, even forgetting what the modern terminology was for some items.

I sat back down again and patted his good hand. "Having a baby is stressful. I think you're holding up very well."

He looked up at me with hope in his eyes. "Really? Because I'm a basket case. I can't really imagine Livy and me as some poor child's parents. I never dreamed this would be possible so late in life. I was unprepared—still am."

"That's the amazing thing about having a baby. It doesn't matter if you're prepared or not. The baby comes along and you figure things out. It works out somehow."

"I've been such a fool with Christine and the others. It's not that I don't care for them. Christine has been very special to me."

"I know. She told me you posted bail for her."

Harry cringed. "Please don't tell anyone else. Finding out about Christine and then about me arranging for her bail sent Livy off the deep end. You know we swore fealty to each other just before we found out she was with child. Neither of us was ever supposed to . . . you know."

"Yes, I know. How did Queen Olivia find out?"

"I don't know. She has spies everywhere. Probably one of them bribed one of my gentlemen or my accountant. It doesn't matter. It's over between me and Christine. I just couldn't let her stay in jail, not with eight children to look after and Chris dead."

"That was commendable, Your Majesty. But I'm sorry the queen stabbed you."

It was a shot in the dark, but I knew from his face that I was right.

"How did you find out? Blasted spies! No matter. I'd appreciate it if you kept it quiet."

"I'd be glad to oblige you. At least it's not part of some large conspiracy going on in the castle." I smiled at him, and he seemed more at ease. Of course, I was holding a very large secret that could be easily shared. He might start sucking up to me. "Could you tell me what you remember about Alice Christmas?"

"Alice. A delightful woman. She was quite funny and flirtatious. I found her fascinating for the short time we knew each other. Adventure Land brought Olivia and me in to replace her and Chris."

"Can you remember how tall she was? Was she thin or heavy?"

"It was a long time ago, Jessie. But I think she was shorter than me. I'm sure she was thinner than Livy. Why do you ask?"

"I think she came back to the Village to kill Chris."

"What ho!! You think she'd still be that angry? Most women seem to get over these things quickly. Women are very resilient, you know. It's what allows them to be the baby carriers."

I ignored that remark.

"Was Alice dark or fair? Do you recall any other marking that might give a clue as to who she is today? I think she's still in the Village but under a different name."

He seemed to consider it, staring off into the recesses of the computer room. "Alice was fair. I can't recall that she had any facial markings like scars or such. She had a relative who worked here, but I can't remember who that was right now. I don't know what the chances would be that the same person would still be here. People come and go all the time."

I knew he was right about that. It would've been helpful if Alice had some striking feature about her like a large mole on her face or some other unusual physical characteristic that could help identify her. All I knew at this point was that she was shorter than Harry, thinner than Livy, and fair. Not much to go on, but it was probably all I could expect after twenty years.

I thanked the king for his help, and he reminded me not to tell anyone who had stabbed him. Now I knew why the wound hadn't been more deadly. Livy had probably barely stabbed him, then fainted. Still, she was capable of more than I'd imagined.

I left the computer room with my printouts tucked into the small purse that hung at my waist. I didn't have my Village mug for free drinks, not necessary inside the castle where food and drink were free all the time. It was about the only perk of serving royalty.

The idea that Alice had a relative working here was intriguing. Although, with all of her records gone, there was no way to know what her maiden name was. It seemed to be a dead end in a long line of dead ends.

Even in the real world outside the Village, tracing someone back twenty years to figure out who they were today was a tall order. The police might be able to do it, or I might be able to find a private detective to do it. I'd have to check on that if there was no other way.

Lady Barbara was coming down the hall toward me. She bowed her head slightly as we met. "The queen is awake now, Lady Jessie. She will see you."

"Thank you." I followed her back to the queen's chambers. Livy was still in bed, wearing a lacy robe over her gown. She was sitting up but looked very pale. I hoped, all jokes at her expense aside, that she would be all right.

"Lady Barbara said you have come with news from the bailiff."

"Yes, Your Majesty." I sat on one of the tiny chairs allotted to the ladies-in-waiting. It was barely big enough for a normal-sized butt to fit on. I assumed that she had seen Harry since he'd come back from the hospital. That didn't seem like news to me anymore.

Instead I told her about how the investigation into Chris's death was going and that it might be possible to identify his killer.

"It hardly seems consequential after everything we have been through," she said. "I am glad Edgar is gone, for good this time. I wish I hadn't been there when he died. It was horrible. But we are alive and our progeny is still kicking. We shall survive, shall we not, Lady Jessie."

"We shall, Your Majesty." I nodded respectfully, then said, "The bailiff wanted me to ask you where you were when Chris Christmas was killed."

"What?" Her eyes were comically large, and her mouth formed an O shape. "I can't believe the bailiff would be so crass as to accuse me of murder while I am pregnant. And you, Lady Jessie, would repeat the question to me."

"With all respect, if you tell me the answer and I tell the bailiff, then you don't have to talk to the police. They think now that Chris wasn't killed by his wife, but they believe it was a woman. And you had a possible motive for killing him. The bailiff and I are only trying to spare you that indignity, Your Majesty."

She started crying and reached for a box of chocolates. "Please tell the bailiff I was here resting when Chris was killed. Lady Jane was here with me. Perhaps that will satisfy everyone. As though I could kill anyone."

I looked at her with her tearstained face and swollen body and agreed. But I also knew she'd managed to put a small knife into her husband. I didn't think Livy was guilty of killing Chris, but she was capable.

I left her there in her bedroom, grateful that she was crying instead of throwing me out of the castle. I decided then that Chase would be doing any follow-up questioning, unless I found a job somewhere else.

Both the ladies were in the sitting room, talking quietly when I came out. Lady Jane smiled and nodded at me. "I hope the queen is well."

"Unhappy," I agreed. "But well."

"Does the bailiff believe the queen is in any danger?" Lady Barbara asked.

"No. Why would he think that?"

"I just thought, with the attack on the king, that Her Majesty might be in danger."

I could see how she might think that. It wasn't my place to tell her what had actually happened. But I did assure her that Livy was safe.

Livy called for Jane and Barbara by name. Both of the ladies fluttered into her bedroom in their best green silk brocade gowns. I'd noticed how often they dressed alike. My gown was very different from theirs—and the queen didn't call for me. That probably didn't bode well for my future at the castle.

I had hoped to have a conversation with Livy about Alice Christmas. That probably wouldn't happen now. Not that my efforts at the castle seemed to be helping anyway. So far everyone I'd talked to about her couldn't seem to remember much. If I hadn't known better, I'd think it was a conspiracy. But instead, I believed it was just a case of out of sight, out of mind.

I decided to go to the kitchen and talk to Rita about Alice. She probably wouldn't recall any more than the others, but I had time to kill. I might as well use it constructively.

Rita was busy supervising dinner for that night. She told me there were several executives from the Adventure Land board of directors coming as well as the usual retinue of cast regulars. As I'd expected, she didn't have much time to tell me what little she could remember about Alice.

"She liked almonds," she said as she took over whisking some eggs from a kitchen drudge who wasn't performing the task to her standard. "I remember that. As far as what she looked like, she was normal looking. Not blond but light brown hair. I think she was tall and thin, maybe taller than you, Jessie."

I frowned. That didn't match Nick's description of the killer at all. Of course, maybe the years had not been kind to her and she'd grown shorter and fatter.

"Thanks, Rita."

"Anytimc. Hcy, do you want to pccl a hundrcd pounds of potatoes?"

I told her that, as much as I'd like to help out, I had a commitment somewhere else. Then I got out of the kitchen as quickly as possible. I might end up working there before Christmas anyway, but not until I'd explored every other job opportunity in the Village. The only thing worse than the kitchen was the laundry.

I was walking back toward the queen's chambers, hoping she might have need of me, when I saw Merlin. At least I thought it was Merlin.

The man was tall and thin with gray hair and a neatly trimmed mustache. His suit and shoes looked expensive. At first, I wasn't even sure why I thought he was Merlin—no pointy hat, scraggly beard, or robe. Then I looked again. Of course it was him. Same pointy nose and chin, and one of his eyes was a slightly different color than the other.

"Merlin?" I asked as I met him.

He glanced around. "Please do not call me that again until the board of directors leaves after dinner tonight."

I laughed. "I knew it was you. Is this what you look like in the outside world?"

"Not any more than I can help." He laughed, too. "Now you know why I live here. Who'd want to look like this all the time and live in some condo or apartment in New York when you can dress like a wizard and live with Horace the Moose here in the Village?"

"I guess I never thought about you having an outside persona like everyone else."

"And I'd appreciate it if you'd keep it to yourself." His eyes narrowed as he looked at me. "I thought you were working at the toy shop during the holidays, Jessie. What brings you to the castle? You aren't pillaging the computer again are you? Bart gets really ugly when someone messes with his computer."

"But everyone uses it," I said. "How can he tell if someone is messing with it?"

"I don't know. I try to stay away from that mundane stuff. He said something earlier about someone losing some information. I'm sure it was just an accident. Who knows how to use the thing that well besides him?"

I thought about that. Obviously someone either had bad luck with the computer or knew exactly what they were doing.

"I'm working for the queen right now," I confessed. "With all the problems at the manor houses, there aren't many toys being made. I'm sure if Adventure Land will let Christine stay on here during the rest of the investigation into Chris's death, I'd be able to make toys with her."

He held up one narrow hand. "Spare me. I've already talked to Chase. I can't say for sure until the board meets, but I'm all right with her staying on. It doesn't sound to me like Myrtle Beach's finest really know if she killed her husband or not. Do you have any ideas on that score?"

I told him about Alice. "Nick says he saw a woman."

"Or at least someone who dresses like a woman." He shrugged. "I know of several men here who prefer women's attire. That doesn't make them killers."

"You must've met Alice. Do you remember anything about her?"

He frowned. "Not really. It was a long time ago. But I'm sure no one could hold a grudge that long. Even my ex-wives are more forgiving. If Nick says he saw a woman, doesn't that put us right back with Christine as the suspect?"

Before I could answer, a group of well-dressed men and one woman walked into the castle headed in our direction.

"Looks like the board is ready to meet," he said. "I'll let you know their decision about Christine after we're through. Carry on, Lady Jessie. Leave the computers alone unless Bart is there."

Twenty-four

No luck with Merlin either. Even worse, by telling him about Nick's observations, I might have made things worse for Christine. Maybe Merlin wouldn't tell the board about the new evidence. After all, it was in their best interest to keep the toy shop open. They may have had an easy time tapping Bart to play Father Christmas, but an experienced toy maker was rare.

I walked out of the castle. It was still drizzling a little, and evening was closing in early. The storm had cooled the air. Smoke was rising from several chimneys in the Village below, making the whole Christmas scene even more beautiful.

Fog was forming over damp grass where the snow had melted. I used my cell phone to take a few pictures that I could keep forever. Who knew what was going to happen after this? The thought was depressing.

I decided to walk over to the manor house to see how

Bart's training was going. Most of the Village residents seemed to be in for the night. The cobblestones were deserted, and no one was out practicing their parts for the next day, as usually happened when the Village closed. It seemed the only thing going on was the decision making at the castle.

I thought I saw someone moving between the manor houses. The narrow walkways between the buildings were rarely used by visitors, but they were a favored shortcut among the residents. Staying away from the cobblestones was often the fastest way to travel. I thought it could be Chase, on his way to check out some other emergency, so I lifted my skirts and ran across the wet ground.

But when I reached the first walkway, I didn't see anyone. I looked through all the narrow paths, but there was no one on either end. Whoever had been there had disappeared quickly.

About a hundred feet away, I caught sight of a woman dressed all in black. Her face was covered by a black veil, and she was wearing black gloves.

My heart started racing. I couldn't get my feet to move. I pulled out my cell phone to call for help—it was after hours. Besides, this could be Chris's killer. She was exactly as Nick had described her.

Of course, Chase's phone went to voice mail. He hardly ever used it when he was working because he had the two-way radio. Of all the times not to be able to communicate with him. The police were too far away to bother with 911. I was going to have to follow her and maybe I'd get a clue as to who she was.

I wished I could confront her, but common sense reminded me that, as much as I wanted to get it over with, confronting her could be dangerous. I had no weapon. If she'd managed to pick up another gun, I'd be sorry. She might not kill me, but, like any other trapped animal, she'd be on the defensive, and I couldn't predict how aggressively she'd react.

I contented myself with observing her. We were only a short distance apart—me standing around the corner at Polo's Pasta. I tried to come up with other details about her that might lead to her arrest, such as her exact height and weight. Nick's description of the black widow had been good. Her waist was wider than mine, and she was shorter. I guessed five foot six, maybe one hundred sixty pounds.

The gown she wore wasn't a Renaissance style either. The skirt had a hoop or some other mechanism making it stand out. It moved back and forth like a bell as she walked. There was more than starch in that material. The design was from the 1800s, instead of the 1500s, maybe a leftover antebellum costume.

The woman was definitely not pregnant. Even though she was heavier set than me, she had no baby bump in front. She wasn't Livy. For all of the queen's faults, I was glad about that.

It was frustrating just following and watching her. It would take only a second to rip away the heavy veil and expose the killer. But thoughts of the consequences of that action were enough to keep me hiding in the shadows. I must be getting old. Usually I was good at confrontation.

So I continued to follow her, staying close behind but hiding by shops and game booths. The daylight was rapidly fading under storm-darkening skies. The black widow occasionally paused to look around her, then she'd hurry on down the cobblestones.

What was she looking for? I couldn't understand what she was up to. She obviously wasn't worried about being seen. It had been a few days since Chris's death. Christine had been arrested. I could see where she might feel she'd gotten away clean.

There was no way for her to know that Nick had seen her and given us her description. She probably felt safe, even invisible, wandering through the Village. Even though her costume wasn't correct, there were thousands every week that didn't fit in. No one would question her.

A few residents came out of Baron's Beer and Brats, sounding like they'd had too much to drink. They were arguing about something that I couldn't quite pick up from my post a few yards away.

The woman in black stood beside the Swan Swing and didn't move until they'd passed. *She's not as confident as I thought.* She didn't want to push her luck by interacting with residents who might wonder why they didn't know her.

I mentally added that information to my growing list about her. She obviously didn't know the Village well or she would've realized that residents weren't that careful about the people around them. They were used to seeing someone new almost every day as employees came and went.

She started walking again, this time in a straight line toward the castle. I followed until my cell phone went off near the privies by Polo's Pasta. I ducked behind one of the portable toilets, hoping she hadn't seen me.

It was Chase, returning my call. "Sorry I couldn't get back with you right away," he said. "I was helping to get a mess cleaned up at the Stage Caravan. I can't believe anyone thought it would be a good idea to bring a bubble-blowing machine onstage with them. The dancers were slipping and falling all over. It would've been funny except two of the belly dancers sprained their ankles."

"I found her," I interrupted his story. "I found the woman in black that Nick described. She was walking around out here in the Village. But she doesn't know we're looking for her."

"What are you talking about? Where are you?"

I explained about seeing Chris's killer. "I'm following her, trying to figure out where she's staying or hiding out so we can catch her."

"Don't move. Where are you now?"

"I'm near Polo's, but I think she's headed toward the castle. The good news is that she's definitely not Livy. I thought no one could miss that belly. But I can't just stand here, Chase. If I lose her, no telling when we'll see her again."

"I understand that, Jessie. But I'd rather lose her than lose you. She's already killed once, if it's the same person. We have to assume she'll kill again."

"I know. I won't get too close. And I won't rush in when she stops somewhere. I have some common sense. Give me a little credit."

"All right. Stay with her until I catch up with you. But please be careful."

I closed my phone and peeked around the corner of the privy. There was no sign of the black widow. My heart fell flat. I'd lost her.

Since it didn't matter, I waited for Chase in the overhang shelter of the Merry Mynstrel's Stage. I kept watch for the figure in black, but she was nowhere to be seen. I even kept an eye out for any woman her size coming out of one of the nearby attractions. She could've gone in the first aid station or the Lady of the Lake Tavern and changed clothes. But no one, male or female, dressed in black or any other type of costume came out in the rain.

A few minutes later, Chase arrived. He sat beside me on

the stage floor, and we commiserated over losing the suspect.

"We don't even know for sure it was the same person," he reminded me. "Sometimes people dress in black. It's unusual around here, but not unheard of."

I disagreed. "With a thick black veil and black gloves? Come on, Chase. It was her and I screwed up. I should've kept my eye on her while I was talking to you. Or not answered the phone. Or something. I don't know."

He put his arm around my shoulder. He smelled like bubbles, blueberry at that. "Let's go get some supper and go home. We'll start again tomorrow. If Chris's killer is still hanging out here at the Village, she's got something else in mind. She'll show herself again and we'll catch her. That's the way it works."

I smiled at him. I couldn't help it. "You've been reading police books again, haven't you?"

"You got it. Also, criminal psychology. The criminal nearly always follows a pattern to achieve her goals."

As if his words were a warning, we heard a scream, and a very young voice shouted, "Help! Someone please come and help my mother!"

"That's Merry Beth." I jumped to my feet. "It sounds like she's at Squire's Lane."

"Great," Chase muttered as we both started running in that direction. "I didn't mean that to be a prediction. Wait for me before you do anything."

We ran through the rain across the wet grass and slippery cobblestones. We weren't the only ones to hear Merry Beth's cry for help. Before we could reach her, Mrs. Potts was there along with Brother Carl from the Monastery Bakery and Roger Trent, who just happened to be walking home from Peter's Pub.

They were trying to understand what Merry Beth was saying. Whatever had happened had stripped away her veneer of adulthood. She was crying too hard to be understood.

"Let's all get inside," Chase said as we approached the crowd on the steps to the manor house.

"Mom's inside here," Jolly yelled out the open door. "We can't wake her up, Chase. Something's wrong with her."

"I can't believe something else is happening," Roger taunted Chase as he passed him on the stairs. "When I was bailiff, things like murders didn't happen under my watch. The whole Village is going to hell in a handbasket, if you ask me!"

Chase ignored him, taking the stairs two at a time until he reached the doorway. Everyone trooped in after him, curious to see what was going on. Hopefully with some intention of helping out, too.

Christine was lying on the sofa, not moving. Bart and the children were standing around her, shaking her and trying to wake her up.

"I took the kids out for ice cream after we were done practicing," Bart told Chase as the kids moved out of the way. "Christine said she wanted some time alone. I should've made her come for ice cream, too."

"What's wrong with her?" I asked. Christine's face was very pale. Her eyes were deeply shadowed, and her lips were white. "Did she have a heart attack, too?"

"I can't tell," Chase said, examining her. "Her pulse is weak and shallow. Pupils dilated." He called 911 on his radio and told the dispatcher who he was. "We need emergency medical assistance here. We're in the brick houses right after the Main Gate. It's the only house with the lights on."

Bart sniffed. "There's the faintest smell of almonds. Can anyone else smell that?"

"Is she going to be okay?" Jolly wrung his hands anxiously, like a scared little boy.

"She'll be fine," Roger told him.

Chase grimaced and muttered, "Roger! You can be the one to tell him if she's *not* going to be fine."

Something needed to be done. Chase and Roger were hovering near Christine—Chase in case she went into cardiac arrest, and Roger, just because. The children stood off to one side, staring at their mother as though they could wake her up with their fears.

The doorway was blocked with Village folk who were well meaning but would slow down the paramedics when they arrived.

"Okay, we need to get everyone off the stairs and out of the way before the paramedics get here to help Christine," I said in my stern professor's voice.

Bart took the hint and began to get everyone moving. I let him have that project and got the children together. They didn't need to see this happening to their mother. Who knew what might have to be done to her when the emergency workers arrived?

"We want to stay," insisted Jolly and Merry Beth, but all eight of the children finally came with me to the kitchen. Faith, Joy, Star, and Holly were sniffling and hugging each other. The older children kept to themselves.

"We can see fine from here," I said, showing them that we could look through the kitchen door and know what was going on. "They need the space to help your mother. We don't want to make things worse."

They agreed but weren't happy about it. I didn't blame them for being scared and worried. I was, too.

Star asked me if she could have a drink of soda from the refrigerator. I was only too glad to turn their attention to something else—drinks would do.

I went to get the soda while I sent Jolly to get glasses. On the front of the white refrigerator was a piece of paper with a threatening message scribbled in red crayon.

You die tonight.

Twenty-five

I knew Detective Almond wouldn't be happy about it, but I took the paper down so the children wouldn't see it and have nightmares for the rest of their lives. I was already approaching that point of no return. How bad was it for them?

I hid the paper under a book on the cabinet and continued to pour soda for everyone. It was all I could do to pretend the paper wasn't there. I wanted to rush all of them out of the house.

By the time each child had a sip of their soda and was thinking about food, the paramedics had arrived. They seemed to diagnose the problem very quickly—probably poison or a drug she'd ingested. They started the IV drip and moved her onto the gurney to take her to the hospital. A doctor would be waiting for them.

Chase immediately took a look around the room. He put some crumbs from the table into a plastic bag and gave them to the paramedics. He also put plastic wrap on a glass that was on the table.

Roger, not to be outdone, also picked up some candy he'd found in a pretty Christmas bowl and gave it to them. Then he ate a couple of pieces of what was left. I shook my head.

"Is there family?" the lead paramedic asked Chase.

"Just her kids are here. She has a sister in Iowa."

"Okay. Maybe you'd like to ride in with her in case she regains consciousness. And there's the paperwork."

Chase glanced at me. I knew what he meant. But even Jolly wasn't ready for that responsibility. If Christine's condition worsened on the way to the hospital, one of them might be there only to watch her die. I shook my head.

"I'll come along," Chase said.

The paramedics picked up the gurney, and Chase followed them out of the house. I could picture them getting in the ambulance and leaving the Village. Traffic wasn't too bad on the roads in Myrtle Beach at this time of year. In the summer, it was hard to move from traffic light to traffic light.

"Are they going to bring Mommy back after they fix her?" Star asked.

"We'll go get her as soon as she's better," I promised, wondering if that would make me a bad person in Chase's book. I had to say something. I couldn't help it. I couldn't leave her dangling, not knowing anything, but I also didn't know what would happen yet. How do you describe beating the odds and surviving a murderous attack to a small child?

Since the food in the house seemed to be in question, I got Bart to help me take all the kids over to Peter's Pub for supper. It was easy to distract the younger children. They didn't really understand what was going on. It was the older ones who worried me. They stared off into the distance, even while a little white terrier did tricks for snacks. They understood how serious the situation was. I hated that for them.

"I don't know how safe it is for them to spend the night in that apartment," I worried out loud to Bart. "If the food was poisoned, what else could the killer have done while she was there?"

"We don't know if Christine was poisoned. Maybe she had some bad peanut butter or something."

"Maybe," I whispered. "But there was a threatening note on the refrigerator. I think the same woman who killed Chris is after Christine now. It might've been better if she'd stayed in jail. At least she was safe there."

He shrugged. "Not from what I've seen on TV. Those places can be brutal."

I couldn't argue with that. I just wasn't sure what to do with eight kids while we waited to find out about their mother. I didn't want to force them out of their home right now, but I didn't know if they'd be safe there.

"The only place I can think of where they could stay the night is at the castle," I said. "There's plenty of room there for them. I'll just have to sneak them in. No one will notice the difference. Then we'll see what happens in the morning."

"Let's tell Rita," he suggested. "She'll help. That woman is all heart."

"So this is where you've been hiding." Daisy Reynolds joined us and ordered a tankard of ale. "Jessie, good to see you. Quit messing with my man, or I'll have to call you out for a duel at sunrise."

I laughed—halfheartedly. Any woman who would try

to take Bart away from Daisy would have to be crazy. She was all muscle from working out with her swords, not to mention making them at the forge for special orders. Daisy was tough, but her curly hair, Kewpie-doll face, and big heart were a reminder of her true nature.

"Even I wouldn't be that stupid," I said. "But it's good to see you, too. I hope you've been keeping busy."

She sat beside Bart and nudged him over for more room on the bench. "Running after this big lug," she said. "I don't know why I put up with him."

Bart smiled and kissed her hand. "Because you love me. That's why I don't mind when you bring a sword to bed at night."

She kissed him and slapped his cheek a little. "That's right." She looked around at everyone watching the terrier. "What's going on?"

Bart explained about the kids. "We have a problem. They need a place to stay since their house might be poisoned. Jessie thinks we should sneak them into the castle."

"I agree with her." Daisy tipped back her tankard and finished her ale. "That's what I like best about you, Jessie. You think on your feet. Let's go. The night's not getting any younger."

The eleven of us left the small crowd throwing coins for the terrier and his owner and started walking toward the castle. The fake snow was spewing out across the Village, maybe with a little less ferocity than the blizzard it had been.

"Why the hell are they wasting the snow at night when no one's here?" Daisy demanded.

"Daisy!" Bart reprimanded. "The children. You can't swear in front of children."

"Sorry. I wasn't thinking." Daisy put her hand to her mouth.

"What's the plan?" Bart asked. "We're like a small army trying to sneak into the castle. I don't think it's going to work."

I hadn't really considered how many of us there were. It might be easy to get one or two in without being noticed, but eleven was a lot. Besides, Joy and Star were tired and whiny. Merry Beth kept telling them they could go home soon, but the two little ones didn't care.

"You're right," I admitted. "I'm ready to hear any and every plan on how we can do this. I just can't think of anywhere else in the Village with the kind of room we need."

Two pirates jumped out at us, ending our discussion. The *Queen's Revenge* was tied up at the end of Mirror Lake near the Lady of the Lake Tavern. That meant mischief was afoot.

"We're here to relieve you of any and all coins, tokens, or other important things you might have." The first pirate was very young. He looked familiar. Then I realized it was Bucky from vegetable justice. This had to be his initiation.

"Out of my way," Daisy said. "Do you know who I am? I'll run you scallywags through if you're not careful."

"Look, we need tokens or something," the second pirate explained. He was new, too, but not as young. "This is a pirate initiation. If we don't come back with something, King Rafe won't let us be pirates. And I'm not working at the frog catapult again."

Having worked the frog catapult, I could sympathize. I started thinking about all the berths on the pirate ship. It would be just like Peter Pan for the kids.

"Belay that, Swordmaster," I said to Daisy. "I think we

have several things these two new pirates can bring back with them tonight."

I stared pointedly at the kids, who were thrilled to be held up by pirates.

"Perhaps you're right," Daisy agreed with a smile. "I'm sure Rafe will be *glad* to see us. Lead on, young sirs!"

We convinced the two new wannabe pirates that Rafe would be very impressed by them bringing people to the ship. They could charge ransom. The other pirates would respect them.

The newbies could finally see how it could work for them, and being hungry and tired of waiting to jump out at stray residents, they agreed.

Daisy and Bart were reluctant to leave me and the kids, but I assured them it would be okay. I could see they wanted some intimate makeup time, not always easy to get around there.

We boarded the *Queen's Revenge* to a raucous chorus of pirates congratulating their two new mates on bringing back something of value. It was a rite of passage for everyone who wanted to join the group.

The two new pirates basked in it, nodding, smiling, and accepting the accolades. At least until Rafe, the pirate king, came up on deck and took a good look at their booty. At that point, all the hardy well wishes came to an abrupt end.

"What's this?" Rafe demanded, arms folded across his leather-clad chest. I noticed that the only holiday garb the pirates had agreed to wear were red and green scarves around their heads or necks. Not such a big change since the scarves were usually red anyway.

"We did as you bid us, King Rafe," Bucky said with a respectful bow and a pretty good hand gesture of respect.

"This is not treasure, my boys." Rafe made a point of walking around me, looking me over as though I were a horse he was about to purchase. "This is trouble."

Rafe and I have a long history. We were once lovers on this very pirate ship for a long summer. But that was years ago during my pre-Chase, love-'em-and-leave-'em days. Since then, we'd pranked each other a few times (the last being the portable toilet incident) but mostly didn't encourage contact. I could understand his hesitancy. That didn't mean he wasn't going to help out. I figured he just needed to understand the situation.

"We seek asylum on your vessel, Captain Rafe," I explained.

He puffed up like a peacock and glared at me. "That's *King* Rafe," he reminded me. His dark eyes looked at me with contempt. "We don't grant asylum to nonpirates on the *Queen's Revenge*. Seek the *bailiff* if you want protection."

I looked at my eight charges, wishing I hadn't told Bart and Daisy that I could handle this on my own. I could have used their backup right about now. Certainly Bart just being himself was enough to scare anyone into submission.

But it was already done. I couldn't let the kids down.

"I can't think of anyone who wouldn't want to be a pirate, right, kids?" I asked them.

I wasn't sure what their response would be, but apparently they had spent enough time in the Village to know what they should say. They all said "*Arr!*" at the same time.

That seriously broke the tension. All the pirates started laughing and slapping each other on the back. It was still hard for Rafe to take in what was happening on his ship. I could see the deer-in-the-headlights look on his lean, handsome face.

The two new pirates, Bucky and Stanly, played up how tough they were, spinning an incredible yarn about kidnapping all of us to hold us for ransom. It made the whole affair take on a different aspect. The pirates were victorious and had proven themselves.

Rafe shouted for quiet. He wasn't through complaining. "I have not sanctioned this action as yet. I have yet to see how this serves us. The Lady Jessie, while a good ransom bet, will be difficult and will not serve *my* needs." He spit on the deck, which caused all the other pirates to begin spitting, too. Before I knew it, all eight kids had joined in. The two smallest ones had the hardest time trying to do what everyone else was doing. But it further endeared them to the crew.

"That may be true," I agreed. "And I'll be glad to leave if you agree to harbor these children. They need you. They'll be safe here. You can protect them. You might be the only ones in the Village who can."

Rafe liked that. I knew he would. He'd had a supersized ego ever since Crystal the Pirate Queen left to reconcile with her husband. Rafe needed his pirates to look up to him and not question his authority. Otherwise there might be mutiny—the old-fashioned way, of course—by throwing him off the plank and into Mirror Lake—and a new pirate king.

I saw Grigg lurking in the shadows by the main mast. I knew he'd tried to do exactly that when Crystal had left. It just didn't work out for him. But he could challenge Rafe again at any time. It was part of the pirate way of life.

I could see Rafe was thinking the same thing. Throwing

the kids off the ship would be unpopular with the crew. He'd risk mutiny if he didn't pledge to protect them.

Finally he gave in with a loud "*Arr!*" and a raising of his saber. "Let them stay. Let them be pirates."

The pirates *arred* and *huzzahed* for a while, then they lifted the kids on their shoulders and took them below deck to the living quarters. There would be hammocks for everyone.

I started to follow them, but Rafe put his hand on my shoulder. "You and I have some unfinished business. Come to my quarters. The men will take care of your precious cargo."

While I'd said I would leave if he wanted me to, I didn't really mean it. I wasn't looking forward to sleeping on the pirate ship again, but I didn't want to leave the kids either. I hoped that wasn't what he wanted to parlay about. Even more, I hoped he didn't think this was some scheme to get his attention and make him want to make out with me in his quarters.

The captain's cabin was exactly as I remembered it. It was like a pirate man-cave, with all kinds of souvenirs from battles he'd fought and treasures he'd found. He was one of the only pirates who slept in a bed—an enormous four-poster covered with black velvet.

"Sit down," he commanded. "Would you like some brandy? I recall you have a fondness for peach brandy."

"No thanks." I sat in one of the ladder-back chairs as far away from the bed as I could. "I'll take some wine if you have it."

"You've gone soft living at the Dungeon with the bailiff," he remarked as he poured the wine. "So what's up with the kids?"

I explained the situation. "The killer is still here, Rafe. She's targeting Christine now. But what if she goes after the kids? They have no other family nearby. Their father is dead, and their mother may be in the hospital for a few days. No one else has enough room for them, or people to protect them. She wouldn't try and get on the *Queen's Revenge*."

"I suppose that makes some sense. I don't mind helping out. You know I couldn't just let them stay without making a big deal out of it for the men."

"I understand and I expected it."

"I was just kidding about you leaving." He handed me my wine, sliding his fingers across mine. "I can't think of anything I'd like better than to have you here again."

We were officially in treacherous waters. I sipped my wine and tried not to look at the big bed. "Thank you for helping them. I'll be glad to stay."

"What about Chase?"

"I'm sure he'd be glad to stay, too." I smiled at him and let the chips fall where they may.

He looked a little uncertain about that and stopped hovering over me, trying to peer down my bodice. "I don't think it's necessary for the bailiff to stay, Jessie. You and the children will be perfectly fine here. We can protect them. Surely you two lovebirds can spend a night apart."

"Actually, Chase will probably be at the hospital most of the night with Christine. She needs someone there with her."

He smiled in a lecherous fashion once he knew Chase wasn't in the Village. It was stupid of me to tell him.

"We'll have to make do without him then, my lady. I would be honored to share my bed with you. No need for you to sleep in a hammock below deck. A woman of your cunning and beauty deserves special attention."

I really wanted to help the children, but if it meant

spending the night in Rafe's bed, we'd have to find another way. I hoped I could circumvent that problem, but it might not be possible.

"I appreciate the offer, King Rafe." I got up and put my wineglass on the table. "But I can't leave the kids alone. Imagine what they're going through after their father's murder and finding their mother poisoned. They need me with them."

I thought for one long moment that he would lose his cool and forget his compassion. To his credit, he did neither. He bowed handsomely to me and smiled. "Then I wish you well, Lady Jessie. Sleep sweet. I shall see you on the morrow."

I curtsied deeply. "We are in your debt. Good night."

Rafe stayed in his cabin while I crossed the deck to the stairs that led below. I breathed a sigh of relief. That problem was narrowly averted. I was surprised how much he'd matured since becoming king.

The night was crystal clear with a small crescent moon hanging above us in the dark sky. The Village slept in holiday splendor while the castle rose stately behind us.

As I started down the stairs into the interior of the ship, I glanced toward the manor houses at Squire's Lane, wishing I'd brought the note I'd found on the refrigerator with me. If I hadn't been so worried about the kids and Christine, I would've remembered it. I wasn't going down there this late. It was just going to have to wait until morning.

The light caught on a dark figure gliding between the shops and attractions. It seemed the black widow was on the prowl again.

Twenty-six

Was she checking to see if Christine was at the manor house so she could finish the job she'd started? I wished I'd thought about it sooner. I could've set myself up, pretended to be Christine, and caught her in the act. Obviously she hadn't been able to replace her gun, so she'd resorted to poison. I'd be safe taking her on. Too bad the time had passed for that deception.

I watched her as she slid up the stairs to the manor house where Christine and the kids were staying. It made my blood run cold to think we could have all been asleep in there, waiting for her to come and do her worst. What kind of person hurt kids anyway? Hurting her ex-husband—I might be able to understand that even though they'd been divorced twenty years. Even Christine. Of course, I had no hard proof that she wanted to hurt the kids—

Enough! No more speculation. It was time to end this. No one was going to distract me from catching Alice.

I looked at my cell phone in the torchlight. There was no point in bothering to put it on silent mode. The battery was dead. Chase wasn't going to be able to get in touch with me.

I didn't need it, or him, for this anyway. All I had to do was follow her long enough to see where she went to roost. After that, I could call in the police from someone else's phone.

For a brief moment, I considered that I could be wrong. This might be some innocent resident of the Village who had been happier with Halloween than Christmas. But if that was the case, I'd just end up feeling stupid. No harm, no foul.

I managed to get off of the ship without being caught by the watch. I still felt safe leaving the kids, even though their security wasn't as good as I'd thought, since I'd managed to sneak out. There were still a lot of pirates to get through if anyone tried to get onboard and mess with them. Besides, I knew the *Queen's Revenge* well. It was doubtful that Alice had spent time there, too.

I tried not to worry about the kids and focused on the black widow. If I lost her again, it might be for the last time.

I sneaked past Eve's Garden and the bright lights the maintenance crew had on to clean out the fountain near Our Lady's Gemstones. I didn't want her to see me and get spooked again.

I moved stealthily past the privies and around the Treasure Trove and Leather and Lace. There was no sign of my quarry. *She could still be inside the manor house.*

I decided to wait near the first aid station. It was only a hunch that she'd want to avoid the bright lights illuminating the King's Highway, too. She had kept away from the residents there when I'd tracked her earlier.

That meant she would have to backtrack, going toward the Main Gate and back up to the castle.

Of course, that would mean she was going to the castle,

as it had appeared when I'd followed her the first time. If she had other ideas, she could come out of Squire's Lane and head down toward the Field of Honor. If that happened, I'd lose her. But I stuck with my hunch and waited where I was.

I listened to the sound of sweet harp music, probably coming from the Merry Mynstrel's Stage where Susan Halifax was practicing. Beyond that, I heard the trumpeting of a restless elephant at the other end of the Village. Though very few lights were on in the shops and resident housing, the Village certainly wasn't quiet.

I was getting restless and bored, wishing something would happen. I didn't exactly relish the thought of spending the night below deck in a hammock with a bunch of snoring pirates, but standing out here waiting wasn't a picnic either.

Maybe I was kidding myself that I had any idea at all about who'd killed Chris or how it had happened, or who had hurt Christine. For all I knew, she had taken too many sleeping pills—maybe she just couldn't deal with everything anymore. Not everyone could face what she was facing.

I was just about to talk myself out of waiting any longer when the Lady in Black glided right by me on the cobblestones. If I'd sneezed, she would've been close enough to bless me.

I held my breath and didn't move. My heart was pounding so hard, I was afraid she'd hear it.

Her veil was so heavy that I couldn't possibly guess whose face was under it, even that close. I had a feeling that she'd be hidden by it even in daylight.

I waited after she passed, counting to one hundred (something I saw a private detective do once in a movie), then stepped carefully out of my hiding place.

I felt the thrill of excitement tinged with fear when I saw

that my hunch was correct. She was making her way toward the castle, slipping to the side of the climbing wall and up close to Mirror Lake.

I held back and caught my breath as she slowed down close to where the *Queen's Revenge* was rocking gently at anchor. It wasn't possible that she already knew where the kids were staying. Even if she did, she was one woman against a large troupe of crazy pirates. They'd protect the kids. Everything would be okay.

The pep talk worked and I started breathing again as she edged up along the lake, past the Lady of the Lake Tavern and the Feathered Shaft.

I was right behind her, hugging the shadows, almost scared to move, my gaze glued on her.

I was surprised when she bypassed the castle gate. *Where is she going?* There was nothing on the far side of the castle except for trees and shrubs. Chase had told me once that the only addition the Village had made to this wilderness area was holly bushes. The spiky leaf bushes would deter most visitors from straying here. The wall that surrounded the Village continued behind the castle, but it was reinforced with barbed wire.

There was nothing back there. I'd gone that way once with Chase when he was looking for a missing child. The back of the castle was a solid concrete wall with no entrances. I wasn't sure if there was even a window.

But the lady I followed was on her own path. She didn't seem to mind the holly bushes and kept going. I had to bite my tongue a few times to keep from swearing when the prickly leaves got me. I didn't remember the bushes being so tall last time. They got me in the neck, face, and shoulders as well as the arms and hands. I hoped they weren't poisonous. Chase hadn't said anything about that.

I continued to follow along the broad base of the old airport control tower turned castle. I couldn't figure out where she was going. I could see the lights from the parking lot beyond the wall and the trees that shielded the castle.

Suddenly I knew where she was going. Though the castle was mostly self-sustaining—the castle staff did all the cooking and laundry—the operation still required deliveries. The trucks pulled in to drop off food and other supplies at the opposite end of the castle entrance. The delivery area was separated from the Village and the cobblestone attractions by a high wall so that visitors never had to lose their illusion about the castle.

I knew there were at least two doors at this end. One was the big loading-dock door. The other was a metal door. Both of them were kept locked, day and night, for fear someone would wander in from the Village and get hurt.

The keys were closely guarded—which was why I hadn't thought about her coming this way. Only a few castle residents had copies of them. One of them was Rita. Gus had one. And so did Esmeralda.

I didn't want to think that any of those three people I knew so well were involved in killing Chris, but it was beginning to seem that way.

The black figure before me didn't have to pause and open anything—the smaller metal door that delivery men used to come in and have their paperwork signed was open. She closed it behind her. I hoped she didn't lock it. I'd come too far and gone through too much pain from the holly bushes to lose her.

I waited, counting to ten this time. I didn't have the patience left to count to one hundred. If she had locked the door, I was dead in the water. It might be possible to search the castle and find the black gown, veil, and gloves, but that wasn't proof of anything. There might be ten costumes like it in the Village, even though it wasn't Renaissance garb. I had to catch the woman in the dress to confront her.

I put my hand on the doorknob and hoped it was regularly maintained so that it didn't squeak. I closed my eyes, said a little prayer, and slowly turned it.

To my surprise, the door swung open easily. Thinking back on it, that should have given me a clue right there.

Quickly, before anyone could spot me sneaking in, I closed the door behind me. With my back against it, I faced the castle supply area.

Every grocery or toiletry that was used in the castle started out here. There were giant-sized boxes of detergent, bales of toilet paper, freezers of frozen meat, and huge burlap bags of fresh vegetables.

It was like a storehouse of necessities that made castle life good for royalty and servants alike. This area was closely monitored to protect against thievery. Even so, there were always missing items that couldn't be accounted for. When I'd worked at the castle, scullery maids and kitchen wenches were frequently accused of stealing everything from food to toiletries.

The bad thing was—the Lady in Black could be anywhere.

There was only the barest lighting in this section. I knew there were brighter lights on the ceiling, but I didn't know where to find the switch. With all the cans and boxes stacked around me, I was an easy target—she could be behind any of them. Or maybe she'd already left the area and gone back to her own room. I was completely convinced now that she lived in the castle.

Fat lot of good it did me. With no proof of having seen her, what could I say to Detective Almond? I knew Chase believed that I'd seen her earlier in the Village, but he couldn't do anything to help either.

I was about to go back outside when I noticed that there were two sets of dewy footprints on the dry concrete floor. Mine were clearly the big ones. They walked all over the smaller prints—but only until I'd reached the huge boxes of macaroni and cheese. Clearly someone in the castle was a fan of that particular side dish.

I stepped back to see where the small footprints led and then followed them, walking behind them this time, carefully preserving them as a trail. They led around the dry goods and the refrigerators. They circled the large cans of chicken broth and finally stopped at a door.

It looked like a closet door or maybe the entrance to another pantry. I carefully opened it (pushing my luck, I know) and found a stairway. It was dusty and full of cobwebs, as though it hadn't been used in many years. But the damp footprints led up the stairs, leaving a trail in the thick dust.

I thought a minute about following the Lady in Black up the stairs. I had no idea where she was going and no way to let anyone know where I was. I considered writing a note in the inch-thick dust, just in case, but that seemed a little extreme. So far she'd stayed one step ahead of me. I probably wouldn't catch her now. She probably knew some secret passage back to the main living quarters.

I was probably safe. I knew she didn't have a gun—we'd found that—although she could have a knife. Obviously I wasn't going to eat or drink anything she might offer me. If it came down to it, I could always tackle her. I was bigger, probably stronger, and younger, if it was Alice. I could take her.

With that cleared up, I crept up the stairs. They were made of wood, so they creaked and groaned with every step. If she was at the top of the stairs, she'd have to know I was coming. But there was no other way up.

As I reached the top floor, I kept my head down, still hoping I might be able to surprise her. It was almost completely dark, the air thick with dust and that terrible musty smell a place gets when it's been closed off for a long time.

I realized that what little illumination there was came from outside, from a window that faced the Village and the large stadium lights. It would've been brighter, but the glass was filthy from years of neglect.

I looked around, suddenly realizing where I was—the only part left of the old Air Force base control tower. I remembered hearing that someone had decided to leave this room intact because it had a bird's-eye view of everything below. The Village was mostly set on the old runways. This spot would've been where the controllers watched for planes and guided them in.

Clearly, the room had been forgotten. No one had been here in a very long time. Some kind of control board with dials ran under the window. Beside it, there was only empty space where machinery had once been installed. An old microphone sat abandoned on a countertop, covered in cobwebs, and charts illustrating different landing patterns hung on the walls.

Other than the stairway I'd just come up, I couldn't see any way out of there—unless the room had access to a secret passageway. I'd heard those existed but had never seen one. This room was in one of the castle's turrets, though. I didn't think it connected to anything else.

In short, I'd walked into a trap.

Twenty-seven

I heard her footstep behind me. *Where had she been hiding?* I stood still, looking out over the sleeping Village.

My strategy was to pretend I didn't see her as I picked up a loose tool of some sort that was on the old console. She was blocking a move to the stairs for escape. I had to be ready to possibly fight my way out of there.

"Lady Jessie Morton." Her voice was deep with a gravelly edge to it, like she had a cold. It sounded affected to me, as though she was purposely disguising it so I couldn't recognize her. That told me I knew her.

I hoped that fact meant she didn't plan to kill me and wanted to protect her identity because she knew we'd meet again. But she had killed before, maybe twice. Zigzags of fear went up and down my spine like I was watching a scary movie. *A scary movie with me in it!*

I started to turn around. Given the dim light, I still wouldn't be able to see her face unless she'd removed her veil. But I'd read that making an attacker more aware of you as a person was a good thing. It would probably work for killers, too.

I put up my hands in the classic sign of surrender but I could feel the old tool against my back. It was close at hand if I needed it. "Okay. You got me. I didn't even know this place was up here. How did you find it?"

"Stay where you are," she warned me.

I didn't know a lot about guns, but I heard a *click* that sounded like the release of the safety. Apparently I was wrong about her not having another gun. I wished I was asleep on the *Queen's Revenge*, listening to the pirates snore. *Why do I always have to do these things?*

"I don't know who you are," I said (trying to make her feel safe and anonymous) in what I thought sounded like a calm voice. "But you won't get away with killing me any more than you'll get away with killing Chris." *Oops! Where had that come from?*

"You're so smart, aren't you? And you have it all. You think you're queen of the Village. You have the handsome bailiff, and everyone loves you. That could all change tomorrow. Where would you be then?"

It was as if the woman had read my mind. I knew she didn't mean what she said in the way I'd been thinking about me and Chase and my life in the Village, but her thoughts about the future were similar to mine.

"You mean like when *you* were queen, Alice?" *Again—where was my brain?*

She laughed, a mean and ugly sound. "That's right. I heard you were researching our history. I suppose you think you have all the answers now, don't you? But you don't understand. You'll *never* understand."

At that point, time seemed to stop or at least slow down.

I heard the gun fire and even saw a flash out of the corner of my eye as I turned my head.

I grabbed the tool behind me but it was too late. She'd anticipated my move or had always planned to shoot me. She laughed and shot at me again. The empty room echoed with the blast. I thought someone had to have heard it and would come running. It was the middle of the night. The castle walls weren't *that* thick.

I knew I was hit. A bullet burned my arm close to the shoulder. It hurt a lot more than I would have expected based on what I'd seen on TV. The impact from it—she was standing so close—pushed me back against the old window.

At one time, the control tower window might have been shatter resistant. But time and weather had weakened it.

In a flash, it was like time had caught up with me. I was outside the window on the castle roof. The only thing keeping me from falling was my hand grabbing an iron icon perched there. I thought it was a gargoyle's head, though I couldn't be sure. I'd never noticed one up here before, and I couldn't see it clearly now. It was just a big blur.

I didn't know if the Lady in Black was gone or not. I didn't really have time to think about it. I'd been lucky to catch myself on the gargoyle (or whatever it was), but I knew I couldn't hold on for more than a few seconds. Already my fingers were slipping.

The pitch of the castle roof at this point was steep but slanted down to the next floor. Rather than falling from that height to the ground, I took my chances and skidded down the roof, hitting the inside connector of another turret, skinning my arms and legs. This turret was smaller, but I was able to hold on with both arms.

I tried to pull myself up onto the part of the turret that attached to the castle roof. I thought if I could get there I'd be less likely to lose my grip and fall. It was a steep drop here, straight to the ground. My feet couldn't find any traction. I realized that my shoes had dropped off and my feet were pushing against the cold, wet roof, trying to find a more secure spot.

I pushed and pulled, grunted and strained, but finally managed to climb behind the fake turret and grab hold for dear life. I hugged it close and closed my eyes, trying not to look down.

Of course that never works. I looked down into the Village. I wasn't above the lake as I'd hoped. I'd considered a drop into the water and a frosty swim to the shore or the pirate ship.

Instead, I was hanging above the cobblestones on the Village side of the wall that kept visitors from reaching the loading dock—the same wall I'd been so happy to creep inside earlier. That seemed like a long time ago.

There was nothing up here. The turret was empty. The living quarters were below me. This was all façade to make the castle look big and impressive.

My arm was in agony—of course, I'd been shot! My shoulder burned like a fiery pit, the pain radiating out into my arm. With that realization of pain came others. I suspected a piece of glass had raked my side as I'd fallen through the window. Something was wrong with one of my ankles, too. I was a mess *and* trapped on a fake turret with nowhere to go but down.

I made myself take a few deep breaths. Panic wasn't going to help. There had to be a way down from here that didn't involve death or dismemberment. I surveyed the seemingly sheer concrete wall beneath me and tried to locate a second place that I could crawl or jump to.

At that moment, the maintenance crew turned off the

stadium lights. They must have finished cleaning the fountains. Usually it was an all-night job. Not tonight. Lucky me.

Then I was in blackness but for the small lights in the Village. My search for a safe way down was over.

I leaned my head back against the rough concrete wall and closed my eyes. I'm not sure how long I sat that way. I hoped some brilliant strategy would come to me. But the wind made me shiver, and snow began shooting out of the castle again, white flakes flying back at me, making my position harder to hold on to.

I looked up, realizing the loud whirring noise was coming from above. I was about ten feet down from the snowmaking machine that had been installed on the castle roof. It seemed close—maybe I could reach it and somehow manage to get inside from its location. There had to be some way to service it, put it up and take it down, repair it if it was broken. Maybe I'd be able to use that to my advantage.

I saw a large hose that had to be piping water to the unit to my left. It was bracketed securely to the roof. I might be able to climb it to the snowmaker. From there, I would be home free. I could turn off the unit, then wait until someone came to repair it.

But the hose might as well have been the moon for as far away as it seemed. My poor body was freezing, covered in icy pellets, and in too much pain to even consider moving. I wasn't sure I could climb up the hose or even move from behind the turret.

Could I just wait until morning when someone would surely notice me up here?

The answer slogged into my brain—if I stayed behind the turret, no one would see me. Even if I yelled for help, I wasn't sure anyone would hear me. Besides all that, I wasn't certain I could hold on the rest of the night. If I fell asleep up here, I'd be on the cobblestones. I wasn't ready for that yet.

I had to convince my body that this was my only plan. I had to force myself up the big hose and pray that there was somewhere to go when I got to the top.

The snow sprayed out on the Village in fifteen-minute blasts. I wasn't sure I could hold on through the snow and the extra wind while I was climbing. I went through two snow cycles before I finally felt geared up enough to take on the climb.

As soon as a fifteen-minute cycle had finished, I pushed myself up to stand on the narrow ridge behind the turret and grabbed the hose before I could talk myself out of it. I put one foot on one of the brackets holding the hose in place, then swung my other foot and arm to the far side of the hose.

I knew there was no going back.

That left me clinging to the cold, damp hose. I reached my right hand, then my left, up to the bracket above me and pulled myself up, advancing about eighteen inches.

I should've been afraid of falling. But I was way past that fear. I was more afraid of being trapped up there. Fortunately, I was so cold, I was numb. Nothing hurt anymore.

I kept pulling and pushing until I was face-to-face with the huge snowmaker. It was like a big, round fan that faced the Village, ready to spit out more snow at any moment. I wasn't sure how long it had taken me to get there, but I knew the snowmaker could blow me down the roof if it started up again before I was on top of it.

Two more pushes. I couldn't feel my bare feet anymore on the frosty metal brackets. I wasn't sure the machine would hold my weight once I started climbing across it, but I was committed. There was nowhere else to go.

I stretched one arm up as far as I could and groaned. Maybe I wasn't as pain free as I'd thought. I grabbed the machine with one hand, then the other, ready to wrestle it, and shoved upward with both legs.

I could hear the blower getting ready to start again as I reached a precarious perch atop it. The metal was cold, icy, as it prepared to shoot snow into the night.

There was nothing here. I wasn't sure exactly what I'd hoped for. There was only the roof and bigger brackets holding the snowmaking machine in place. I'd climbed all that way for nothing. If there was someplace up here from which to work on the machine, I couldn't find it. I couldn't find any switch to turn the snowmaker on or off either. Maybe it was the darkness, or maybe I'd reached the end of my endurance.

It suddenly came to me that maybe there was something else I could do.

The blower was maneuverable. The fan part moved from side to side. That's why the snow kept coming down in different directions. If I could force all the snow into one place, maybe someone would notice.

But what would be a likely target? Who would still be up and outside to notice they were in a blizzard?

The pirates.

The pirates kept a twenty-four-hour watch on the *Queen's Revenge*. Someone was always on deck, not just because of their own code of conduct but also for insurance purposes, to keep nonpirates from getting hurt.

If the snow started zeroing in on the ship, the watch would notice. He'd tell Rafe, who'd call maintenance, and maybe someone would check on the snowmaker and get me off of the roof.

It was a good plan. The fan started whirring, and I

angled it toward the pirate ship. But it was harder to hold the fan in place than I'd thought. I had to wrap my arms and legs around it to keep it where I wanted it to be. It got steadily colder as it worked. The wind still blew the ice crystals back at me. I shut my eyes against the stinging bite of them against my face

It was a long fifteen minutes. I was scared I might not be able to last the whole cycle without losing feeling in my arms and legs. Just when I thought I couldn't hold on any longer, the machine turned off. I slumped down on it, hoping I was doing the right thing.

I held the blower in place through two more cycles before I noticed lights coming on far below at the pirate ship. Then, they must have stood out on the deck through two more cycles before they felt certain something was wrong—pirates can be a little slow.

On the next cycle, the accent lights situated across the castle walls came on. Hope bloomed in my frozen limbs. It seemed someone had noticed there was a problem.

Then nothing happened. I was sure it was time for another cycle of snow. But the snowmaker stayed ominously quiet. Had they turned it off rather than deal with the problem at night?

I was ready to give up. I didn't know what else to do. I was all out of clever ideas for one night. I just wanted to go home and be with Chase.

Then I heard a strange sound, a squeaky hinge noise like the sound of a rarely used door being opened.

"I don't know why this can't wait until morning," an angry male voice said. "I don't think it's safe for us to be out here. There's fake snow all over. We could slip and fall."

I was never so happy to hear an angry Village maintenance man's voice.

"This whole snow idea is stupid anyway," a second voice said.

I laughed and cried at the same time. "I could use some help out here."

My voice stalled out on me, and sounded more like a croak than actual words.

"What's that?" the first man asked.

"I think it came from whatever that is on the unit." He shone a flashlight beam on me. "No wonder it's not working right. Is that some kind of big bird on it?"

I cleared my throat and tried again. "It's me, Jessie. Can you help me down?"

"Chase's girlfriend?" the first man asked. "Jessie Morton? Is that you?"

"What the hell are you doing up here anyway?" the second man asked. "Chase will have our hides if you don't get inside right away."

I was too relieved to respond.

Getting to the real parapet, where the small door was located, about twenty feet to the side and another ten feet down, took some maneuvering and rope. The two men used the brackets attached to the roof that I hadn't been able to see. They tied the rope around me then helped me reach that wonderful warm room. I dropped on the floor and didn't bother getting up.

"Call 911," the first worker said in a scared voice. "Jessie, can you hear me?"

"No. Don't call anyone," I rasped. "We can't do anything like that—not right now. She'll get away. She knows that I know. She knows who I am."

"She's delirious," one of them said.

"I guess her weight must've tipped the snowmaker so the snow blew down on the pirate ship."

"It wasn't my weight," I explained. "It was the only way I could think of to let you know I was up there."

"That was smart," the second worker said as he coiled up the rope that had saved my life. "But you don't look so good. I think you should go to the hospital."

"I will later." I sat up slowly. Everything hurt at the same time. But I was afraid the Lady in Black would get away unless I acted as soon as I could. She probably thought I was dead—which was good. She'd feel safe carrying on as usual.

I was in a suite of rooms on the second floor, which was rarely used. Still, everything was immaculate, not a dust bunny to be seen. Too bad housecleaning didn't make it to the old tower room. It was amazing to me that I had lived at the castle without ever realizing that area existed. Part of me couldn't wait to find out if Chase knew about it.

The other part said thanks but no thanks to an offer from one of the maintenance men who asked if I wanted to call Chase and let him know what had happened. I told him it was because Christine needed him at the hospital and I didn't want him to worry. But the real truth was I wanted to finish this, and I didn't want him to run back here and try to coddle me.

Although God knew I needed some coddling. The idea of having him put his arms around me and tell me it was okay, that I was safe, was almost irresistible.

But I resisted.

Lucky for me visitors often leave a few clothes behind when they check out. Housekeeping rarely gets rid of them, just shoves them back in the closet. It's come in handy more than once to have some spare clothes available for those times when someone arrives without a suitcase.

I found a shirt and some trousers, both left there by

some nameless man, who knew how long ago. I could make them work with an ugly tie for a belt and by rolling up the blue-striped shirtsleeves.

It could've been worse—it could've been a troll costume from last Halloween.

The maintenance men finally shrugged and gave up trying to convince me that I needed medical attention. Now that the snowmaker was throwing the icy crystals across the Village again, they gathered up their rope and other tools and left me in the suite.

I was glad they were gone. I didn't have to pretend to be capable of anything besides falling on the floor and crying. I looked at myself in the full-length mirror and was frightened by what I saw. No wonder they'd wanted me to go to the hospital.

I was covered in blood from my head to my feet. My clothes were torn and soaked in it. My feet looked like they'd been skinned.

But I had to find *her*, the Lady in Black. She might feel safe tonight, but tomorrow she'd be looking for a way out of the Village. She might already be packing and plotting where she'd go.

At least that was the theory that got me moving. I had to push myself as hard to get into the warm shower as I had to reach the snowmaker. I groaned and suffered through the first few minutes. Each drop of water was like a knife pricking my skin.

Eventually, the pain subsided as the water began to wash the blood down the drain. I examined my arm—it looked as though the bullet had gone in one side and out the back. Through and through, they called it on one of my favorite cop shows. I couldn't be sure, of course, but it was going to have to wait for a more thorough examination. I found a first aid kit and got to work on it.

The shower gave me a little surge of energy that got me through the grim job of bandaging my wounds. I found some socks for my feet that made them feel better. I also drank one of the mini bottles of whiskey from the liquor cabinet. That made *me* feel *a lot* better. I ate a couple of the chocolate pillow mints, which jump-started a second energy surge.

I tidied up the room as best I could, then crept into the dark hall and down the stairs.

I suppose I could've gone after Gus. He had a key to the delivery door. But I knew he wasn't the Lady in Black. It could've been one of Chris's girlfriends, but I was staking my reputation on either Esmeralda or Rita.

Something about the way Esmeralda had acted the last time we'd spoken sent me to her room first. No one ever locks their doors in the castle, so it was easy to get inside.

There was no sign of her, which seemed odd. Maybe she'd been called downstairs for a laundry emergency, but that seemed unlikely. She had staff on duty at night to handle late-night royal housekeeping needs when they occurred.

I wasn't sure what I would have said if she'd been in her suite. I guess I would've made something up. But that was not the case, which made me even more suspicious.

She had a nice suite—bedroom, sitting room, and even a little kitchen. Most of the staff who lived in the castle had only a bedroom. But she'd worked here forever.

I looked through every room, but there was no sign of the black dress. That could mean she was still on the prowl—if she actually was Alice Christmas—maybe even looking for the kids. I was still doing okay from the whiskey and the chocolate, so I walked a little faster toward the basement stairs where Harold had fallen.

It was about three A.M. No one was around. Everything was quiet. Even the most humble kitchen and laundry servants had gone to bed, with buzzers to wake them if they were needed. It was only me—and the Lady in Black.

I hated that she had a gun and I didn't. I borrowed a fake sword from a suit of armor against the wall. It wasn't a good sword like Chase's—it didn't even have a real edge—but it would have to do. Considering that she thought I was dead, I might be able to sneak up on her. I could at least hit her in the head with the heavy hilt.

I crept quietly down the stairs, pausing at each stair to make sure I still didn't hear anything. I'd left the light off so she wouldn't see me coming if she was down here. All I had in my favor was the element of surprise. I hoped it would be enough.

The laundry area was dark, darker than the stairs where some light was still coming from the dim sconces in the hall above. It wouldn't do to have a castle visitor fall and get hurt.

There was laundry everywhere, from sheets to underwear. Esmeralda and her crew were responsible for making everyone from royalty on down look presentable. The room smelled of detergent and bleach.

I walked through the whole area, pushing some of the laundry out of the way until I could see the floor. I was wasting my time. She wasn't here.

I tried to think where else she could be. After the snow incident, there was probably too much excitement on the *Queen's Revenge* for her to attempt to board. If she had it in mind to hurt Chris's children, she'd probably wait until later when things settled down.

She would've been in her room packing if she were trying to escape. I hoped all that time I'd spent trying to get off the roof hadn't given her an opportunity to get away. If that was the case, I'd be sorry I didn't let the maintenance men call 911. Maybe they could've caught her. I was fresh out of ideas and my chocolate–alcohol high was wearing off, leaving me exhausted and in pain.

A groan came from a big pile of laundry near the dryers. I had to hear it again to know exactly where to look. I flipped on the lights and started going through the laundry.

As I got closer to the concrete floor, I noticed blood on the sheets and towels that I moved. The groaning became louder, more insistent. This was someone else injured and in pain. Maybe I'd been wrong about Esmeralda. Maybe she was a victim in this, too.

I finally reached her. It looked like she'd been shot in the side, but it was hard to tell—there was so much blood. I was amazed she was still alive.

Esmeralda grabbed my hand when I touched her. She opened her eyes and tried to smile at me. "Jessie. You were right. Alice never forgave Chris. I think she influenced Olivia to invite Chris here. She wanted to kill him."

"How? How did she influence her? Where is she?"

"I don't know. We argued. She told me she tried to kill Chris's wife. I couldn't believe that was my little sister, Ally, talking. I couldn't believe she could hurt anyone."

I knew it was hard for her to talk. But I had to find Alice before she hurt anyone else. "Where did she go, Esmeralda? Where is your sister?"

She coughed and held a hand to her side. "She's with Livy. You have to stop her, Jessie."

She passed out again. I wasn't sure what to do. I had to find Alice, but I still wasn't sure who Alice was. At the same time, Esmeralda needed help. I needed to do both things. For the hundredth time that night, I wished my cell phone was working.

There was an intercom that ran from the laundry to the kitchen. I wasn't sure if it went anywhere else, but I thought I might get lucky. I pushed the button to talk. A sleepy voice answered, telling me it was too early for breakfast.

"Is that you, Rita?" I asked. "I need your help. Esmeralda has been shot. She's in the laundry room. Call someone."

"Jessie? Is that you? Is this a prank? If it is—"

"Just do it. I have to go. Help her."

I knew Rita would at least take a look. She could handle it from there. I limped up the basement stairs, clutching my fake sword, and headed for the queen's chambers.

Twenty-eight

Alice was with Livy. I wished I could get in touch with Chase. Did she mean to harm Livy or was there something else going on?

Clearly Alice was one of Livy's ladies-in-waiting. Who else (besides a man) would be with Livy at three in the morning?

I could hardly believe it. Both Lady Jane and Lady Barbara had been at the castle for at least the last ten years. How could Alice stand it all that time? It was easier to imagine her coming in as a new hire than living here for so long, plotting her revenge.

Of course, maybe it was a crime of convenience. Chris and Alice split up. She came back to the Village but didn't tell anyone who she was. She'd only been there a short time to begin with. So many people had come and gone over the years. Only Esmeralda knew. She lived here as Livy's companion, and when she had the chance to have Chris hired as Father Christmas, it was too good an opportunity to pass up.

My aching arm and other painful body parts had little sympathy for her plan. I understood about holding on to anger, but she'd hurt other people besides her ex-husband. She was going down. I hoped.

There was still the matter of her gun. She'd clearly lost her mind if she was willing to shoot her own sister. She knew she couldn't go back from that. Esmeralda wouldn't allow it to go on. At least I hoped she wouldn't. Family could be strange. She'd obviously harbored Alice even after she'd shot Chris.

So why would Alice go back to Livy? Why not head out of the castle as soon as she could?

Livy's chamber door was open when I got there. I clutched my fake sword closer. I pushed the door open all the way and looked around. The sitting room was empty—not surprising since it was still the middle of the night for most people.

I didn't want to cause any undue alarm. Maybe Alice would give herself up without a fight. Maybe she'd realize that she'd gone too far.

The queen's bedroom door was ajar as well. I carefully pushed it open all the way. A dim light was on at the side table. Lady Jane sat near the window in one of the tapestry chairs. She was in her nightgown, her long brown hair spilling down her shoulders. When she looked at me, I saw the fear in her eyes and I knew it wasn't over.

"So you found me." I recognized that voice now. The Black Widow. "Good. Let's have a party. Shut the door."

I closed the door. Barbara stood with the gun she'd used to shoot me and Esmeralda trained on Livy's head. Livy sat in the opposite tapestry chair near the fireplace. She was very quiet, silent tears streaming down her face.

The element of surprise wasn't on my side after all. I'd given Alice/Barbara another target.

"Take a seat, Jessie," Barbara instructed. "You don't give up easily, do you? I was expecting they'd find you dead on the cobblestones in the morning. You must have nine lives."

I sat on the edge of the bed facing the three ladies. "You know there's no way out of this for you, Alice. I just had Rita call the police for Esmeralda. How could you shoot your own sister?"

She waved the gun around, not so intent on holding it against Livy's temple now that we were all locked in the room. "She's always thought she could tell me what to do. She never understood how much I hated Chris. 'Get over him,' she always told me. 'Get on with your life.' Well you know what? I can do exactly that now. I got rid of Chris and his stupid wife. I'm only sorry it has to end before I wiped his progeny off the map."

"So now what?" I asked, still holding the fake sword at my side. She obviously hadn't seen it when I walked in. The room might have been too shadowed for her to notice it.

"Now I get rid of the three of you and get out of the Village." She shrugged her shoulders, still wearing the black gown. "I think that's doable."

"I'm pregnant," Livy begged in a voice I had never heard her use before. She sounded sane and rational for once. There was no royal we—no ego. "Please don't hurt my baby. You can leave right now and no one will catch you. Jane and I won't say a word. Jessie won't either."

Alice laughed. "You must be kidding. I've been with you almost since you began as queen. You're a selfish, arrogant fool, Olivia. You'd do anything to make things better for yourself. You'll never convince me that you care about that poor baby you're carrying except as a way to raise stock prices for Adventure Land shareholders—you and Harold being two of the biggest."

"You're wrong." Livy pushed herself to her feet. It wasn't easy. But she stood with her head held high, facing the woman threatening her life. "This baby means more to me than anything I've ever done. You don't know me as well as you think you do."

Alice looked a little surprised. It would've been hard to ignore Livy's sincerity. Then she tossed the gun around again, making Jane wince and close her eyes.

"I don't care. What's done is done. I'm not giving up my life for you, any of you. I've waited a long time to get on with my life. I can finally do that. I'm free from Chris."

I hadn't noticed until that moment that Livy had grabbed the fireplace poker from beside her as she'd struggled to her feet. She held it draped in her huge nightgown, resting her body against the tapestry chair.

Alice faced me, the gun steady again in her hand. "I think the second time might be the charm, huh, Jessie? I don't know how you survived when you fell off the roof, but I'm sure you won't have that kind of luck this time."

Okay. I admit it. I was even more scared than I had been on the roof. There was no way she was only going to wound me this time. The gun was pointed at my head. She was obviously crazy, but her aim looked pretty solid to me.

I thought about Chase and all the times he'd asked me to stay with him at the Village. I thought about how much I loved him and wanted to share the rest of my life with him. I had wasted so much time. If I didn't die tonight, things were going to be different. I wasn't going to be so worried about the future because I knew that there might not be one.

If I can just make it through the night. I closed my eyes as she squeezed the trigger.

Then I heard a dull thud and a loud groan.

Livy had hit Alice with the fireplace poker. She stood over Alice's body, looking like she was ready to do it again. Alice was quiet and still on the plush carpet.

Lady Jane fell out of the tapestry chair in a dead faint.

Livy moaned and dropped the poker so she could put both of her hands on her huge stomach.

"I think the baby is coming. Oh God! What do I do now?"

There wasn't time to think or question where help could come from. I heard sirens coming toward the Village or already on the cobblestones. I wasn't sure which. All I knew was that Livy's water had broken. She was going to have her baby right there in the castle despite all the preparations to get her to the hospital.

I slapped Lady Jane lightly to wake her up. She was upset but understood that I needed her. I sent her to look for help or call someone who knew how to deliver a baby. My knowledge of giving birth consisted of what I'd seen in movies and on TV.

"What about *her*?" Jane pointed to Alice with a shaky finger.

"I'll take care of her," I promised. "You go for help."

Though Jane was obviously dedicated to her queen's welfare, she was more than happy to comply.

Livy was breathing hard and yelling every so often. "What do we do? What happens now? Will the baby be okay?"

"The baby will be fine," I assured her as I stripped all but the bottom sheet from her bed and threw the pillows on the floor. "You're not hurt. Neither am I, thanks to you. Just lie down and help will come. It's going to be okay."

"Well I couldn't let her hurt the baby, could I? This baby means everything to me and Harry. It represents a whole new life for us."

I wasn't sure about all of that, but she climbed up on the huge, old four-poster and did as I said. As she kept talking, I tore her sheets and used the material to tie up Alice. I didn't want any surprises from her, though she was clearly out of it. Livy had done a heck of a job.

I wished there was someplace to boil water. I had no idea what for, but it seemed like the thing to do. Livy's cries were getting louder. I pulled up a chair close to her face and encouraged her to breathe. I kept hoping Lady Jane would get back sooner rather than later.

After one bone-clenching grasp of her hand as she went through a strong contraction, the bedroom door flew open and police officers ran into the room, weapons drawn.

"Is everyone all right?" the lead officer demanded. "What happened here? A woman told us someone had tried to kill her."

I explained as quickly as I could before Livy started another contraction. "We need a doctor or someone who can deliver a baby. I don't know how close she is, but I don't think there's time for the hospital."

Detective Almond scrunched through the line of cops. "And here you are." He laughed. "Look for Jessie, look for trouble. So who's the killer?"

"You found Esmeralda in the basement. This is her sister, Alice, who was married to Chris Christmas once a long time ago. She killed him and tried to kill Christine. That was before she tried to kill me and her sister."

"I thought this was the queen?" Detective Almond queried.

"She's—"I looked toward the tapestry chair where I'd left Alice—"gone. I don't know where she went."

"Edwards, Taylor." Detective Almond barked out orders. "Take a few men and look for her."

"She's wearing a long black dress," I told them. "I think she's probably the only one up and around at this time of the morning."

"And she's got a big bump on her head where I hit her with the poker," Livy ground out before her next contraction.

"I'm looking for the pregnant woman," someone yelled from the sitting room. "Let me through."

"That should be the paramedic," I said, gratefully giving up my place at Livy's bed.

Lady Jane, a true friend to Livy, led the way with the paramedic.

Detective Almond and his men left the room to start searching for Alice. I knew it was going to be like looking for the proverbial needle in the haystack. They didn't know the Village. There were plenty of places to hide.

I passed King Harold as he made his way into the bedroom. He paused as Livy let out an ear-piercing shriek, but to his credit he kept going.

Maybe Livy was right. Maybe this baby would change everything for them. I had no vested interest, but I sincerely wished them the best.

I limped out into the well-lit hallway to find the kitchen staff and everyone else in the castle running from place to place trying to figure out what had happened and what part they could play in it. Paramedics and police were talking with Merlin, who was back in his starred robe minus the pointy hat.

And I wasn't sure if I could take one more step. Everything that had been hurt was throbbing painfully. There was no chocolate or whiskey in sight to help.

Worse, I knew where Alice would go to ground. I knew where the rest of her mission would take her. I couldn't rest yet. Too bad I hadn't realized before all the police were gone.

I knew I couldn't face Alice alone, even if she was woozy from a hit in the head. I wasn't sure if I could move my arm that had been shot.

I didn't see anyone else available, so I took some kitchen wenches, a few fools, and a knave or two with me. I wished I had time to find Gus or Bart. I wished Chase was here. But it looked like it was going to be only me and those stalwart Village folk on the trail of the Black Widow.

The pirate ship was dark and quiet. Even the safety lights, required by OSHA, were off. I knew that wasn't right. Could Alice have overtaken the watch and made her way below deck to the children? My heart started pumping hard as my small group climbed onboard the *Queen's Revenge*.

The pirate who should have been on watch was splayed out on the deck, unconscious. Not a good sign.

"What now, Lady Jessie?" a buxom kitchen wench whispered, a large urn in her hands.

"I don't know. All of you stay here for a minute. If you see a woman in a black dress, take her down, but be careful."

I hugged the shadows, trying to see through the darkness, listening for any unusual sounds. The rigging sighed in the slight breeze, and the ship made familiar noises as it bobbed in the water.

The outside lights at the castle came on again at the

same time that Rafe opened the door to his cabin, took a look around, and said, "What the hell—?"

Alice was rushing toward me, a look of pure hatred on her face, a large pirate knife in her hands. Blood was dripping down from her hair. She looked like one of my worst nightmares come to life.

I took a deep breath and waited for her to reach me. I really had no strength left. I had to be devious.

Rafe yelled out my name and started toward me. My band of wenches and peasants surged forward. They would all have been too late.

But just as Alice reached me, I stepped away from my place at the rail. She kept going, and when she smacked into the side of the ship, I used her momentum to push her up and over the edge. There was a satisfying splash a few seconds later as she ended up in Mirror Lake.

"Use your radio," I said to Rafe. "Call someone. There are police all over the Village."

"Jessie, you look awful," he said, putting his arm around me. "Can you walk?"

"I just need some coffee and a cinnamon roll," I told him, sounding delirious even to my own ears.

I don't really recall what happened after that. Rafe said later that I smiled at him and closed my eyes before I blacked out. I never made it to the coffee.

Twenty-nine

I woke up in the Myrtle Beach hospital the next morning. I was covered in bandages and some kind of foul-smelling antiseptic. The sun was shining. It seemed we'd finally made it to morning.

Chase was asleep in a chair beside the bed. He was wearing street clothes, jeans and a Ren Faire T-shirt. The sunlight from the window was golden on his handsome face. I was grateful just to be able to sit there and watch him for a few minutes.

I felt pretty good considering everything that had happened. I was rested and ready to get out of the hospital. There was so much I needed to know, so many questions to ask. I figured I'd lost about eight hours. I needed to know what was going on.

I was about to wake Chase and ask him about Christine and Livy and Alice when a young doctor with very serious gray eyes came in to talk to me. He introduced himself as

Dr. Steve Brown and said he was glad to see me awake finally.

"You were quite a mess last night, Ms. Morton." He picked up my chart as Chase woke up and looked around. "But I think you'll be just fine. Stay off of castle roofs and away from loaded guns. I'm sure there's a story to tell out of that. Maybe sometime you can get me free tickets to the Ren Faire. My wife and I went a few years ago. We had a great time."

"Just give me a call," I said with a smile. "I'll be glad to set you up. When do I get out of here?"

"I'll see what I can do about that." He nodded to Chase. "Mr. Morton. I'm sure you'll be glad to hear that your wife is going to be just fine."

Chase shook his hand and smiled but didn't correct him. "Thanks. I'll try to keep her away from dangerous things in the future. It's not easy."

"Just one question," Dr. Brown said. "I thought guns weren't allowed at the Faire. I take it some foul villain was doing his dastardly worst."

Chase and I both laughed at that. Dr. Brown did, too, but probably for some reason other than his terrible British accent.

When we were alone, Chase took my hand, wrapped in a big white bandage, and kissed it. "Don't ever scare me like that again. I leave you alone one night and you're climbing the castle roof and finding the killer. You didn't leave a thing for me to do."

"Believe me, if my cell phone battery hadn't run out, I would've called you. And once I was up in that control tower, it was too late. Did you know that thing was still up there?"

"Yeah. They left it there on purpose. The door going up

there was supposed to be locked. Some Adventure Land person wanted it to hang out in occasionally."

"Does he dress like a wizard and like to flash the ladies?"

"I believe he does." He kissed me very carefully. "You saw her and followed her again through the Village, didn't you?"

I nodded. "I think she knew and that's why she was ready for me. But your guys were on the spot as soon as I figured out how to make all the snow fall on the *Queen's Revenge*. It was just a question of time before I caught up with Alice after that."

"You were just lucky. She could've killed you."

"Never mind that." I moved stiffly in the bed to see him better. "What about Christine? Is she okay?"

"She's fine. She went home to the kids this morning." He smiled and ran his fingers through my hair. "She called me for advice on how to get her kids off the pirate ship. It seems they've all gone rogue."

That was completely incredible. I laughed even though it hurt. "And Esmeralda? Is she okay?"

"A little repentant. She knew her sister killed Chris and didn't say anything because she thought Alice was only gunning for him. But she's going to be fine, too. The bullet missed anything major. She got out of surgery a couple of hours ago."

"And Livy? How's the baby? Did she and Harry make it through the whole ordeal without killing each other?"

"Livy's fine and so is the baby. She's forgiven Harry for sleeping with Christine while she was pregnant, and he's forgiven her for stabbing him in the back because she was angry. Just their usual drama."

"What are they calling the baby?"

He smiled and kissed me again. "You'll love it. Princess Henrietta Olivia Jane Jessica Martin. I think they're calling her Pea right now. She's cute, for a wrinkled little human."

"She gave her *my* name, too?" I couldn't believe it.

"You might've saved her life. Even Livy can be grateful."

A pretty nurse came into the room with a wheelchair. "Mrs. Morton? It's time for us to get you packed up. Maybe your husband could excuse us for just a minute." She smiled at him, and Chase let go of my hand.

"I'll be waiting right outside," he said. "We have a lot to talk about."

The statement had an ominous ring to it. I was worried about where it might lead.

We went through the nursery and saw Pea before we left the hospital. She was kind of cute for being all wrinkled and squished looking. I talked about her all the way out to Chase's Mercedes.

I purposely kept the conversation light and fluffy while we were driving back, talking about the Village and how great it was to be there for the holiday.

I knew what Chase wanted to talk about, and I wasn't sure if I was up for it. I'd sworn things would be different between us—but that was last night when I wasn't sure if I was going to live or not.

Today, everything seemed fine and I was just as scared of making the commitment that Chase wanted. Why couldn't we go on as we always had?

But what if this was it between us? It had never happened to me, but I'd known couples that had broken up because one of them didn't want to get serious.

When we finally reached the Village, I jumped out of

the car and hobbled as fast as I could to the Main Gate. The sun was shining and the cobblestones were full of visitors. There was a long line stretching from the manor houses on Squire's Lane, so I knew Father Christmas was in session.

"Where are you going in such a hurry?" Chase asked, catching up with me.

"I just want to see everything," I gushed as though my brain had been injured with the rest of me. I felt terrible acting that way. Chase deserved better. I just seemed incapable of giving him what he needed.

To my surprise, I had a reprieve waiting for me as soon as I got past all the well wishes from the greeters at the Main Gate. Christine and all the children, out of pirate gear now and back in elf costumes, were there to see me. They all rushed up and hugged me, almost knocking me over in the process.

"We're so glad you're all right," Christine said. "I'll never forget what you've done for me and the kids. Detective Almond told me that Alice had actually planned to kill the children, too, after she got rid of me. He also dropped all charges against me, and the insurance company called to say that our money has been cleared."

I hugged her back. "That's great news. Are you leaving the Village?"

"No. As a matter of fact, that nice man from Adventure Land offered us an empty shop and house so we could stay here and sell toys. Can you imagine? It's all the kids can talk about."

"Wow. That will be awesome, Christine. And the kids can go to a real school, although I have a feeling it won't be as exciting as it sounds."

"None of it would've happened without you and Chase,

Jessie. I hope you'll consider finishing your toy-making apprenticeship with us."

There were no sweeter words to my ears. It meant I wouldn't have to walk around looking for work or deal with the drama that was sure to come when Her Royal Princess Pea came home.

"I would love to do that," I assured her. "Thank you for asking me."

Christine hugged me again, then said she and the kids had to get back to helping Bart. All the kids hugged me again, and Merry Beth hugged Chase, too.

Then we were alone again, Chase and I, in a crowded Village.

"I got the Dungeon all set up for you," Chase said. "I'll take you upstairs, then check on you every so often. I'll leave a two-way with you in case you need anything."

"You know, I think I'm well enough to start making toys again. Why don't I just meet you for lunch."

"I'm not even sure you're well enough to be out of the hospital. Your release papers say you're supposed to rest for a few days, then go back in for a checkup."

I stopped hobbling and faced him. I couldn't stand it anymore. "Just say whatever it is you have to say. I can't take the pressure."

He kind of moved both of us out of the flow of visitor traffic, close to the hatchet-throwing game. "I really hadn't planned on doing this out here, but if you insist."

I braced myself. This had gone beyond where it was supposed to. I expected him to ask me to marry him. What was I going to say? I wasn't sure how to say yes, or no, to him. Either one felt like it could break my heart.

Instead, he pulled some papers out of the leather purse

he carried on his belt. "I want you to feel secure for once, Jessie. I spoke with a friend at USC-C. They are going to let you have your job back in January. They're willing to offer tenure work as soon as you complete your doctorate."

He put a copy of the e-mail from the university board in my hand, and I gawked at it. This surely wasn't what I was expecting.

"And I don't feel comfortable with you driving that old car anymore. These are the keys to your new car."

I could barely feel the car keys in my hand. I'd gone numb all over.

"And the solution to your apartment problem." He handed me another key. "I bought your apartment, which is now your condo, last night."

"Chase." I could hardly get the word out. "I can't take all this from you. You know how I feel."

He shrugged. "That's fine. We'll arrange payments, if that makes you more comfortable."

So many thoughts were going around in my head that I could hardly keep track of one. "But I thought you wanted me to stay here with you."

"Not because you don't have anywhere to go. I want you to stay here with me because you want to. This way, you have a choice."

Then it happened. He dropped down on one knee and took out a ring.

By that time, a crowd had begun to form. And not just of visitors. It seemed as if half the Village was there looking over Chase's shoulder as he offered me the beautiful, antique ring.

"Lady Jessie Morton, will thou take my hand in marriage and live here with me? I pledge my undying fealty and love to you. You have only to say yes."

What else could I say to this perfect man that I loved? "Yes, Sir Bailiff. I will marry you and love you forever with all my heart."

I wondered how long it would take to plan a real Renaissance wedding and how I was going to get back at Wanda while I was doing it.

Ye Olde Village Crier

Greetings!

The holiday season has changed a lot through the centuries. Christmas as we know it is much different than the Christmases celebrated during the English Renaissance.

Twelfth Night was the name of the festival lasting through December to Epiphany. The churches battled each other over how festive this celebration should be, what days it should be held, even what food should be eaten. Many people were afraid to openly celebrate the holiday for fear of getting into trouble with one faction or another.

Carols were born during the 1500s. Saint Francis of Assisi is said to have written many of the original carols as a way to celebrate the season

Of course, the rich celebrated the season with much more ceremony, food, and gifts than the poor. The servants and peasants were allowed only half days to celebrate, after which they had to return to their work.

For the rich, there was music and lavish gifts. No amount of food was too much or too unusual. There would be stuffed peacocks, pounds of marzipan, and hundreds of roasted, boiled, and baked dishes. Wine flowed freely, and the guests at these feasts were treated to amazing splendor. A dessert course during the holidays might have two hundred different fruits, sweet cakes, and jellies.

Boar's head was always the centerpiece of the main meal during the season. It was garnished with fruit, rosemary, and other costly herbs and presented as though it were to the king himself.

The legend of Father Christmas has grown and evolved over hundreds of years. In the late nineteenth century, his persona started to merge with that of Saint Nick, who was himself a compilation of several saints named Nicholas famed for their good deeds. Depictions of Father Christmas adopted Saint Nick's red and white color scheme, which is said to have been appropriated from bishop's robes. Father Christmas's once brown beard was changed to white as the myth continued. Because Christmas was celebrated in all parts of the world, in one form or another, the various incarnations of folkloric holiday gift givers meshed together, so much so that Father Christmas, Saint Nick, and Santa Claus are virtually interchangeable today.

Fruitcakes are said to have originated in ancient Rome, but they became widely popular during the Renaissance. Recipes were greatly prized and rarely shared between families. Church regulations forbade the use of butter in the recipe until Pope Innocent VIII issued a letter known as the "Butter Letter," allowing it. He also decreed that honey could be used.

These cakes were different than what we would expect of a cake today. With their rough flour and log shape, they were more like bread, though they were decorated with marzipan and other rich icings.

Traditional English Fruit Cake, sometimes known as spice cake, was a celebration cake, one of the few sanctioned by the Church during the Renaissance. While today we think of it as ordinary or even plain, during the Renaissance, it was anything but.

RENAISSANCE FRUIT CAKE

This recipe produces a close likeness of a Renaissance fruitcake. The cake is better the longer you let it set. During the Renaissance, it was made six weeks or longer before it was eaten.

12 ounces plain flour
2 tablespoons mixed spices (listed below)
1 teaspoon cinnamon
1 teaspoon grated nutmeg
1 pound butter
1 pound brown sugar
2 tablespoons black treacle
1 dozen eggs
2 pounds mixed dried fruit
6 ounces chopped mixed fruit peel
6 ounces chopped nuts (your choice)
1 bottle brandy, whiskey, or sherry
6 ounces chopped glacè cherries

Sift the flour with the spices. In a separate bowl, cream together the butter, brown sugar, and treacle. Beat in the eggs. Stir in the dried fruit, peel, and nuts, and then add half of the brandy. Stir well. Fold in the cherries, and transfer the batter to a greased and floured loaf or bundt baking pan; smooth the top with a knife. Bake for 4 to 4 1/2 hours until a skewer inserted in middle of cake comes out clean. Let the cake cool slightly, then turn it out onto a wire cooling rack.

When the cake has cooled completely, wrap it in aluminum foil and store in a cool dry place. Once a week, for six weeks, unwrap the cake and use a brush to cover it with some of the remaining brandy, then rewrap it. The cake is ready to eat when all the brandy has been applied. Makes multiple servings.

Huzzah!